Dear Reader,

To me, this isolated island off the coast of Maine represents rest and recovery. I need seclusion and solitude, not that constant ministrations of a woman who wants to give me liberal doses of her tender loving care.

But inhabitants are scarce at this end of the island, and Jeannie MacPherson isn't happy unless she's helping others. Suddenly, she thinks I'm the answer to her prayers.

What do I think? That the sea air has affected my mental processes. Because Jeannie MacPherson's not even my type—and yet, I'm finding myself bewitched by her big blue eyes and dark red hair.

Matthew Connelly

ANNE STUART

Anne Stuart has written over sixty novels in her twenty-five-plus years as a romance novelist. She's won every major award in the business, including three RITA® Awards from Romance Writers of America, as well as their Lifetime Achievement Award. Anne's books have made various bestseller lists, and she has been quoted in *People, USA TODAY* and *Vogue*. She has also appeared on *Entertainment Tonight,* and, according to her, done her best to cause trouble! When she's not writing or traveling around the country speaking to various writers' groups, she can be found at home in northern Vermont, with her husband, two children, a dog and three cats.

Anne Stuart

Rocky Road

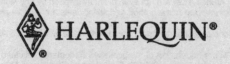

TORONTO • NEW YORK • LONDON
AMSTERDAM • PARIS • SYDNEY • HAMBURG
STOCKHOLM • ATHENS • TOKYO • MILAN • MADRID
PRAGUE • WARSAW • BUDAPEST • AUCKLAND

ISBN 0-373-36022-3

ROCKY ROAD

Copyright © 1985 by Anne Kristine Stuart Ohlrogge

Published Harlequin Enterprises, Ltd. 1985, 1993

www.eHarlequin.com

Printed in U.S.A.

To Ben and Jerry's Ice Cream, with thanks for the inspiration and the Heath Bar Crunch

Chapter One

"What the hell are you doing in my kitchen?"

The words were gruff, threatening in the stillness, and Jeannie MacPherson whirled around. The blazing-hot casserole in her hands slipped past the pot holders, touching her skin, and with a small shriek of pain she let go. The earthenware casserole plummeted to her bare feet, smashing into shards of pottery and chicken Marengo. The steaming sauce splattered her legs, and she shrieked again, this time using words that seldom escaped from her usually serene lips. The pungent swearwords, more inventive than obscene, faded in a haze of pain as Jeannie stood there, unable to move for fear of embedding the pottery in her feet. The man who had startled her into the sudden disaster just stood there in the kitchen door, watching her.

Then he moved into the dimly lit, low-ceilinged kitchen of the old Maine cottage, and she noted his limp through her own dizzy pain. "I repeat," he said in that low, unfriendly voice, entirely unmoved by her situation, "what the hell are you doing in my kitchen?"

No help from that quarter, Jeannie thought philosophically. She should have known better than to have played the Good Samaritan; it would be up to her to extricate herself from the current predicament. She ignored him, surveying the uneven floorboards of the old kitchen. Most of the mess was in a tidy pool around her feet. The pain in her scorched ankles and calves had subsided to an unpleasant throbbing, and she could see the red streaks that were either from the burn or the red-wine sauce traveling up toward her knees. This would have to be one of those times she only wore aging cutoffs on her legs, she thought. It was very definitely not her day.

Pieces of pottery were scattered over the rough flooring, but if she were uncommonly agile she could jump clear. Unfortunately the closest spot untouched by the broken casserole was where her accuser stood.

Too bad for him, she thought with a shrug of her shoulders, and leapt, landing beside him with only a small grimace of pain. Pieces of mushroom clung to her bare feet, and the room was redolent of chicken and wine and French cooking. Ignoring the pain in her legs, she managed a game smile.

"Hi, there."

Matthew Connelly, if that was who he was, didn't respond to her friendly smile. He just continued to look down at her, with that grim expression on his face. "Do I have to ask you a third time?"

Jeannie shook her head, giving up. "I'm your neighbor, Jeannie MacPherson. I was just bringing you a casserole to welcome you to Muscatoon Island. Sorry about the mess. It'll just take me a minute to clean it up."

"Don't bother."

"Really, it's no trouble. After all, it was my fault." It wasn't, of course. It was his, for scaring her like that, but Jeannie MacPherson was a generous soul.

Matthew Connelly glowered. "Don't bother," he said again, and there was no doubting that was an order. "How did you know I was coming?"

"Your sister told me when she was here last week," Jeannie said guilelessly. What Sally Connelly Riccetti hadn't mentioned was how very attractive her artist brother was. And how very unfriendly.

He was tall, but then, most men were when they stood next to her five feet two inches, which was actually five feet one and three-quarters, but she counted every inch she could. He was probably somewhere around six feet, with long legs, shaggy, wheat-colored hair and disapproving gray eyes. He had a scar across his stubborn chin, a hard, unfriendly mouth and a strong nose that had been broken at least once. He looked distant, cold and just a little bit mean, but beneath the light layer of early-summer tan she could see the grayness of pain, and the grimness of his mouth radiated past and current physical discomfort. Jeannie's momentary irritation faded in sudden concern.

"Sally asked me to keep an eye on you, make sure you have everything," she continued blithely, uneasily aware that her artless friendliness wasn't going over at all well.

"That won't be necessary."

"Oh, but it's no trouble," she protested.

"I don't give a damn whether it's any trouble or not," he said. "I came to Muscatoon Island to be alone; I had my sister rent on the east side because she promised there'd be no neighbors. If I wanted people around I wouldn't be on a remote island in Maine."

"But—"

"I don't need anyone making me welcome; I have everything I need; I don't want you to clean up the mess you made," he said, the words bitten off like bullets. "I want you to go away and leave me alone."

Jeannie MacPherson opened her mouth, then shut it again. There wasn't really anything she could say. She had trespassed, even though her motives were pure, and apparently the last thing Matthew Connelly needed was a ministering angel.

"All right," she said with an effort at matching his coolness. "If you won't let me help..."

He shut his eyes in sudden weary anger. "I don't need any help."

Jeannie hesitated for only a moment longer. "You have no telephone, you know."

"No one does on Muscatoon," he replied. "And no one has any electricity outside of the village. I know all that. I don't need a travelogue or a welcome wagon, lady. I just need to be left alone."

This time there was nothing she could say. Without another word she turned and walked out of the low-ceilinged kitchen, past the small, cozy living room with its aging mishmash of summer cottage furniture, out the front porch and into the summer evening twilight.

It was a beautiful night, she thought with a sigh, wrapping her arms around her slender body as she headed down the narrow path to the sea. Too beautiful for a man to be so miserable, so angry, so unhappy. She could see that physical pain was part of the cause, but definitely not all. The pain reflected in Matthew Connelly's cold gray eyes went beyond the discomforts of the recent operation Sally had warned her of. It went straight to the bottom of his soul.

"You'll like my brother, Jeannie," Sally had said. Was it only a week ago, as they sat on the porch overlooking the bluff? "I'm counting on you to make sure he doesn't overdo. He's had surgery, and if I know Matthew, he'll try to do too much too fast. I better warn you in case he collapses at your doorstep some morning."

"We look after each other on Muscatoon," she had replied, serenely pleased at the thought of a new victim for her to mother.

Sally had laughed. "You sound as if you've lived here forever."

"Sometimes two years seems like forever," Jeannie said with a peaceful sigh. "I can't imagine what life will be like when I go back."

"Back?"

"Back to reality. To cities and crowds and stress and burnout and all the ills that flesh is heir to." Jeannie grimaced.

"Who says you have to?" Sally had asked, one eye always kept on the romping figures of her three-year-old daughter and her five-year-old son.

Jeannie followed her gaze. "*They* say I have to," she said, nodding in the children's direction. "I'm thirty-three years old and my biological time clock is ticking away. I need babies, and I need a man to love, and I've finally come to the conclusion that I can't just sit around waiting for it to happen. If I want a family I'm going to have to do something about it. And my options on an island inhabited by seventy-five people year-round aren't overwhelming. Everyone's either old or gay or married."

Sally hadn't even seemed surprised. "There are options, you know. Artificial insemination, a judicious one-night stand—"

"No!" The words sounded almost anguished, and Jeannie quickly lightened them with a laugh. "No," she repeated in a softer voice. "My father left us when I was six years old. I grew up without a father, and I would never willfully put a child of mine through it. Besides, I'm not about to settle for second best. I want it all—children, husband, love forever after. The works."

Sally had shaken back her wheat-colored hair, the same thick blond as that of her unfriendly brother. "Well, maybe Matthew will provide the answer."

Jeannie had laughed then, and even now she snorted at the memory. If Matthew Connelly was the answer to her prayers, she was in deep trouble. As she scrambled down the steep path, the way was rough beneath her bare feet and the skin on her legs was painfully warm. Maybe she'd learn her lesson and not take on the troubles of the world. Matthew Connelly was obviously determined to take care of himself; he didn't need Jeannie MacPherson to mother him. She would have to decide, sooner or later, exactly who or what she was going to mother, and she'd have to decide by autumn.

In the meantime she was going to enjoy her island life to the fullest. She reached the bottom of the path and strode past the rocks into the ocean, breathing a sigh of relief as the chilly salt water lapped around her knees, stinging, then soothing the burns. It was high tide, and the fresh sea smell tickled her nostrils as the breeze ruffled her thick hair.

"Matthew Connelly will have to fend for himself," she said aloud in the darkening stillness. "He's not going to have Jeannie MacPherson to kick around anymore, Sally or no Sally."

The lapping of the water on the clean white beach sounded just the slightest bit like disbelieving laughter.

MATTHEW CONNELLY WATCHED her go. It was amazing how dignified she looked, in her cutoff jeans and bare legs splattered with food. He should have at least offered her the use of the bathroom to wash it off. He should have thanked her for her effort, even as he made it clear that he needed no help. He'd even opened his mouth, to try and temper his harshness, but only anger had come out, driving Ms Jeannie MacPherson away.

Thank God. Ignoring the mess on the kitchen floor, he limped back into the living room, letting his weary body sink carefully into the mission oak couch, which was more comfortable than it looked. It had been a hell of a day, and the sooner it was over the better. Tomorrow his damned hip would feel better, and he'd clean up the mess the casserole had made. His stomach growled in reminiscent hunger, but his hip put up an answering serenade, and he stayed where he was. He'd lost too much weight since the surgery, but that was just as well. He'd had to be so damned sedentary he would have developed a beer gut if he had eaten like a normal human being.

The hip was improving, slowly but surely. All he needed was a couple of months' peace and quiet to get his strength back, and then he could come to some decision about his future. Forty was a rotten age to try to change careers, but he'd had no choice but to quit. He sure as hell wasn't going back, not in the same way.

His hip throbbed warningly. Matthew knew he should pull himself off the couch and find the painkillers Doc Kellogg had sent along. But they always knocked him out, and he woke the next morning feeling fuzzy-mouthed and cotton-headed. Maybe he could doze off before the pain got really bad.

The damnable thing about it was that each time the hip acted up, each time the pain grew in intensity like this, he'd remember four months ago, when the bullet had slammed into his leg, and he'd stared down at the pooling blood in amazement before toppling forward in the only faint of his life. And the torn, slowly mending muscles would clench up, sending his body into spasm, just as it was doing now....

Sweating, he pulled himself into a sitting position and limped painfully over to the bags he'd dumped inside the door. He might just as well take some of those damned knockout pills. He needed all the sleep he could get right now.

He was back on the couch, just drifting off into a drugged, pain-racked sleep, when he remembered Jeannie Mac-Pherson. His sister had to be out of her mind. He liked statuesque blondes, Amazons, with large breasts and soft bodies. Jeannie MacPherson, with her small, lithe body, looked more like a teenage boy than a woman. And he hated red hair—always had, always would.

Still, she had a nice mouth. And those blue, blue eyes of hers looked as if they could see through a man's soul and beyond. It should have been an uncomfortable feeling, but it wasn't. It was a good thing he had no intention of getting involved with anyone right now. Jeannie MacPherson would be nothing more than a pack of trouble. His instincts warned him of that, and his instincts seldom failed. They had kept him alive for the last seventeen years. If they had faltered four months ago, then it was only a warning that he'd pushed his luck too far, for too long.

Damn, but he hated red hair. Hers was more auburn, though, a deep, dark russet. And he did always have a weakness for blue eyes.

With a weary sigh and a wince of pain, Captain Matthew Connelly, late of the Chicago police force, head of the detective squad, fell into a drugged sleep.

THE COLD SEAWATER had done wonders to Jeannie's wounded legs. "Bastard," she muttered cheerfully, thinking of Matthew Connelly's cold gray eyes, as she picked her way down the beach. Her rambling old Victorian summerhouse perched just above the ocean, not more than a quarter of a mile from the tiny cottage Connelly had rented. Well, she could keep her distance, and she damned well would. Sally Riccetti must have been out of her mind to think that Jeannie would want anything to do with her nasty brother.

For one thing, he was too old. She always thought women

did best with men a couple of years younger than they were. Tom had been twenty-five to her twenty-seven when they first met. Granted, his new wife was five years younger than he was, and it seemed to be working out fine. But Matthew Connelly looked as if he was in his mid-forties. An exceptionally good-looking mid-forties, to be sure, but that would make him more than ten years older than she was. And she was feeling old enough right now.

For another thing, he was too tall. No, that excuse didn't hold water; she'd been seriously considering taking Hal Vreeland up on his constant offers of companionship, and he was six foot three. Was Connelly too handsome? No, Hal was a perfect Harvard-type beauty, with three ex-wives being his major drawback.

But there was something about Matthew Connelly that was extremely dangerous to her hard-won peace of mind. Jeannie knew that with sudden certainty, and the thought sent a flash of mournful longing across her narrow backbone as she neared her darkened house. Sally's brother wasn't the man to give her love and babies and "happy ever after," and the thought brought her sudden, slashing grief.

"Are you out of your mind, Jeannie?" she demanded out loud in sudden disgust as she climbed the wide front steps of her house. "You don't need to worry about getting involved with the likes of Matthew Connelly. He won't be getting within ten feet of you. He's not your type, he's not interested, he's too old and he's no problem."

Her voice echoed in the stillness, clear and light against the constantly soothing rush of the ocean in front of her house. This time she laughed at herself. "Of course," she mused, crossing the wide porch, "he does have wonderful eyes. I wonder what that mouth would look like if he smiled." As she closed the door behind her and made her way into the darkened house, she knew the answer. His mouth would look very sexy, very sexy indeed. Without bothering to light the kerosene lamps, she headed up the wide front stairs to her bedroom, still astounded at her own idiocy.

Chapter Two

"I hear you've got a new neighbor." Hal Vreeland came up behind Jeannie, wrapping his long arms around her waist, his breath tickling her ear. The kitchen of the Muscatoon Inn was a hectic place in the midst of the breakfast rush, but Jeannie's sometime employer ignored such practical matters. "Who is he?"

"Hmph," Jeannie replied in an unencouraging voice, resisting the impulse to step on Hal's size-thirteen feet. "It's not the proper time to grab your cook while she's making an omelet, boss. Timing is everything."

"I've always said so." Hal released her, stepping back from the already steaming black stove as Jeannie continued to work, unperturbed. "Let me take you away from all this, Jeannie MacPherson. You were made for better things."

"You're the one who got me into all this," she said in a reasonable tone of voice, flipping the omelet over and sliding it onto a thin china plate with the deftness of long practice. "Have you found someone else to fill in for Doris and Bernard?" She handed the plate to the fresh-faced college-age waitress who always made her feel positively ancient, and turned back to flip the blueberry pancakes.

"You don't need me to cook anymore?" she continued,

unruffled, as she slid twelve perfectly browned blueberry pancakes from the griddle.

"Darling, I would love to have you do nothing but smile at me, but I desperately need you to cook breakfast three mornings a week."

Jeannie smiled sweetly, stopping for a moment. "Then I suggest you remove yourself from the line of fire. Halfway through the breakfast rush is not the time for propositions or island gossip."

"No respect," Hal mourned, reluctantly moving away from the work area to perch on the chest freezer. "Don't you remember? I'm the boss, you're the employee."

"Don't you remember—" she was pouring a cup of coffee "—that I work here as a favor, not out of financial necessity? You want to end up cooking scrambled eggs again?" She added cream and sugar to the coffee and handed it to him, and he fell upon it with pathetic eagerness.

"No, thank you, precious. I nearly had every guest walk out on me the last time. I need you, darling, in more ways than one."

There was a momentary lull in the rapid activity. Jeannie poured herself another cup of coffee and leaned back against the counter. The first wave of ravenous tourists who came to sample Muscatoon's fabled beauty and Hal Vreeland's astonishingly overpriced hospitality was momentarily appeased. It would likely be only a few moments before the next bunch straggled down from the brass beds and ruffled eyelet sheets that adorned each room, and Jeannie needed every second of it.

"I told you, Hal, no propositions before eleven in the morning. It's only eight, and I've been up since five." Some of her dark red hair had escaped the kerchief she wore when she worked, and she knew her usually pale skin was flushed with the heat. How Hal could still look at her with that hopeful, lustful expression in his gorgeous brown eyes was beyond her. It must be sheer instinct.

"Have you really been up that long, darling? For heaven's sake, why?"

"To feed your damned tourists," she snapped. "They're expecting fresh Maine blueberry muffins and pancakes, fresh-ground coffee, fresh-squeezed orange juice...."

"But I have machines to do all those things," he protested.

"Machines don't run themselves."

"Have you seen the ice-cream machine, Jeannie?" he asked eagerly, changing the subject. "State of the art, the restaurant supply man assured me. When do you want to christen it?"

Jeannie allowed herself a momentary glance at the gleaming metal machinery that had been so great a part of her life for five years. "Maybe next spring."

"But darling, I bought it for you!" he protested, deeply wounded, and Jeannie relented.

"It's just that I'm still a little weary of ice cream," she confessed.

"Jeannie MacPherson, late of Tom and Jeannie's Ice Cream, is tired of the stuff! Here you are, half of the culinary and marketing success story of the eighties, and you tell me you're sick of it. I don't believe you."

"Believe away, Hal," she offered, draining her coffee and adjusting the heat under the warming pan. "If I never make ice cream again, I think I'll survive."

Hal just sat there, his long legs swinging, a dubious expression on his handsome face. "I think we should start with blueberry ice cream during our blueberry festival."

She snorted. "You don't take no for an answer, do you, Hal?"

"I've taken it from you for far too long."

She grinned, pushing away from the counter and dumping her mug in the sink. "So you have. I'll make your ice cream, Hal."

"Since you're being so reasonable, will you go to bed with me once the breakfast rush is over?"

"I'll make your ice cream, Hal."

"Damn. I won't give up, you know." He climbed down off the freezer and advanced on her. For a moment Jeannie found herself wondering how she could resist the light-hearted advances of such an admittedly handsome specimen.

"Hands off, Vreeland, or you'll be scrambling eggs," she warned.

"It might be worth it," he said. But he stopped short. "So what's this about your new neighbor?"

For reasons that Jeannie didn't even want to begin to analyze, she was loath to tell him about Matthew Connelly, which was ridiculous. On an island this small and deserted, the permanent population ran into one another at regular intervals. "His name is Matthew Connelly; he's an artist and a hermit." If her voice wasn't encouraging, Hal chose to ignore it.

"An artist? Every artist I've ever known has rented on the west end of the island. Artists never get up to paint sunrises; they always prefer sunsets. Why would an artist want to be on the east side of the island?"

"Maybe because he's a hermit, too."

"Still and all..." Hal shrugged, then cast Jeannie a suspicious look. "How old is this hermit?"

"Your age," she said, countering that look with a dulcet smile. "About forty-five."

"I'm forty-three!" Hal snapped. His age and the well-hidden thinning at the crown of his leonine mane of hair were his two sore points. "Is he gay?"

"I haven't asked. You changing your habits, Hal?"

This time he didn't rise to the bait. "Just sizing up the competition, Jeannie."

Jeannie opened her mouth to protest, then shut it again. Hal had been chasing her in earnest for the past three months, ever since the latest of his live-in lovers had decamped, and she'd been just as determined to keep her distance. Hal's track record was less than encouraging, including three ex-wives and countless less-permanent companions since he attained puberty. In the past two years since Jeannie had come to Muscatoon, he'd been through the latest of his wives and four lovers. Jeannie didn't fancy being the next in line, no matter how enforced celibacy was nagging at her. Hal Vreeland was nothing but *mucho* trouble.

As was Matthew Connelly, for that matter. It was a fortunate thing they had no interest in each other.

"Oh, oh, here it comes again," Hal said, backing away from the determined advance of three waitresses. "The second wave is demanding its breakfast." Skirting the stove, he poured himself another cup of coffee and headed out into the dining room, his charming "mine-host" smile plastered to his tanned, handsome face. Jeannie watched him go with a dubious shake of her head.

"The Curtises want more blueberry muffins, Jeannie," announced Karen, the oldest and most efficient of the waitresses. "And you've got three omelets."

"Damn. Why did I ever agree to do omelets?" Jeannie grumbled. "Why did I ever agree to work here in the first place?"

"Because you were bored," Karen said. "And because it's very hard to say no to Hal Vreeland."

Jeannie allowed herself the luxury of a quick glance at Karen's face as she cracked eggs into a stainless-steel bowl. Karen was in her late thirties, divorced, and had lived her whole life on the island. She was pretty-plain, warmhearted and loyal, and in love with Hal Vreeland. Everyone on Muscatoon knew it, except the man himself.

That was another reason for Jeannie to keep her distance. "Hal Vreeland is a good man to say no to," she muttered, whipping the eggs with more enthusiasm than was strictly necessary. "See if you can limit the Curtises to three more muffins; I'm running low."

"Yes'm," Karen murmured, not missing the message as she moved back toward the dining room, fresh coffee in hand.

Jeannie allowed herself enough time to watch her leave, then breathed a weary sigh. She really had to get over her tendency to mother anything in sight, particularly when it was a very capable woman five years older than she was. But damn, she wished there was something she could do about Karen and Hal. If, indeed, something should be done.

Omelets, she thought with a grimace; and all the damned yuppies thronging Hal's dining room wanted them. At least she'd put a stop to croissants, insisting muffins with real Maine blueberries were the better choice. She shouldn't be so cynical; it was yuppies who'd made Tom and Jeannie's gourmet ice cream such a success, yuppies who accounted for the atrocious sums of money that kept flowing into her coffers every month, rain or shine. The least she could do was make them an omelet.

She looked up, her blue, blue eyes trained on the distant horizon. The Muscatoon Inn overlooked the ocean. The kitchens were relegated to a landlocked back view over the alleyways of the picturesque little village. There was still a trace of early-morning fog in the air, and she found herself wondering if Matthew Connelly was going to enjoy painting on an island that spent half the time covered in fog.

And she found herself wondering if he liked blueberry ice cream.

MATTHEW CONNELLY DISLIKED everything and everybody at that moment. He was reluctantly, damnably awake, his head still fogged with the aftereffects of the painkillers, his stomach putting up a violent protest. The pain in his groin had subsided to a dull roar, and he had a shallow slice in his foot from having stumbled onto the remains of last night's casserole still decorating his kitchen floor. It was on his right foot, his good leg, and he'd tracked blood all around the first floor of the tiny cottage as he'd cleaned up the cold, gluey mess. By the time he had made some instant coffee and put an essentially useless Band-Aid on his foot, his mood had traveled from foul to furious. Scalding his tongue on the horrible-tasting brew didn't help matters.

The store would be sending over the supplies he'd ordered sooner or later, but in the meantime he'd have to make do with instant coffee and packaged toaster pastries, which didn't seem worth the effort. Particularly since he couldn't find a toaster.

He moved back into the living room, walking slowly, testing himself. It was getting better, slowly but surely. It had been four months, four long, grueling months. Most days now he could manage with only the trace of a limp, except for yesterday, with the endless journey that had brought him to this tiny little oceanfront cottage on a blessedly empty island in Maine.

He could have, should have, had someone carry the battered leather suitcases that had served him since he was in college. He could have, should have, taken a seat to rest between planes, accepted the fact that he was temporarily diminished in physical strength. *Always out to prove something, Connelly,* he mocked himself, sipping at the watery, bitter stuff that dared call itself coffee. *You only end up paying for it in the long run.*

The toaster pastry tasted of chemicals and cold lard, and he tossed it back on the scarred coffee table with a grimace of distaste. He was starving, but there were limits to what a man could do to his stomach. Cold toaster pastries were beyond that limit; so, by God, was instant coffee.

That long, long journey that had started out yesterday morning at O'Hare Airport and ended on Muscatoon Island was a limitless hell. At one point it had seemed almost promising, when he'd gotten for a seatmate a nubile female in her late twenties who had sized up his gray eyes and not-too-battered frame and decided he might be worth the effort. He was used to that look; he'd seen it often enough during the last twenty years to recognize it when he saw it. He had settled back, prepared to enjoy himself for the flight from Boston to Portland, when the pleasant flirtation had abruptly turned to ghoulish fascination on her part and a determination to escape on his.

"You were a detective? In Chicago?" she'd exclaimed, shallow blue eyes alight with morbid fascination. "Did you work on the Springside Strangler case?"

He had considered telling her the truth—that the last two years of his life had been spent chasing down leads, tracking down a demented killer whose modus operandi had been particularly grisly. He had spent two years viewing bodies and parts of bodies, asking questions, making educated guesses, haunting the most squalid, depressing parts of an essentially squalid and depressing city, and had ended with a bullet in his groin and a sickness in his soul. The last thing he saw before he passed out had been George Kirwin, alias the Springside Strangler, being disarmed by his partner. He had waited long enough to make sure that George Kirwin would never see the light of day again before tendering his resignation.

They didn't believe him, of course. Fred and Tony wouldn't take no for an answer; the commissioner told him to consider it a leave of absence. But he was never going back. Seventeen years spent cleaning up after the scum of the earth was long enough; you started to forget that there was anybody decent or good or caring left anymore.

His ex-wife had warned him. Long after she had stopped caring, had stopped sharing her highly vaunted goodness and decency with him, she had told him what he'd have to look forward to. Cold, lonely nights, with his only companions the horrifying memories that crept into his sleeping brain when he could no longer keep them at bay. And there wouldn't be anyone for him to turn to in that sagging double bed, which he had never gotten around to replacing. He'd wake up, sweating, terrified and alone.

She was right, of course, and he couldn't blame her for leaving. Their marriage had been a mistake, right from the start, but it had been 1967 and when a man got a woman pregnant, they got married. If fate had decreed the unwanted pregnancy would end early in a miscarriage, well, that was too damned bad. You toughed it out.

Children would have helped, maybe distracted Matthew from the insidiously seductive horror of criminal investigation, but children were out of the question. The miscarriage turned into an infection that turned into a hysterectomy, and Margaret had turned to a church that had never had any place for him. She drifted farther and farther away, until the divorce four years ago. He'd hardly noticed she was gone.

He had made an effort in the last year as he felt himself slipping deeper and deeper into the morass of crime and despair that surrounded him. He'd discovered a taste for other tall, buxom blondes, all looking somewhat like Margaret. They had provided him with momentary forgetfulness, a momentary release that made the next day more bearable. His sex life with Margaret had always been the one area in which they were compatible; her rather stern God had insisted that wives submit physically to their husbands' carnal demands, and Margaret had submitted enthusiastically. The next morning she'd be cold and distant, while her replacements had been cozy and clinging, and he'd wonder which was worse as he headed out into the mean streets again, on his quest for the Springside Strangler.

God, he felt like a piece of crud. He needed a shave, his mouth felt like the inside of a lion's cage, and his clothes had the damp, constricting feeling of having been slept in. He was hungry, bad-tempered and miserable. He should drag himself upstairs, shower, shave and brush his teeth, and then see if he could get his wounded carcass back across the island to the store and find something decent to eat. At this rate he doubted his empty stomach could wait for the eventual arrival of the delivery van. Maybe he would even have lunch at the inn his sister had told him about.

He could still smell the remnants of the chicken, and his stomach growled in protest. Privacy was one thing, starvation was another. He'd probably been much too quick to order Jeannie MacPherson from his house.

The sound of light footsteps broke through his grumpy abstraction, and he looked up, startled. The sun had broken through the early-morning fog. Standing in his doorway, surrounded by dazzling sunlight, stood the lady herself, a basket over her arm, apparently as undaunted by last night's disapproval, though a trace of wariness lingered around those unfathomable blue eyes of hers.

He didn't move. He sat there on the mission oak sofa feeling grubby, hostile and hungry. He glowered at her, about to order her out once more, when a seductive scent tickled his nose. Not jasmine or roses or lilies of the valley, not Joy or Anaïs Anaïs or even Nuit de Paris. It was the demoralizing scent of coffee and something else that just might, if the gods were disposed to be merciful, be blueberry muffins.

Hunger warred with temper and wisdom, and hunger won. "All right," he said wearily. "I give up. I'd sell my soul to the devil himself for a decent cup of coffee."

Jeannie MacPherson's answering smile was even more dazzling than the sunlight off the ocean. As Matthew watched her approach he had the gloomy conviction that he would have been safer starving.

Chapter Three

"It's better out on the porch." She had a light, pleasant voice, with that faintly upper-class East Coast phrasing that always used to irritate him. "The sun's baked off the fog, and there's a light breeze. I've always liked the porch here." She still kept her distance, like a slightly fearful lion tamer entering a maneater's cage. From somewhere deep inside, Matthew Connelly felt the stirrings of a long-lost amusement.

"I'm not going to bite you," he said, pulling himself out of the sofa with more effort than he let her see. "If you've brought me something to eat, you'll find I can be downright pleasant."

She still didn't move any closer, but he could see the thin shoulders beneath the oversized cotton shirt relax slightly. "How would you respond to fresh blueberry muffins?"

Maybe there was a God, after all, Connelly thought, his uncharacteristic amusement deepening. If she wasn't getting any closer he might as well bridge the gap. *Not too close, though,* he warned himself. Despite her small, boyish body, despite that dark red hair, despite the fact that she was nothing he'd ever found attractive in a woman, she had the uncanny ability to stir him. That was something he needed to watch out for.

"Blueberry muffins might even get an apology for last night out of me."

She grinned then. "Don't bother. You meant what you said, didn't you?"

It was his turn to be startled. Those blue eyes of hers were just as observant as he'd thought. "Yes."

"And you want to be left alone, right?"

"Yes."

She shrugged. "So I'll leave you alone. Once I make sure you aren't going to starve." He'd gotten within touching distance of her now, and the intoxicating scent of blueberries and coffee were making him light-headed. She held out her hand, and he looked down at it. "Truce?"

He took her hand in his. It was a small hand, strong, calloused, with short, efficient nails. Not what he was used to, not what he wanted. He shook her hand solemnly, then released it. "Truce," he agreed. "Now can I have some coffee?"

"Sure. Go out on the porch while I get some mugs. That is...if you don't mind my having a cup with you?"

"No, I don't mind." It was a lie, but what else could he say? She was being so damned careful not to encroach. Little did she know that her very presence, moving through the small cottage, was a psychological encroachment that would haunt his dreams if he wasn't ruthlessly strong-minded.

But, God bless her, she knew when to be silent. She handed him the mug of steaming dark brew and sat in peace while he drank half of it. There were a couple of rickety wicker rockers out on the small front porch of the cottage, and he sat there, not rocking, not moving, staring out to sea and concentrating on the necessary wonder of real coffee. She handed him blueberry muffins, still warm from the oven, dripping with butter, without a word. He ate four of them, feeling more and more kindly disposed toward his unwanted visitor as the hunger pangs passed.

Wind was ruffling through her russet-colored hair, blowing across the pale face that watched the ocean with the same concentration he'd shown. He knew she was keeping her gaze from him on purpose, and he resented her for it. It would be a hell of a lot easier if she were pushy instead of sensitive.

She must have felt his eyes on her, for she turned and smiled at him. "Are the rest of your things arriving soon?"

"Rest of my things?" he echoed.

"Your painting stuff. Easels, canvases, you know. Sally said you were a painter."

Damn, already he was getting involved in lies and excuses. He considered telling her the truth for a brief moment, then abandoned the idea. The luscious blonde on the airplane had fallen on him with morbid delight; Jeannie MacPherson with her restricted social life would be even more fascinated.

"Yes, I'm a painter," he said repressively. He said nothing more but drained the coffee, forcing himself not to request a refill. The sooner she was gone the better.

Those blue eyes must have read his mind again. "Been too curious, haven't I?" she murmured ruefully. "It's one of my besetting sins."

He should have let it go, let her go, but he couldn't. "What are some of your others?"

"Matchmaking, gossiping, my inability to make up my mind until it's too late, interfering in other people's lives, junk food, absentmindedness...I could go on forever."

Gossiping and interfering in other people's lives. That was the last thing he needed right now, he warned himself. He said nothing, keeping his eyes cool and distant, unencouraging.

Jeannie rose, and he had to admit she was graceful enough in that little boy's body of hers. "I bet you don't want me to wash the mugs."

"You're right." It was ungracious of him, but he wanted her out of there, and fast.

Jeannie shrugged. "Well, let me tell you what you need to know. I'll do it quickly, efficiently, and then leave you alone."

"I don't need—"

"Listen, Matthew, we're neighbors. You may not need a damned thing, but I do." She was getting a little nettled, he noticed. He found himself liking the way her blue eyes snapped.

She started in, like a schoolgirl reciting her lessons. "The ferry to the mainland comes twice a week, bringing mail and fresh food to the store. The store makes deliveries, but you'll have to hike over there to place an order. As you already know, there are no telephones on the island, but Hal Vreeland over at the inn has a shortwave radio if it's an emergency. The only television on the place is also at the inn. It gets no reception, but he has a VCR and lots of tapes. Everything from *The Wizard of Oz* to *Dirty Harry*."

She paused for breath, and he had to ask her. "Do you like Dirty Harry movies?"

If she was surprised at the sudden question, she hid it well enough. "I love them. The only problem with living without television is missing 'Hill Street Blues.' I have a real weakness for cop shows."

Great, he thought grimly. *Another ghoul.*

"You have a gas refrigerator, gas hot-water heater and kerosene lights. The store delivers propane and kerosene every other week. If you find you're going through it too fast, let them know and they'll come more often. You and I are the only people on this end of the island. High tide's around eleven in the morning, low tide is in the afternoon. The path to the beach is to your left; it's a little tricky, so be careful.'' She took a deep breath, then plunged back into her catalog. ''I'm your only neighbor, but I like to walk, so if you don't stay completely housebound you're apt to run into me. Sorry about that, but them's the breaks. I also swim every morning. When I'm cooking at the inn I swim around ten; when I'm not working it's closer to eight. Sometimes I wear a bathing suit, sometimes I don't. If you don't want to stumble over a possibly naked lady, I'd suggest you keep away from the beach before eleven. Unless you want to join me?''

It was a challenge, wryly spoken, and she clearly expected no answer. She went on, undaunted. ''I have three cats, and they may visit. Do not throw things at them, and don't feed them unless you want them moving in on you. They're insatiable. I will leave you alone unless you let me know otherwise. My house is about a quarter of a mile down the beach, up on a bluff. You just follow the path along the water for a few hundred yards and you'll see my house. Come anytime. I won't be expecting you.'' She took another breath. ''Any questions?''

He wanted to smile at her. He wanted to tell her to sit back down and have more coffee with him. Some small, stupid part of him wanted to pull her down into his lap and kiss that wide, breathless mouth until her blue eyes glazed over and her endless spate of words faded away. ''No questions.''

''Then welcome to Muscatoon Island.'' Without another word she turned and left him, bounding down the porch and heading off toward the sea without a backward glance.

He watched her go, the wicker basket swinging on her arm. Reaching for his coffee mug, he found she'd refilled it when he wasn't watching. And she'd left the rest of the muffins.

With a weary sigh he tipped the chair back and took an appreciative swig of the coffee. If only it were ten years ago. If only life really consisted of blue sky and green ocean and rocky beaches and a redheaded tomboy with the bluest eyes he'd ever seen.

But it didn't. Not for him, anymore. It consisted of people like George Kirwin and his random victims. Suddenly he remembered Elizabeth Harris; she'd been the worst of the bodies he'd had to view, looking for elusive clues. She'd been in her early twenties, sweet, innocent-looking even in death. Jeannie MacPherson, damn her friendly little nature, reminded him of her.

Well, he'd take her warnings seriously. He'd keep away from the beach before eleven o'clock; he'd take his solitary walks in the opposite direction of her house. After a while he'd even forget he had a neighbor. Maybe.

WELL, SHE'D DONE HER DUTY, Jeannie told herself briskly as she scrambled down the steepest part of the path. She'd at least made sure they'd be on speaking terms when—if—they ran into each other. And she'd warned him about her swimming habits. Not for anyone would she curtail her early-morning swim, and if Matthew Connelly chose to get in her way that was his tough luck. The bad-tempered, unfriendly old grouch.

It would be so nice if she could simply put him out of her mind, the way he so clearly intended to put her out of his. It would have been nice if he were old and ugly, instead of damnably attractive. Instead of mooning about those cold gray eyes and that grim, unsmiling mouth, she should consider whether Hal might not be the answer to her problems. It would almost be worth it, just to see the look of shock on Hal's handsome, Ivy League face when she finally said yes. Almost, but not quite. Hal was incapable of the kind of love and commitment she needed. There was Karen to consider, too.

Not that she was responsible for Karen's well-being, Jeannie reminded herself for the umpteenth time. Just because once, two years ago, she'd been devilishly clever in matching her extraneous fiancé with her administrative assistant at the ice-cream factory was no reason to think she'd meet with similar success. If Hal had been interested in Karen, he would have done something about it long ago. He certainly seemed to have done something about every other presentable female on the island.

She stopped when she got to the little inlet that provided a perfect crescent of sandy beach, dumped her basket on a rock and began to pull off her clothes. This time she had a bathing suit underneath, just in case Matthew proved either more difficult or friendlier than she had expected. He was neither; he simply was...not there.

The ocean was icy cold swirling around her ankles, but she ignored it, striding into the water, diving under when she got waist-deep. She swam steadily and purposefully, out past the ledge of rock till she could see the spit of land that curved around to the harbor, and then back again, pacing herself, breathing evenly, using every muscle in her body.

She was pleasantly tired when she walked out of the sea, and she could be grateful there was still some coffee left in the bottom of the pot she'd brought over to try and appease the dragon. She poured it into the Styrofoam cup that lay on the bottom of the basket and sat there, nursing it and watching the waves.

Was her absorption with Matthew Connelly a mistake? She had made more than her share in the last few years. The only thing she knew wasn't a mistake was coming here, to Muscatoon Island. Everyone needs peace at some point in their lives, and at the age of thirty-one Jeannie Mac-Pherson had needed it desperately. Still, at times like these, when nothing but the incessant sound of the ocean vied with her memories, doubts began to trickle through.

She'd been working too hard, of course. Had been working since she was twelve years old, helping her mother make ends meet. She'd worked her way through college, through graduate school. She had taken her proudly acquired M.B.A. and gone to work for a factory making little steel rings for large steel machines. It had been soulless, deadly work, its only advantages the steady salary, the beautiful Vermont location and Tom Mickelson.

Tom had been assistant foreman, an aging hippie with long hair tied underneath his hard hat. He'd hated the factory, hated being boss, hated everything to do with Renner Tool and Die. He and Jeannie had been soul mates, who found they shared a passion for Celtic music, Greek food, detective stories and ice cream. Together they had gone to Dirty Harry movies and Chieftains concerts in the small city of Burlington; together they had cooked moussaka and stuffed grape leaves and traded Ed McBain novels. Until the infamous day they made ice cream together for a group of friends during a Fourth of July picnic.

History had been made, Jeannie thought with a wry grin. Their friends had been ecstatic, their own delight unlimited. They had started making ice cream as a sideline, to augment the sparse salaries Renner Tool and Die paid them. They found they were making more money in a weekend of ice cream than a week of hard labor. With great trepidation they quit their jobs, borrowed a sizable sum of money from a sympathetic bank and went into business for themselves.

They had always planned to be married. To be sure, the two of them always had a little more passion for Heath Bar

Crunch and Heavenly Hash than they'd had for each other. But they were well matched, compatible enough so that they enjoyed each other in bed.

Life seemed secure until Tom and Jeannie's Ice Cream exceeded even their wildest dreams and became a nightmare. Even with her M.B.A. Jeannie was run ragged trying to keep track of all the profits, reinvestments, expansions and stocks. The new factory had been the final straw. The ground-breaking ceremony had followed a blistering fight, with Tom trying to set a date for the long-postponed wedding and Jeannie still hedging. The dedication of the new building had followed Tom's final ultimatum. The first day of production had followed Tom's introduction to Daisy, his wife and future mother of his two babies.

If she had just been certain, Jeannie thought, pushing a hand through her wet hair, *those could have been her babies.* Instead, she had left her job and retired to the most remote island she could find, taking with her the almost indecent profits that came to her as cofounder of Tom and Jeannie's.

No, it hadn't been a mistake. She and Tom had grown apart years ago; they had simply been too busy to notice. Daisy was perfect for him, sweet but hardheaded, a wonderful mother and cheerfully adoring; just the kind of woman Tom needed.

What kind of man did she need? Not decent, hardworking Tom. And not charming, handsome Hal Vreeland. And certainly not someone like Matthew Connelly, chasing away demons and Jeannie MacPherson with equal abandon.

When it came right down to it, she needed a man who needed her. One who wanted her and babies and everything that entailed. It was clear that Matthew Connelly wasn't that man. It was also clear that that man didn't exist, at least not on the circumscribed acres of Muscatoon Island.

So she'd have to look farther afield; except that she knew from experience that whenever you went looking for love, that was when you were least likely to find it. You quite often came home and found it waiting in your own backyard.

Hell, no! That was something out of *The Wizard of Oz*. It had been a long winter, and Jeannie had been reduced to seeing that film almost weekly for lack of something else to do. She already had the Dirty Harry movies memorized.

The only thing in her backyard was Matthew Connelly. If he was the answer to her prayers, she was in deep trouble. As soon end up with Dirty Harry himself. She didn't need an artist, and she didn't need a grouch. She just needed someone to love.

She had till autumn. No, a little later than that, she hedged. Till the last of the leaves fell, till she had to begin the endless banking and winterizing that made the rambling cottage remotely habitable in the winter.

Tom had been talking expansion last time she had been in touch. A branch on the West Coast, a branch somewhere in the resort areas of Colorado or New Mexico. Maybe Texas. He'd been begging her to come back and take over some of the endless work, and that might be the answer. After two years she knew the answer wasn't on Muscatoon, much as she longed for it to be.

No, leaving Tom hadn't been a mistake. Coming to Muscastoon wasn't a mistake. And leaving Muscatoon wouldn't be a mistake, either.

She just had to make absolutely certain that she didn't get sidetracked along the way. Matthew Connelly would be a very big mistake indeed. Enough to counteract all those right decisions that she was still worrying about.

With a sigh she put the pot and the Styrofoam cup back in the basket, pulled her clothes on over her wet bathing suit, and started back toward her house. If she just kept busy, she told herself. The front parlor needed painting. It had waited patiently all spring. Today it would wait no longer.

MATTHEW FINISHED the final muffin, washed it down with cold coffee that was still miles better than the horrible-tasting instant he'd mixed, and basked for a moment in an unaccustomed sense of well-being. He was pleasantly full, tired and at peace with the world. Much as he hated to admit it, Jeannie MacPherson had a great deal to do with it.

He'd better watch his step. Feeding a man when he was hungry was the first step toward undermining his resolve. He had gone hungry before and had not given up his principles. Surely he wouldn't be seduced by blueberry muffins and coffee.

And blue eyes, he added dreamily. He found himself wondering whether today was one of the days she wore her bathing suit; and whether she still looked like a boy when she was naked.

Damn. He slammed the chair legs down on the porch. Time for a long, cold shower. Then maybe a walk along the beach, in the opposite direction of Jeannie MacPherson's house. Maybe, if she just kept out of his way, he could keep her out of his mind. Maybe.

Chapter Four

"So tell me about the hermit of the east end," Karen said, folding her spotlessly clean apron in her strong tanned hands and laying it on the shining countertop.

Jeannie gave the stove one last desultory wipe with the aging sponge. The last of the kitchen help had long since departed for the Saturday night frolics, Hal was zeroing in on a bored divorcée who was vacationing with her aged mother, and only Karen and Jeannie were left in the deserted kitchen of the Muscatoon Inn.

"Who calls him that?" Jeannie dropped the sponge into the sink, pulled off her own filthy apron and took the kerchief from her hair.

"Just about everyone who's even aware of his existence, and there aren't too many of them," Karen answered. "You're his only neighbor, and as far as I know you're the only one who's met him, outside of Ernie at the store. Come on, I'll buy you a cup of coffee and you can fill me in."

"I thought gossip was a winter sport," Jeannie grumbled.

"Listen, kid, it's quarter past nine on a Saturday night in June, and you and I are the only people on this island without a date. What else can we do but gossip?"

Jeannie laughed. "If I hadn't had to fill in for Doris I'd be very happy at home, thank you. The Crime Club sent me a Joseph Wambaugh, an Ed McBain and a John D. Mac-Donald. I can't think of any man who could even begin to compete with that.''

''I warned you when you let Hal talk you into doing breakfasts that he'd have your soul before long. Didn't you tell him you never wanted to cook dinners?''

''I did,'' she said ruefully.

''What were you doing tonight instead of reading your bloodthirsty novels?''

''Cooking dinner for thirty-seven people,'' she admitted. ''So I'm a sucker. Hal knows me too well. All he has to do is bat those eyes at me and act as if he needs a mother, and I'm hooked.''

''Hal's too damned good at it,'' Karen said, and there was just a trace of grimness beneath her light tone. ''I've seen him do it for years now. Anything he wants just falls in his lap.''

''Not quite. He's gotten my cooking, not my lily-white body.''

''Just wait.''

''You just wait. I think, at the advanced age of thirty-three, that I am past falling for men that are no good for me.''

Karen sighed. ''Why should *you* be? I'm not past it at age thirty-eight.''

''Karen...''

''So tell me about the hermit. What's his name, Cunningham? Do you ever see him?''

''On occasion. His name is Connelly, Matthew Connelly. Listen, I've had too much coffee tonight already, and I want to go for a walk before it's dark. Why don't you come with me?''

Karen shook her head. ''Love to, but my feet are killing

me. I'll walk you to the end of town if you promise to tell me about the hermit.''

It was a still night. All the courting was being done indoors or along the western edge of the island, and the main street was deserted except for the two women.

"No, he's not tall, dark and handsome, Karen," Jeannie said irritably in response to her incessant questions.

"Short, blond and ugly?"

Unbidden, the memory of Matthew Connelly's rangy body materialized in Jeannie's unwilling brain. She sighed, not even realizing he was doing so. "All right, all right. He's tall, blond, reasonably good-looking, spectacularly unfriendly, unattached as far as I know and nothing but trouble. He spends all his time either painting, sitting on his front porch or walking by the ocean."

"If he's so unfriendly, how do you know how he spends his time? I thought hermits kept away from other people."

"Oh, he keeps away from me, all right. I just don't keep away from him."

"Jeannie!"

"Don't sound so horrified. I promised his sister when she was here that I'd look out for him. He doesn't even know I'm there. I just make sure he's back home when I take my walk at night. I leave him stuff sometimes—a loaf of home-baked bread or muffins or the like. I put the stuff on his porch while he's asleep, and the next night the empty plate is waiting for me. I figure he's either Santa Claus or an elf."

"I figure you're crazy."

"He needs someone to watch out for him," she defended herself. "Everyone needs a little mothering every now and then, whether he wants it or not. I'd never be able to look his sister in the eye if something happened to him."

"You're probably not going to be looking his sister in the eye again anyway, Jeannie. You're just making excuses, and you're asking for trouble. If the man wants to be mothered he'll say so. It sounds to me as if all he wants is to be left alone.''

Jeannie sighed. ''That's it, of course. And he isn't limping much anymore. I suppose he's well enough to make it on his own.''

''I suppose so,'' Karen said wryly. ''You need something else to concentrate on, kid. I think maybe you'd better give in to Hal. At least it would give you some good exercise.''

They'd reached the end of the narrow village street. Somewhere in the distance Jeannie could hear the sound of a buoy tolling mournfully.

''I wouldn't think of it.''

''Don't reject him for my sake, Jeannie. I know far too well he'd be no good for me. You can have him with my blessing.''

''No way.''

''Think about it. I think he'd be safer than the hermit.''

''Trust me, Karen. Matthew Connelly's the safest thing around. You can't even get within twenty feet of him.'' She stretched lazily. ''God, I'm tired. I may even forgo my walk tonight. Thirty-seven people are too many to feed. G'night, Karen. See you Tuesday if not before.''

''Sleep tight.''

This time she wouldn't do it, Jeannie promised herself as she veered toward the left, down the narrow path that led through the stand of towering white pines, past Mallet's abandoned boat yard with its eerie pyramids of lobster traps, through the fields that once boasted ripe corn but had for long years lain fallow. This time she'd walk straight home, feed the cats and climb into bed with Ed McBain. Doubtless he'd be much better company than...than...well, than whoever it was she'd contemplate going to bed with. More entertaining and a helluva lot more reliable. At least Ed

McBain and the Eighty-seventh Precinct were going to be there, good times and bad, year after year after year. What man could you make the same guarantees about?

Certainly not Matthew Connelly. So why the hell had she taken to haunting the windswept acres around the tiny cottage, why did she check his propane supply when he was gone to make sure he didn't run out, why did she always manage to end up in his direction when she went for her walks? Why had she been unable to sleep until she knew he was safely settled for the night?

I mean, the man is a fully grown adult, she told herself sternly. *So he limps a little. He can take care of himself. He doesn't need a mother hen bustling around him.*

But telling herself was one thing. Believing it was another. Damn, but her feet hurt. She may not have been racing back and forth between kitchen and dining room at the behest of the thirty-seven well-heeled guests as Karen had, but just moving around the kitchen used up a fair amount of energy. And it was just under a mile from her house to the inn; surely that was exercise enough for one night. She needed a shower and her bed, not a stroll along the cliffs to make sure Matthew Connelly was settled for the night.

Tonight, damn it, she was going to listen to her better judgment. Tonight she'd go straight home, and maybe break herself of this neurotic fascination for the hermit of the east end.

Two hours later she tossed Ed McBain on the floor, threw back the covers and pulled herself out of bed. Principle was one thing, she told herself as she pulled on a pair of soft, faded jeans, insomnia was another. Bad as checking on Matthew Connelly's well-being was, spending the night wide awake worrying about him was even worse.

She yanked the forest-green chamois shirt over her head, shook back her still-damp hair, and headed down the narrow front stairs, stopping long enough to pull on a pair of running shoes. The moon was almost full and the sky was clear, so the path was illuminated. It would take her ten minutes to climb down the cliff, run along the ocean to Matthew's beach house, peer in his window if need be and race back. Fifteen minutes for the whole expedition, tops. Then maybe she'd have learned her lesson.

It took the entire fifteen minutes and more. The pathway that she knew so well proved to have a surprising number of roots and stones and twists and holes. She tripped once, cursed roundly and continued on. The tide was going out, and the smell of rotting sea vegetation was a little unsettling. Or maybe it was being out alone in the middle of the night on a fool's errand, Jeannie chided herself.

"What the hell do you think you are, Jeannie?" she muttered to herself. "A witch? A psychic? Nothing's wrong with Matthew Connelly that a good shot of cheer-up pills wouldn't help. He's not lying in some ditch, waiting for you to rescue him."

The wind had picked up, and Jeannie shivered for a moment. She hadn't bothered with any underwear for her midnight sortie, and the shirt was loose enough to let the breeze sneak underneath. Her damp hair blew in her eyes, and she shoved it out of the way impatiently as she started up the incline toward Connelly's cottage. Sunshine Cottage, the owner had once termed it, and a cracked and faded sign attesting to that fact still hung askew over the front door. Not an aptly named vacation spot for the likes of Matthew Connelly, who would doubtless be sitting in the living room where he always sat, nursing a dark amber glass of something suitably lethal and painting his mysterious picture.

She would have given years off her life to see what he was working on with such an intensity that almost bordered on desperation. She'd begun weaving the most ridiculous fantasies about the man as she hovered around him. She had the instinctive feeling that he never did anything halfway. His paintings had to be like him, dark and passionate and almost violent and...

"Good grief," Jeannie said out loud. "Dark and passionate and violent? Give me a break, Jeannie. He probably does pastels."

An errant cloud swept in front of the moon as she topped the hill in front of Sunshine Cottage, and Jeannie swore lightly under her breath. She felt a sudden cold prickling in her spine as she realized there was no light coming from the ramshackle little cottage.

"Don't be ridiculous," she said aloud, and her voice was a nervous thread of sound. "It's almost midnight; he probably just went to bed early."

But she had walked by later than that and he'd always been up, sitting in that chair, drinking his drink in grim and solitary splendor, or working on that painting of his.

"Maybe he's gone out on a date. No, he would have left a light burning for when he came back. Besides, who would he go out with? The only person he knows on this island is me, and he's fool enough not to want me." The words sounded even more ridiculous spoken out loud, but the sound of her voice on the cool night breeze was curiously reassuring, and she continued as she edged toward the cottage, almost whispering, in case he really had gone to bed early.

"Or maybe he's gone off island and no one bothered to tell me. He could have taken the morning ferry out. He may have moved out for good, dummy. You must have driven him away!" The thought left her curiously desolate. Her sneakered feet making no noise at all, she crept up the steps to the sagging front porch, tiptoed across and peered in a darkened window just as the moonlight spilled across the stark landscape.

His canvas and easel were still in the corner. There were dirty dishes on the table, a half-empty glass on the mantel, and the front door was open.

She had no choice. Her sixth sense was acting up like crazy; it was better to be caught in the act than risk having him...God, she couldn't even begin to imagine all the horrible catastrophes that could have befallen him.

"Matthew?" she called, her voice a thin thread of sound. She pitched it a little louder. "Matthew?"

Only the thick, dark silence answered her. She started into the cottage, then whirled around and headed back out without checking. Her instincts had been right so far; she was going to go with them one more time. She knew his habits pretty well by this time, knew that when he went for his solitary walks he always headed as far from her house as he could. Her only choice was to head along the cliff, out toward the eastern bluff, and hope that the moonlight stayed bright enough until either she found him or felt certain he wasn't out there at all.

The rocks were slippery beneath her feet, cold and damp from the night mist. The wind whipped past her, picking up in speed and intensity with an almost demonic force, and Jeannie wrapped her arms around her narrow body, hugging the chamois shirt closer as she followed the worn path with dogged determination. She thought back to Ed McBain and the clean white sheets of her narrow iron bed, and a wistful longing swept over her. Matthew Connelly was probably bending an elbow with Ernie down at Sharp's Tavern, or up in his bed, dead to the world, and she hadn't bothered to check. He was probably perfectly all right, whereas she, poor fool, would likely fall to her death.

He was no more than two hundred yards from the cottage,

but she might have missed him if she hadn't stopped long enough to retie her shoe. She saw his hand first, lying in a tuft of grass, and for a moment the scream rose in her throat like bile as she remembered all sorts of gruesome tales Ernie told to terrify the flatlanders.

But the hand was attached to a wrist that was attached to an arm that was still attached to Matthew Connelly's unmoving body. Jeannie swallowed the scream and crept forward, whimpering slightly with sudden fear as she reached out a tentative hand to see whether he was still alive.

His skin was cold and wet from the heavy sea mist. Jeannie sat back on her heels, trying to figure out where she could check his pulse, when his eyes flew open, staring up into hers with his usual ill grace, and that grim, oddly sexy mouth opened.

"Are you just going to kneel there and stare at me," he growled, "or are you going to help me to my feet?"

"What happened?" She was too concerned to let her irritation get the better of her.

"What the hell do you think happened?" he shot back. "I fell. You intend to do anything about it?"

Jeannie said not a word for a long moment. "I think," she said in a judicious tone of voice, "that I will let you freeze to death."

"I'm not going to freeze to death at the end of June, even in this frigid climate," he said tersely, and Jeannie could hear the thread of pain beneath his sarcastic drawl. "However, if you're going to leave me here you might consider lending me that shirt. I didn't dress for spending a night on the cliffs."

Indeed he hadn't. He was wearing khakis and a thin chambray shirt, suitable enough wear for the earlier, sunshine hours, but woefully inadequate once the sun went down. Which meant that Matthew must have been out there for quite some time.

Jeannie reached a hand out to unbutton her shirt, then dropped it as she remembered just how little she wore underneath it.

"Sorry," she said in her briskest voice. "I don't fancy freezing, either. I guess I'll just have to help you up, much as it goes against the grain. Anyone with your charm of manner deserves to spend the night on a cozy bed of granite." She slid her strong arms under his shoulder, squatted back on her heels, and prepared to pull. "Ready?" she inquired politely.

"Ready."

She yanked; he bounded to his feet and immediately collapsed on top of her small frame.

It took all her strength to remain upright beneath his weight. She could feel the muscles clenched in his larger body as it leaned against hers; she could almost feel the pain radiate through him. She knew that he'd want to go back to the house, that he wouldn't give in to the pain long enough to rest, to try again, so she didn't even ask.

She gave him long enough to catch his breath and then rearranged herself, sliding her arm around his waist, leaning her body against his to give him better support. She felt his arm go around her shoulders in a crushing grip, and as his considerable weight pressed against her it took all her strength not to waver.

"You wanna just stay here and cuddle, Connelly," she drawled, "or do you want to go back to Sunshine Cottage?"

She surprised a laugh out of him, a weak one, but a laugh nevertheless. "I think Sunshine Cottage is the place to be. Once you haul me there and pour us both a drink you can tell me what you were doing wandering around here at...what time is it?"

"After midnight. How long have you been out there?"

If she hoped to distract him from his original question, it was a vain hope. "Too long. Don't worry, neighbor. It's going to take us a while to get back to the cottage. It should give you plenty of time to think of a good excuse. Let's go."

His voice was grim, implacable, and for once Jeannie didn't begrudge him that grimness. She could feel the pain coursing through the big, strong body pressed up against hers, could feel the battle he was waging against it. Beneath the cold, damp skin was bone and muscle and heat that should have had no effect on her whatsoever, given the seriousness of the situation. So why was she wanting to turn to face him and slide her other arm around that narrow waist? Why did she want to reach up and kiss him on that grim, sexy mouth?

Two years was too long, she told herself with equal grimness. She'd finally snapped.

"Okay, Connelly," she said. "Anchors aweigh."

Chapter Five

It took them a long time to travel that two hundred yards across the rocky outcropping above the beach. Matthew Connelly was lean enough, owing no doubt to his recent surgery, but he was still a hell of a burden for a five-foot, almost two-inch woman with only average muscle power. They lurched forward, Jeannie's sneaker-clad feet slippery on the rock, Matthew barely able to support himself with her dubious assistance. The moon chose that endless time to be stubborn, hiding behind the only cloud in the inky black sky, and the wind whistled around them, whipping Jeannie's shirttails against her and teasing her teeth into a relentless chattering.

With a grimness that matched her reluctant neighbor's, Jeannie pushed onward, her muscles shivering and cramping beneath his weight, stumbling over the tufts of beach grass, her knees and ankles buckling. She'd spent most of her life wishing she were taller, but never more so than at that moment, when another few inches and another few pounds would have made her task so much easier. She could only hope that Connelly had the strength to make it; without his minimal help there'd be no way at all she could budge him.

The three wide steps leading to the front porch almost signaled their downfall. Matthew wavered, and for a moment Jeannie wondered whether she'd have to settle him down on the stairs for the rest of the night.

"C'mon, Connelly," she said briskly. "Don't give up on me now. If you made it this far you can make it to your bedroom."

"How the hell do you know?" The words were a thin thread of pain, but he kept moving, one foot after the other. "You sound like some...goddamned head nurse. Next...thing I know you'll be...asking, 'How are we today?'" They made it up the first step.

"Stop wasting your strength trying to insult me," she shot back. The second step was theirs, and then the third.

"I like insulting...you," he said hoarsely. "It keeps my mind off the pain."

Sudden sympathy flooded through Jeannie's encumbered body. "Does it hurt terribly?"

"Only when I laugh. Can you get the door?"

"You left it open." They lurched through, and for a moment they both leaned against the doorframe. "Where's your bedroom?"

"Second floor, of course."

"That's a ridiculous place to have a bedroom," Jeannie snapped. "Why didn't you take one of the downstairs rooms?"

"Because I don't believe in giving in to the pain."

"You're going to tonight."

"Wanna bet?" He pulled away from her to stand alone, and for a moment he swayed. "Thanks for your help, neighbor. Now go away."

"You're very welcome," she said sweetly. "I'll go away the moment I get you in bed."

"I should have known you'd have that on your mind," he grumbled, still in that echo of his rough voice. "Forget it, lady. I haven't the energy tonight."

"You know perfectly well my name is Jeannie. The longer you fight me the longer I'll be here. Which bedroom do you want to use?"

He swayed again, and she moved swiftly, sliding her arm around him and propping him up with the last vestiges of her strength. "Come on, Connelly. Stop being such a damned baby! Which room?"

His eyes closed, and she noticed in the dimly lit living room that his lashes were absurdly long and thick, wheat-colored like his hair. His face was the color of parchment, marred by shadows of pain. "Off the kitchen," he whispered.

He'd obviously been using it as a storage room. There was an extra easel, empty cardboard boxes littered the sagging double bed, and the entire room smelled of oil paint and turpentine and grease. She had to lean him up against the wall while she cleared off the bed, and her muscles screamed in pain as she lowered him down as carefully as she could.

"Pills," he whispered. "Get my damned pills."

"Yes, sir. Anything you say, sir. And where would I find your damned pills?" she snapped.

A ghost of a smile flitted over his weary features. "On the mantel, Big Nurse."

Jeannie opened her mouth to suggest he perform an anatomically impossible feat, and then shut it again, contenting herself with stomping loudly through the cottage, grabbing the pill bottle and heading back into the bedroom, pouring a glass of rusty-looking tap water on the way. She had to help him lift his head to swallow two of the huge pills, and when he fell back he lay there unmoving.

"Are you going to die on me, Connelly?" she inquired evenly.

He didn't bother to open his eyes. "Probably not," he

murmured. "And it wouldn't be on you, MacPherson. Unless you're planning on crawling into this bed and maneuvering me into indecent positions. I already told you I wasn't in any shape..."

"I get the message."

"No, you don't." He did open his eyes then, and Jeannie could see they were glazed with pain and something else, perhaps the beginning effects of the drug. "I've been telling you for the past week to leave me alone. I don't need you, I don't want you around...."

"You'd rather have spent the night out on those rocks?" she interrupted.

"I would have survived. I've survived worse," he said simply, and she believed him.

"Next time I'll leave you there."

"Next time you won't even know I've fallen," he corrected her, and his voice was beginning to slur. "You won't be prowling around like some damned voyeur, hovering over me like a chicken hawk...."

Jeannie laughed, the sound rusty and surprising in the dimly lit cottage. "And what do you see yourself as? A sitting duck?"

"Not a damned roast capon," he murmured sleepily, his eyelids drifting closed over his glazed gray eyes. She could see the pain leave his body as he relaxed into the power of the drug.

"More like a wild turkey," she murmured softly. "You want a hot compress, Connelly?"

"Leave my body alone, lady," he said on the breath of a sigh. "Go away." And he began to snore.

Jeannie stood there in the doorframe, watching him. "Connelly?" she whispered. "Matthew?" A little louder. "Hey, turkey." He only snored louder.

She moved forward into the room. The dim kerosene light

from the kitchen cast strange shadows over the room; the sound of the wind and the ocean outside was curiously depressing. *"Wuthering Heights,"* Jeannie murmured wryly, reaching out a tentative hand to touch Matthew's shoulder. "Damn!" The chambray shirt was wet and icy cold from the sea mist. There was no way she could leave him there in those freezing clothes; he'd have pneumonia by morning.

"Sorry, Connelly," she said under her breath, beginning to undo the buttons on the shirt. "But I'm going to have to have my wicked way with your body after all. I'm not going to have your death on my conscience." Yanking the shirt from his pants, she pushed it back over his chilled shoulders, trying to raise him high enough to slide it off. "Oof, you weigh a ton, Connelly. Did you know that?"

He continued to snore. "You wouldn't be pretending, would you?" she inquired, tossing the shirt on the floor and reaching down for his pants. She had to climb onto the sagging bed, but the addition of her weight didn't disturb him in the slightest. "No, you wouldn't," she added with a sigh. "I'm sure you wouldn't put up with these indignities if you could help it. I hate to think what you're going to say tomorrow."

Thank God he was wearing loose-fitting khakis and not jeans. Wet denim was one of the hardest things to peel off even a willing body. She worked quickly, efficiently, pulling the pants down over his narrow hips and long legs and tossing them on the floor beside the shirt. Then she sat back and looked at him.

"Well, well, Matthew," she murmured softly. "Who would have thunk it?" He was wearing tiger-striped jockey shorts, an absurdly fanciful choice for someone of his usually grim demeanor. But her own humor vanished when she saw the scar.

It ran up from the top of his thigh, underneath the shorts,

and ended up just under his hip. It was raw, red and nasty, and it was no wonder he'd been in pain.

"What in hell did you do to yourself?" she whispered. "A hernia? Appendicitis?"

He snored in answer, his breathing shallow, slow and drugged, and slowly Jeannie leaned forward. "You're going to kill me for this, Connelly," she said, and hooked a finger inside the jockey shorts to get a better look at his scar.

It was nasty indeed, but at least it hadn't left him a roast capon after all. That possibility had sped through her mind the moment she'd seen the scar, but it had traveled along the outside of his groin, leaving him intact. Quite spectacularly so, as a matter of fact. Forcing her mind back to medical matters, she turned her gaze back to the scar, sucking in her breath with sudden empathic pain.

It looked for all the world like a gunshot wound. Something large and nasty had torn into his groin, and Jeannie had read enough detective novels to jump to the obvious conclusion. "But who would have shot you?" she whispered, letting the shorts rest gently on the scar once more. "A jealous husband? More likely an angry neighbor."

Connelly only snored. Jeannie moved off the bed, careful not to waken him from what was the soundest sleep she'd ever encountered. She picked up the pill bottle, peering at it in the dark. "Well, no wonder, Connelly. These pills would knock out a horse. I don't blame you for not wanting to take them." She set them back on the table, looking down at him with sudden curiosity.

"God, Matthew, you're absolutely beautiful." It was an extremely uncomfortable revelation. When he'd been glowering at her, dressed in baggy clothes and stomping around, she hadn't had that much time to notice him as a man. But as he was lying there, dead to the world, she could look her fill, and it hit her with the force of a blow in the stomach.

He was without doubt the most gorgeous man she'd seen in years, maybe in her entire life.

She particularly liked his chest. It was smooth, strong, lightly tanned, with only a tiny dusting of golden hair. His shoulders were slightly on the bony side, his arms strong and muscled, his stomach flat above those absurd jockey shorts. His legs were long, lean, with the long corded muscles of a high jumper. Jeannie had always had a secret lusting for Dwight Stones, the rangy Olympic athlete, and the man lying in the bed had almost as nice a body. Maybe even nicer.

"This complicates matters, Matthew," she said wearily. A sudden exhaustion washed over her. It had been a long, long day, starting with the breakfast and dinner crowds at the inn, and ending with her race across the bluff and her struggle with getting Matthew's large, strong body back to the cottage and safely into bed. She swayed slightly, and her legs trembled with the accumulated strain.

Her house was almost half a mile away. Down one hill, across the sand, and up another hill in the dark, and she was too damned tired to go scrambling right now. There were at least two other bedrooms in the dark confines of Sunshine Cottage, but she didn't fancy stumbling around looking for them. Besides, the bed and its practically comatose occupant were undeniably inviting.

"Might as well be hung for a sheep as a lamb," she said, looking down at the glorious body with a sigh of lust. "And you're too drugged even to notice. I'll be home long before you wake." And moving around to the other side of the sagging iron bed, she stripped off her own damp jeans and sneakers and crawled into the bed beside him, wearing only the voluminous chamois shirt.

Connelly didn't even move. She flipped the covers up over them, burrowing down into the concave mattress, care-

ful not to touch the large, warm body next to hers. The dim
light of the kerosene lamp filtered into the darkened room,
and for a moment she considered getting up and putting it
out. But her body refused to move, utter weariness finally
taking command, and she shut her eyes with a blissful sigh.
There was no danger with the lamp, it would just burn itself
out. For now, all she wanted, all she needed, was a few
hours of uninterrupted sleep.

It would have been nice if she could have gotten it. She
woke with a start. The house was pitch-black; the lamp had
burned itself out, but it was still well before the first lightening streaks of dawn. She was lying pressed up against
Matthew Connelly's almost naked body, her chamois shirt
pulled way up above her waist, and his long arms were
around her, holding her against him, as his rough, calloused
hands cupped her breasts.

"Connelly," she whispered. His breathing was still shallow, drugged, and he didn't even move as she stiffened in
his arms. "Matthew," she said again, trying to move out of
the tight prison of his arms.

He shifted, but the arms stayed around her, holding her
against the furnace of his body. There was no way she could
break away without waking him up.

That wasn't something she was prepared to do. He was
going to be mad enough when he woke up tomorrow and
found she had undressed him. God only knew what his reaction would be if he knew she'd slept with him. It wasn't
something she had the energy to witness right now.

With a sigh she forced herself to relax against him. "You
and your stupid ideas," she whispered to herself. She should
have known better.

Who did she think she was kidding? She'd climbed into
Matthew's bed thinking it was a harmless way to get a decent night's sleep, but there was no way she was going to

get it. She could try to convince herself that it was simply the unaccustomed presence of a warm male body next to her, but it would be a waste of time. It wasn't any male body that aroused her, it was Matthew's. And it wasn't just his body. She was drawn to him, body and soul, when she knew she should have run in the opposite direction. He wasn't going to give her the commitment and babies that she needed, and she didn't want to settle for less. Although, feeling Matthew's heated skin against hers, she had to admit she was sorely tempted.

The hands that were cupping her small, soft breasts were moving. She could feel the nipples harden against him, and she groaned softly. If ever the man wanted revenge, he was getting it in full. She was lying there, more turned on than she'd ever been in her entire life, and the object of her desire was a drugged, bad-tempered man who hated her.

"For God's sake, Connelly," she pleaded in a desperate undertone. "Go back to sleep."

But the problem was that he was asleep. His hands were moving instinctively, with a cleverness that spoke of long practice. "Damn you, Matthew, don't do this to me," she whispered.

He snored softly, shifted and moved even closer. She could feel him, hard and massive against her bare hip.

"Oh, no, Matthew," she groaned miserably. Matthew only snored in response, his grip around her unbreakable. He was a damned strong man, even in a drugged stupor, Jeannie thought with despair. It was going to be a hell of a long night.

When she awoke again it was dawn. Sometime during the night Matthew had released her to roll over on his back, and his breathing sounded more normal. She had no idea when he had released her, but it had provided no release from the erotic dreams that plagued her. She looked down at his sleeping face, noting with surprise how very young he looked, and revised her estimate of his age downward. He couldn't be much more than forty, despite the lines around his eyes and his mouth, not and still have such a delicious body.

The face was fairly delicious, too, Jeannie thought sleepily. When he wasn't frowning at her, his mouth looked impossibly sexy, and those gray eyes of his had always attracted her. And what the hell was she doing lying in his bed when he could wake up at any moment?

He didn't move as she slipped out of the bed. Scooping her clothes up from the floor, she tiptoed out the door, through the kitchen and out onto the front porch before she put her jeans back on.

Dawn was streaking across the eastern sky in glorious shades of pink and purple and crimson, and not for the first time Jeannie felt a pang of grief that she had to leave this place. Gulls were wheeling around overhead, their raucous cries mocking her early-morning doubts. They knew what a fool she'd been, she thought, moving down the steps toward the sea.

The sea mist was light that morning. Her bare feet moved over the rocky path with sureness and speed. If she'd had her doubts before, now she finally knew better. She'd better keep her distance from her sexy neighbor if she knew what was good for her. Matthew Connelly, of the curious scar and grumpy nature, wasn't the answer to her problems. He might well be the cause of a great many more.

The sun was heading up above the horizon when she reached the small crescent of sandy beach. No bathing suit today, but at least Connelly was still lost in his drugged sleep, and he wouldn't be going anywhere today if his hip was still acting up. She ought to check on him, but that was the last thing she had planned. She'd have Ernie send someone out. The less she saw of Matthew Connelly the better.

The sea was icy cold against her nude body, and just what she needed to clear the cobwebs and doubts and lingering, lascivious longings from her besotted brain. She moved out with long, slicing strokes, reveling in the feel of the ocean around her. She made it to the spit of land with energy to spare, wheeled around and headed back, pacing herself. She saw him standing there on the beach, watching her, before she was halfway back.

She didn't slow her pace as she considered her alternatives. She could always turn around and head for the bluff, but there was a treacherous current, and she might very well end up in the Canary Islands. She could try and make it around the island to the harbor, some two miles, but her emergence from the sea in her birthday suit was a scene she didn't care to contemplate. She had her choice of one glowering, unsympathetic witness or the entire town. She chose Connelly.

The trick to it, she warned herself as she stood up and started walking the last few feet out of the ocean to her pile of clothes and the man towering over them, was to be relaxed. After all, it was just a body.

She strode casually, reached down and picked up the chamois shirt and pulled it around her wet, naked body. It hung to her knees, and it wasn't until she'd finished buttoning it up that she looked up into Matthew's face.

"I didn't know you were a voyeur," she said calmly.

"I figured I might as well return the compliment," he drawled, but that easy tone didn't fool her. Matthew Connelly was blisteringly angry. "Did you have a good night's sleep?"

Damn, she thought. *He knew.* "Of course," she managed breezily. "What about you?"

"I had nightmares," he snapped.

"You did not, Connelly. You slept like a baby." Not quite like a baby, she thought with a sudden blush, remembering the feel of his hardened body pressed up against her.

He was standing there, watching her, far too close for her peace of mind. He'd put on fresh clothes, jeans this time and a flannel shirt that he hadn't bothered to tuck in. She could no longer ignore the fact that she found him overwhelmingly attractive, glower and all. Especially when he was standing there, watching her out of those gray eyes that held a mixture of anger and something far more elemental. She wondered how much he remembered of last night.

He moved then, swiftly, gracefully, so fast that she couldn't avoid him. "You forgot to kiss me goodbye," he said, and pulled her into his arms, his mouth coming down on hers before she had a chance to duck.

One of his strong hands held the nape of her neck in a viselike grip, the other arm slid around her waist and pulled her up against him as he kissed her, a long, slow, erotic insult of a kiss. She'd opened her mouth to protest and he'd taken possession of it, with a deliberate, sexual kiss that brought her blood racing to her loins and flames of fury racing to her brain. His tongue explored her mouth with a casual completeness that left her unable to resist, unable to respond. All she could do was stand there in the prison of his arms and let him kiss her, and fight the overwhelming temptation to kiss him back. She ought to bite him; she ought to knee him in the groin. But then she remembered that aching scar, and she shuddered.

He released her immediately. The fury had gone from his face, leaving a cynical curiosity that was hardly more appealing. "So that's clearly not what you're interested in," he drawled, misinterpreting her shudder. "What is it you want from me, then, Jeannie MacPherson?"

"I just wanted to make sure you were all right...."

"I don't need a mother, I don't need a lover, and I don't need a friend," he snapped. "And I most certainly don't need a nosy neighbor. If I want to drop dead on the cliffs, that's up to me."

"The hell it is!" Her red-haired temper, usually held in firm control, snapped. "I don't give a damn if you want to litter this end of the island with your corpse. It's my end, too, and I don't want to have to stumble over dead bodies. So as long as you're here you're going to have to put up with my making sure you're still in one piece. If you want to drop dead with no interference, go someplace else."

"Are you finished?"

"No, I am not finished. If you just managed to be a little bit more pleasant, then I wouldn't have to skulk around checking on you. You'd have a lot more privacy and I'd have a lot more peace of mind. How's your hip?"

That last had been thrown in as an afterthought, and he blinked in sudden confusion. "What?"

"I said how's your hip? And who shot you? I'm assuming it was a gunshot wound."

"Checked that out, too, did you? You had a very busy night."

"Too busy," she shot back, when the sudden memory of those ridiculous jockey shorts crept back. A smile tugged at the corners of her mouth, and she tried in vain to banish it. "Tell me, Connelly, do you always wear underwear like that?"

If she'd hoped to stop him, she was bound to be disappointed. "Tell me, Jeannie, do you always sleep in nothing more than a chamois shirt?"

"You bastard," she hissed. "You weren't asleep at all."

"I was asleep. I just wasn't comatose. I tend to notice

when nubile young ladies climb into my bed, no matter how drugged I am.''

"I'm sure you have a lot of experience with such things."

"With nubile young ladies trying to take advantage of me?'' he echoed, and she could see the unexpected light of amusement in his eyes. "You overrate me, Jeannie. You're the first one who's seemed absolutely desperate. Maybe you've been on the island too long."

Enough was enough. "Connelly," she said in a low, dangerous voice, "buzz off."

"MacPherson," he replied in just as dangerous a voice, "I have already said the same thing to you far too many times. Leave me alone."

"This time," she said, "I will."

Chapter Six

He stood there and watched her leave, without moving a muscle. It was hard to stalk with dignity when one was a short, barefoot redhead wearing nothing more than a chamois shirt, but Jeannie MacPherson could manage it. She didn't look back, didn't hesitate, just marched up that rocky path like a haughty matriarch. Matthew watched her go with mingled irritation and appreciation.

She had nice, long legs for such a small person, he mused. And without any clothes on she hadn't looked at all like a boy. She had very definite breasts; he could still remember the feel of them from his drugged sleep. Nice hips, not too round but nice. And clearly her red hair was natural. She hadn't turned around, so he couldn't judge her butt, but he imagined it was just as cute as the rest of her. "Cute" was definitely not an adjective he tended to apply to ladies he was attracted to. She was definitely not his type, he told himself for the thousandth time. But that body was very nice, nonetheless.

Not that he could even begin to understand what went on in that dizzy brain of hers. He could have sworn she was attracted to him, that beneath that smothering, motherly concern was an elemental interest that had nothing to do with being a good neighbor. Or he had thought so, until he felt that shudder pass through her body.

Maybe she didn't like men. Maybe she'd moved to this island to get away from the craziness of modern city life, just as he had. Though he certainly didn't want to keep sex out of his life. He just wanted to keep it in its place.

Clearly Jeannie MacPherson was no Maine native. Just as clearly she was something more than a fill-in cook at the local inn.. He still wondered why she looked so familiar, why the sound of her name should ring a distant bell. He usually prided himself on his memory, on his ability to summon forth obscure facts from the back of his brain and put them all together to come up with a conclusion that could hold up in court. But not this time.

Jeannie MacPherson was a damnable mystery. Or maybe she was no mystery at all, maybe he was just imagining it because he wanted a case to solve. He needed to concentrate on his painting, not on his surprisingly desirable neighbor.

He must be getting better, he thought as he slowly climbed the path back up the cliff. Not just his hip, which had survived last night's setback with surprising ease. No, his misanthropic state of mind seemed to be improving. Slowly, surely, he was coming out of the fog of anger and disgust that had been plaguing him during the past six months.

The Springside Strangler had been enough to give even the most optimistic person a disgust of mankind, Matthew thought, limping across his front porch. He'd devoted the last two years of his life tracking him down, had lived, eaten, slept and breathed with his quarry. But George Kirwin was locked away forever. When the next one took his place, sooner or later he'd be caught, too. Matthew was finally remembering that not everyone was like that.

He turned around, moving to the edge of the porch to

look out over the ocean. He could see the dim blue outline of Monhegan Island in the distance, still misted in a light fog. The sun was just beginning to burn through the haze; the smell of the sea was fresh and clean and invigorating in the early morning. Suddenly Matthew smiled, for perhaps the first time in six months. It was going to be a glorious day. And maybe, just maybe, if his benevolent mood held, he might make it over to Jeannie MacPherson's rambling cottage and tender a very tentative apology. Not enough to encourage her, mind you. If he didn't watch it, she'd make a habit of shadowing his every footstep. But a little delayed neighborliness might not be too bad an idea. It sure was a shame she had red hair.

HER TEMPER CARRIED HER through most of the morning. By the time it tapered off she'd taken a shower, scrubbed her already spotless kitchen, baked six loaves of bread for the inn, finished painting the front parlor, and washed half the windows in her bedroom. Not a bad day's work, she thought, peering out her second-floor window to the crashing blue ocean. Matthew Connelly certainly had an energetic effect on her.

It wasn't until early afternoon that she stopped long enough to remember. That kiss had been beyond devastating. It had shattered her to the very essence of her soul, and once she allowed herself to dwell on it she couldn't get it out of her mind. Over and over again she replayed it in her mind, trying out different responses, different things she could have said, could have done. No matter how she tried to avoid it, she had to face the fact that what she'd most wanted to do was kiss him back.

"Damn the man anyway," she muttered, remembering his long, lean body clad only in those ridiculous jockey shorts. Why couldn't he look like Woody Allen instead of Harrison Ford?

It was a hot day, but there was enough of a sea breeze blowing across Jeannie's porch to make it comfortable. She made herself a thick cheese and butter sandwich with the fresh-baked bread, and a glass of iced tea, and settled herself in one of the old wicker chairs, determined to banish Matthew Connelly from her thoughts for at least an hour while she made it through another chapter of Ed McBain. Travis McGee was waiting up beside her bed, and she was impatient to get to him. Much as she loved the Eighty-seventh Precinct, she'd always had a weakness for ol' Trav.

"Ahoy there, Jeannie MacPherson," a voice broke through her abstraction, and she looked up, startled, to see Hal Vreeland's limpid blue eyes looking down at her. "It's too nice a day to sit on your porch reading," he said severely. "Why aren't you out lying in the sun?"

"Because I have red hair, remember? It's taken me weeks to build up even this much color, and it'll be weeks longer before I get a tan." She leaned back to look at him with a jaundiced eye. "What do you want, Hal? If you think you can talk me into cooking tonight or at any time in the next few days, you can forget it. I'm not scheduled till Tuesday and this is Sunday. Go find some other sucker."

"Jeannie, you wound me," he protested, looking like a very handsome sheepdog. "Would I try to take advantage of you?"

"Of course you would. You always try to take advantage of anyone you can. You especially like to try with me, because I'm such a difficult mark. You like the challenge. Well, forget it, Hal. I'm not in the mood."

"I didn't walk a mile and a half from the village to try to talk you into cooking, Jeannie," he said mildly enough.

"And no, I don't want to go out with you."

"That wasn't it, either. Not that the offer isn't always open, but actually there's a very nice guest..."

Jeannie grinned. "Karen and I noticed her. So if you haven't come for work or sex, what have you come for?"

"Matthew Connelly."

Jeannie's good humor fled. "You won't find him around here," she snapped.

"I know that. Karen calls him the Hermit of the East End. I just wondered how much you knew about him." He sounded merely curious, but Jeannie wasn't fooled. Something was going on; her intermittent instincts told her at least that.

"Not much," she admitted. "He's an artist. He paints, he goes for long walks and he hates people. That about sums it up. Why?"

"The police are looking for him."

"What?" It came out as a shriek. "You're kidding!"

Hal shrugged, perching on the white spindled railing that surrounded the porch. "Apparently not. It's been unofficial so far—just a few friendly inquiries to Enoch about new passengers on his ferry run. He didn't tell them a thing, of course. You know Enoch; ever since his nephew Jamie was arrested for stealing cars he hasn't trusted the police. He can't get it through his thick old Down East skull that Jamie is as sleazy as they come."

"So who was asking? Do you know?"

Hal shrugged. "I think the locals. May have been the state police, too, I'm not sure. I just wondered whether you noticed anything. You've seen more of him than the rest of us. Do you think we've got a dangerous character in our midst?"

There was the gunshot wound, of course. There was his almost pathological need for privacy, besides. There was his refusal to say anything about his past, present or future.

There was also his completely normal sister Sally, with her open friendliness and her two children. "I haven't seen anything suspicious," Jeannie lied promptly, not knowing why she did it. "If he is wanted by the police I'd be willing to bet you it's something minor enough. Maybe five hundred traffic tickets or dodging the draft. We haven't got a criminal in our backyard."

Hal looked doubtful. "I'll take your word for it. I asked Ernie, but he said Enoch was probably making it all up. You know the two of them never got along."

"Enoch doesn't get along with anyone. He and Connelly would make a good pair."

"As long as it's not you and Connelly," Hal said morosely.

"I beg your pardon?" Jeannie stared up at him in amazement. Hal had never struck her as particularly observant. What was he doing noticing something she'd refused to recognize herself?

He shook his head. "Never mind. Just being paranoid, I suppose. You know, I could tell my lovely lady guest to find someone else if you felt like changing your mind. We could go out on the yacht and have a quiet dinner. Open the hatch and look at the stars."

"Hal, if we opened the hatch to look at the stars we'd have to be lying in the front cabin. I know the layout of the inn's yacht very well, and I'm not in the mood for it."

"You haven't been in the mood for the two years you've been here."

"What can I say, Hal?" She smiled up at his tall, ridiculously handsome form. "It's just a shame you're so ugly and unpersonable. If you were just a little taller and a little more charming..."

"Witch," he said genially, ruffling her dark red hair. "I won't give up. Fifty years from now I'll still be waiting, alone and lonely on my island, waiting for a lady with a heart of ice cream.''

Jeannie laughed. ''You'll be ninety-three, Hal. Beyond worrying about the condition of anyone's heart but your own.'' She rose, stretching luxuriously, and Hal rose beside her, towering over her with his six-foot, three-inch frame. She always felt like such a shrimp beside him. At least Matthew was just the right height. Tall enough to be interesting, but not too tall. ''Enoch going in tomorrow?'' she asked in a deceptively bland tone.

''He always does. Mondays and Thursdays, regular as clockwork. Why, are you thinking of going to the mainland? Don't forget I'm counting on you for Tuesday morning. If you don't come back I may lose half my guests.''

''I was thinking of just a day trip. I have some shopping to do, a little business to take care of. I'll come back with him on the afternoon run.''

Hal nodded. ''Sounds as if it will do you good. You haven't been off-island in months.''

''Yeah, I thought so,'' Jeannie said brightly.

''And that way you can check with the police yourself,'' he said with that shrewdness she could never quite accustom herself to.

She grinned. ''Maybe. I thought I'd telephone his sister first. No need to go jumping to conclusions when it's so easy to find out what's going on.''

''You're smart,'' Hal said, ''and you're gorgeous. Why can't you be on the make, too?''

Oh, God, Jeannie wailed inwardly. *I am, I am, but not for you.* ''Tell Enoch he's got a passenger tomorrow,'' she said instead. ''And take the bread I baked. It'll save me a trip in.''

''Bless your heart, Jeannie. I wish to God Doris could bake.''

"She does everything else well, Hal. Don't be greedy." She opened her book pointedly. "The bread's in the kitchen. Leave me the half loaf."

"I'm dismissed, eh?" He paused long enough to look down at her, and she could see the sudden worry in his eyes. "You'll take care of yourself, Jeannie?"

"Why shouldn't I?"

"I don't like the idea of your being alone out here with someone who might be a dangerous criminal. Why don't you come back to the inn with me until you talk to his sister? We've got plenty of rooms." He grinned ruefully. "I'll even let you have one to yourself if you insist."

"Hal, I'm fine. Matthew Connelly wouldn't hurt a fly. He's just a bad-tempered hermit; he's certainly no hardened criminal. Trust me. If I had any doubts I'd go with you."

"I don't suppose I have any choice in the matter," he grumbled. "You're sure you'll be okay?"

"I'm sure." She watched him go, out of calm, blue eyes, finally turning back to Ed McBain.

It was half an hour before she started looking over her shoulder every few minutes. It was an hour and a half before she went in search of a flashlight and some sort of club she could use to protect herself. It was two and a half hours before she went inside and locked all the doors and windows. Not for one moment did she consider going to check on her neighbor to make sure he was safely bedded down for the night.

It was another night of disturbed sleep, full of dreams in which Matthew Connelly performed deliciously erotic acts upon her body before turning into Ed McBain's latest bloodthirsty killer. She woke up several times, bad-tempered and full of all sorts of frustrations she refused to name. She woke up for good at dawn, grumpy, wide-eyed and ashamed of the previous day's nerves.

"He's harmless," she said firmly, sitting up in bed and staring around the neat, pretty confines of her bedroom overlooking the ocean. "Completely, perfectly harmless. I don't need to call his sister, I don't need to go to the mainland, I know there's no problem." She nodded a couple of times, threw back the covers and headed for the bathroom. Enoch's boat, the *Morning Star*, left at six-thirty sharp every Monday and Thursday morning for the two-and-a-half-hour trip to the mainland. And he waited for no one.

IT WAS ONE of her favorite times on the island: six o'clock in the morning, with no one around but the lobstermen heading out to haul and the gulls wheeling and cawing overhead, the mist rolling in off the ocean, and the salt smell of rockweed and fish and clear, clean water made for a heavenly state of bliss. It was half the reason she did breakfasts for Hal three times a week. She certainly didn't need the money, not with Tom and Jeannie's Ice Cream sending her huge checks every month. But she liked the break in her daily routine, and she liked having a reason for walking across the island at six in the morning.

When she'd first come to Muscatoon she'd tried lobstering with Enoch's brother-in-law—just once—and it was the hardest work she'd ever done in a life filled with hard work. It had been an unending nightmare of pulling up the heavy traps that were weighted with ballast and, they hoped, several pounds of lobster, pulling out the lobsters and less-welcome captives, spearing the herring in the bait bag with the bait hook to rebait the trap, and tossing it back overboard. Then she had to measure and peg the lobsters so they wouldn't lose their claws while they thrashed about, desperate to escape, and Jeannie had tears running down her cheeks, freezing them to ice as the endless day wore on.

She hadn't eaten lobster for her entire first year on Muscatoon.

She could thank the summer guests for her current occupation. Muscatoon had a fair-sized summer community, mostly artists and writers, with a few university professors thrown in. Jeannie had immediately made friends with a cookbook editor and her husband, and had spent the past two years testing recipes for such exotic cuisines as Peruvian, East Afghanistani and Laplandish. She'd had to make do without llama, camel or reindeer meat, but she'd done surprisingly well. Every weekend from October through May she had dinner parties for everyone from Enoch and his brother-in-law, to Ernie at the store, to Karen and her teenage son, to some of Hal's more congenial guests. It had given Jeannie a constructive outlet while she decided what she was going to do with her life.

She'd miss the cooking. Sooner or later she was going to have to go back to Tom and Jeannie's and face her responsibilities. Besides, she still had a sneaking fondness for ice cream. That was one of the first things she had planned, once they landed in Bellingham. She'd had a craving for Heath Bar Crunch for the last three weeks, and she was going to satisfy that craving. Right after she talked with Sally Riccetti.

The *Morning Star* was lying at anchor in the small harbor. She could see Enoch's grizzled form moving with silent deftness on the deck, shifting boxes, his yellow slicker a bright splash of color in the monochromatic mist. She probably should have brought her own foul-weather gear, but she knew far too well how quickly the sun would burn off the haze. She had settled for a skirt, the first she'd worn in months, a silk shirt and the cotton sweater Karen had knitted for her last winter. She'd even been able to unearth a pair of panty hose from the back of her underwear drawer. She felt positively sophisticated, and she greeted Enoch with her customary good cheer.

He peered at her from beneath his beetled brow. "You look some fancy, Jeannie," he grumbled. "You turning your back on island ways?"

She laughed. "I'm in disguise as a thirty-three-year-old woman, Enoch. Are you going to let me on board, or do I have to go back and get my jeans and sneakers?"

He seemed to consider it for a long moment. "You can come on board. I didn't say you weren't a fair treat for the eyes. Besides, you can keep m'other passenger company."

"Other passenger?" she echoed curiously.

"Me." Matthew Connelly was directly behind her, and his voice was its usual laconic drawl. "Any objections?"

That blew her chance of pumping Enoch about the questioning police, she thought. How in the world had he managed to come up close to her so silently when he had such a limp? Though he didn't appear to be limping much at all as he moved past her to the boat. He paused at the gangplank, looking back at her, and he raised an eyebrow in inquiry. "You coming?"

Well, she clearly had no choice in the matter. She'd simply have to force herself. There was only the slightest bounce in her step as she followed him, only the slightest lilt in her voice as she answered him. "I'm coming."

Chapter Seven

"Watcher step, Jeannie," Enoch grumbled as she practically skipped aboard the lumbering old *Morning Star*. "Those shoes are worthless on a boat. I thought you had more sense than that, girlie. High heels on a boat...." He wandered off, muttering under his breath, to cast off, and Jeannie had no choice but to face her fellow passenger. The last time they met had not been under very promising circumstances. She'd been wearing nothing more than a shirt, and he'd been murderously angry. *Wrong choice of words, Jeannie,* she warned herself, eyeing him warily. He certainly didn't look like a criminal.

He also didn't look quite as threatening as usual. "Affable" would be going too far, but at least he didn't look as if he was going to bite her head off. And he hadn't moved away from her. He just stood there, leaning against the bulkhead of the unprepossessing little cabin, watching her out of those distant gray eyes of his, waiting.

Waiting for what, she wondered uneasily. *Was he going to toss her overboard once Enoch got going?* She decided it was more than time to break the silence that was unnerving her. "The seating arrangements on board are nothing to write home about. Enoch believes the cargo deserves more comfort than the passengers. But I forgot, you came out to

Muscatoon on the *Star*. You must have already dealt with the shortcomings.''

''Ain't no shortcomings,'' Enoch growled from the front of the boat. ''If you don't like the transportation you can swim, missy.''

''I love the transportation, Enoch,'' she replied, smiling over her shoulder at him. ''I just wasn't sure whether Matthew was tough enough to take it.''

''Oh, he's tough enough,'' Enoch muttered obscurely. ''You can count on that.''

Before Jeannie could follow up on that, he started the noisy old engine, drowning out any response she could have made. She turned back to Matthew, bracing one hand against the railing as the old tub pulled away from the dock. ''Are you tough enough, Matthew?''

He still hadn't moved. ''Who am I to argue with Enoch?'' he said. ''He seems a fair judge of character.''

''Enoch?'' Jeannie echoed in surprise. ''He hates everybody. He thinks all human beings are rotten.''

Matthew Connelly actually smiled at her. A cynical smile, to be sure, but a smile nonetheless, that deepened the grooves beside his sexy mouth and even lit his usually cold eyes. ''As I said, a good judge of character.''

At that moment the *Star* lurched, and Jeannie's moderately high heels collapsed underneath her ankles, tossing her against the bulkhead. She managed to miss Matthew, but not by much, and the strong hand that caught her elbow was warm and slightly calloused and capable of bringing back a host of unwanted memories. He'd cupped her neck with that hand, holding her still while he kissed her. Even through her ridiculous panic of the night before that memory, the tactile feel of his mouth on hers haunted her.

She righted herself with a shaky laugh, and his hand fell away instantly. ''Enoch's right. These are no shoes for a boat. Are you going to throw me overboard?'' *Damn,* she thought. *Why did I give in to temptation and ask him that?*

If she had hoped to startle him, she failed. ''Not with a witness.''

''Oh, Enoch wouldn't mind. One less interefering female, one less summer complaint wintering over.''

''Summer complaint?''

''You and me, buddy. Any non-Maine person coming to spend summers on the coast. Spending winters makes a visitor even less welcome. Fair warning if you're planning to stay long.''

''I'm not.''

That ended that topic of conversation, she thought dismally. ''You want to call a truce again?'' she inquired.

''That depends.''

''Depends on what?'' she asked suspiciously.

''On whether there's coffee in that huge bag you're carrying.''

''It's in a sealed thermos bottle. You must have a remarkable sense of smell,'' she said.

''Just good powers of observation. The bag's far too heavy to hold just the usual paraphernalia.''

''No sexist remarks...'' she warned.

''Did I make one?'' he inquired innocently. ''Any muffins?''

''Doughnuts. I thought I might bribe Enoch into being a decent human being.''

Matthew glanced over in the old man's direction, and Jeannie found herself gazing dreamily at his strong profile, which was far too appealing. He turned back, shaking his head. ''Nope, don't bother. He's too far gone.''

''What about you? Are you too far gone to be a decent human being?'' Why should his answer matter so much to her, she wondered. But it did.

Matthew considered it, and then he smiled again, that

tentative, wary smile that still held a trace of cynicism. "We'll have to see, won't we?"

She didn't hold out much hope. There were times when she was afraid he was farther gone than old Enoch, who, as far as she knew, had never broken a law in his sour life, had never been wanted by the police. But then, she didn't know that Matthew Connelly had actually broken a law, either. She shrugged. One more time, she thought wearily. No one ever said Jeannie MacPherson was a quitter. "I guess we will. Hope springs eternal." She threaded her way among the boxes and barrels to the lopsided bench in the lee of the cabin and dumped her bag down beside her.

Despite her warning to Matthew, she did carry an astonishing assortment of stuff in the tote bag that doubled as a purse. Cultch, the locals called it. Any weird assortment of flotsam and jetsam that might have some possible future use. There was a thermos of coffee, two Styrofoam cups, a package of homemade doughnuts, a Swiss army knife, an Ace bandage for the sprained ankle she was courting with those damnable shoes, a pair of ballet slippers, two scarves, three packages of tissues, a bag of ancient makeup, three combs with teeth missing, a dog brush, lollipops for any stray children she ran into, aspirin, tranquilizers, antacids, cystitis medicine, allergy medicine, three paperback murder mysteries, every credit card known to man, an extra pair of panty hose, a sewing kit, and a thousand other things that had since dissolved into lint at the bottom. "I had some cream and sugar in here somewhere," she muttered, scrabbling around.

"That's all right. I drink it black." To her complete amazement he dropped down beside her, seemingly at ease in her presence for the first time since he'd come to Muscatoon Island. His long legs were encased in tan corduroys, and he was wearing a flannel shirt and ragg sweater against the early-morning chill, and he looked warm and solid to

Jeannie's starved eyes. She quickly turned her attention back to the coffee.

"So what are you going to the mainland for?" she asked, then could have bitten her tongue. As always, she'd been too inquisitive, and she waited for him to snap her head off again.

But he only smiled lazily, accepting the coffee. "None of your business," he said pleasantly. "You have to be the nosiest woman I have ever met in my entire life, and I've met a lot of nosy women."

"Then why are you sitting here with me?"

"Because you make great coffee." He leaned back against the bulkhead, stretching his legs out in front of him. "Why are you going to the mainland?"

Now it was Jeannie's turn to feel uncomfortable. She could feel a blush rise to her face, a light blush that always signaled the advent of a lie. Fortunately, Matthew didn't know that. Though he did seem to be looking at her out of uncommonly observant eyes.

"Oh, I just had a few things to do," she said artlessly. "Some shopping, some phone calls to make." She dropped her gaze to her own cup of coffee. "I guess I just needed to get off-island for a change. I haven't left in months."

If he didn't believe her he didn't say so, but she could feel his skepticism as if it were a tangible thing. "Enoch says you're the nun of Muscatoon Island," he said after a moment. "While everyone else spends the off-season bedhopping you remain supremely chaste. Why?"

"Enoch isn't usually so loquacious. What in the world made him wax so elegant?"

"I asked him about you. I couldn't figure out why you were shadowing my every move."

Jeannie laughed. "You asked him that? Gossip on Muscatoon is going to take a fascinating turn the next few weeks. People are already wondering about the Hermit of the East End. Now they'll think we're having an illicit affair out there, and my reputation will be ruined. Though I hadn't realized I was considered so nunlike.''

"The Reverend Mother of Muscatoon Island. So what made you become so determinedly celibate?''

"This is a hell of a conversation for six forty-five in the morning,'' she complained.

"You don't seem to have any qualms interfering in my life,'' Matthew drawled. "I just thought I'd return the favor.''

She looked up at him. She was never the sort who needed much secrecy about her life. She had an unfortunate habit of confiding all sorts of things to complete strangers, which wasn't that awful, unless it was other people's secrets she was artlessly confiding. But for the first time in her life she didn't feel like making her life an open book for the cynical stranger sitting beside her. Knowledge was power, and he already had far too much power over her, just by his mere physical presence.

On the other hand, if she were completely, artlessly open, he might very well relax enough to tell her something about what he was doing there. Enough to set her mind at ease, to know he wasn't a master criminal or dope dealer, enough to know that he wasn't about to dash himself to death on the rocks below Sunshine Cottage or blow his brains out if his painting wasn't going quite right.

"What's going on in that devious mind of yours, Sister Jeannie?'' Matthew murmured. "Trying to avoid answering?''

She flushed again. "You're too observant.''

"I would say the same thing about you,'' he murmured. "Those blue eyes of yours look right to the center of a man's soul.''

She turned to stare at him in complete astonishment, but his gaze was fixed on the blue-gray swell of the sea as the ferry plowed onward through the chop. "What was the question?" she said finally.

He grinned. "Short attention span, eh? I asked you what made you run away from sex."

"I haven't run away from sex, as you so crudely put it. I'm just hard to please."

"Are you waiting for true love?" The cynicism was back in full force, and Jeannie wanted to shake him.

"Don't you think it exists?"

"No." It was short and unequivocal, with no room for argument.

Jeannie didn't bother trying to change his mind, not right then. "Well, I do," she said calmly. "I need to feel more than simple sexual attraction when I jump into bed with someone. I need to feel a connection, a pull, a possibility of..." Her voice trailed off as he turned to look at her, and those distant gray eyes were unreadable.

"Why'd you jump in bed with me?"

There was a loud crash behind them, as Enoch dropped the carton he was shifting. His grizzled old face was wreathed in astonishment, and there was no doubt he had heard Matthew's words. And there was no doubt Matthew had known he was in hearing distance.

With deceptive calm Jeannie waited, her attention on the old man. Enoch stalled as long as he could, settling the box in place with all the care of Leonardo placing the perfect finishing brush stroke. Then he lit his pipe, an act that required a large amount of time and deliberation. Jeannie still watched him, her blue eyes unclouded, and finally he had no choice but to head back to the bow of the boat, grumbling all the way.

She turned back to the unrepentant Matthew. "Pig," she said calmly. "The nun of Muscatoon Island has now fallen from grace."

"You didn't answer my question. I know it wasn't unrequited lust, nor was it your mythical feeling of connection.''

"How do you know?"

"Because of the way you shuddered on the beach when I kissed you. That wasn't the reaction of a woman overcome with lust.''

Jeannie screwed the top on the empty thermos, her movements deliberate. "Not that we can claim a long relationship, but have I ever struck you as a woman overcome by lust?''

"No," he admitted. "More's the pity."

"What?" Her shriek brought Enoch's attention back to them, and she watched with sudden despair as he hefted another box and started back in their direction. The *Morning Star* was not noted for its privacy.

"Ignore that," Matthew ordered. "It was instinctive."

"It must have been. If I'm so observant I could see through a man's soul, I couldn't have missed that," she said wryly. It was taking Enoch a blessed long time to reach them. "I climbed into bed with you because I was exhausted and I didn't feel like wandering over the cliffs in the darkness. I wasn't planning to take advantage of your innocence, I was just planning to rest up. For God's sake, I left before you woke up.''

"So you did." Enoch was in earshot again, and Jeannie gave Matthew a warning look, one he blithely ignored. "So if you're not interested in me sexually what do you want from me?''

Enoch stopped dead still, his rheumy old eyes avid. The Reverend Mother of Muscatoon Island drew herself up, a difficult task when one was sitting on a ramshackle bench on a pitching and rolling mail boat. "I didn't say I wasn't interested in you sexually," she said in dulcet tones.

Enoch dropped his pipe. "I'm just not interested in all

the strange things you suggested we do,'' she continued blithely.

Enoch started to choke. Jeannie bestowed her best, nun-like smile on him. "These off-islanders," she said sweetly. "They have the strangest notions of courting."

It was too much for poor Enoch. Muttering under his breath, he shuffled back to the bow of the boat, and Jeannie turned that serene smile back to her tormentor. "Now your reputation's in shreds, too."

If she had hoped to disturb him, she had failed utterly. His answering smile was without cynicism, and it reached those stormy gray eyes of his, warming them. "I won't underestimate you again."

"It would be unwise to do so," she murmured. "So why are you going to the mainland?" She waited to see whether that closed look would come over his face again, but apparently the truce was well and truly called.

He laughed. "Would you believe I'm traveling two and a half hours for ice cream?"

She stared at him as if he'd gone mad. "I beg your pardon?"

Matthew shrugged. "What can I say? I have a craving for Heath Bar Crunch. Muscatoon is full of wonderful things, fresh fish and lobsters, sea air and seclusion. Frozen foods from the mainland are not part of its many charms."

"Heath Bar Crunch?" Jeannie echoed weakly.

He looked down at her in surprise. "It's simply the best ice cream in the world. Don't you like ice cream?"

"Oh, yes, I like ice cream," she said.

"Then you must have tried Tom and..." His voice trailed off, and the sudden astonishment in his face took years off his age. "My God, that's why you look so familiar. I've seen your face on the top of ice-cream cartons." His voice was accusing, and she nodded.

"Guilty as charged." But why did she feel so guilty, she wondered. What was he looking so angry about?

"What are you doing on Muscatoon Island, Jeannie of Tom and Jeannie's?" he demanded. "And where's Tom?"

"I've retired. Tom's running the company in Vermont, living very happily with his wife and two babies," she said in a tranquil tone of voice. "What's it to you?"

The tension seemed to vanish from his wiry shoulders. "You aren't married to him?"

He couldn't be jealous, she told herself. He didn't even like her, much less give a damn whether she had a husband stashed away someplace. Still, it was an enticing thought. "Never have been married to him," she replied. "Never will be. Why?"

If she hoped to elicit some emotion, some reaction from him, she was doomed. That blank expression shuttered down over his face, and he leaned back against the bulkhead and shut his eyes. "Just curious," he said blandly. "You know what curiosity is, don't you, Jeannie?"

She liked the way he said her name. "Yes, I know what curiosity is," she replied. "Are you taking a nap?"

"Yup. Any objections?"

She smiled sweetly. "None at all. I'll wake you when we get to Bellingham."

"Do that." And he shut his eyes.

She stared at him for a long moment. The chop had settled down, so that the *Morning Star* was moving through the waters at a reasonably decorous pace. She was tired herself. Her last two nights' sleep had been crammed full of the man dozing peacefully beside her. They had another hour to go. Maybe if she closed her own eyes, it might just be possible to catch a few minutes' sleep....

Chapter Eight

"I believe we're here." The soft breath was tickling her ear, blowing into it gently. Her hair ruffled around her. It was a nice voice, she thought dreamily, and it went well with the strong, warm chest beneath her cheek. Strength and warmth, that was what she needed. She snuggled closer.

"Jeannie?" The voice was pitched low, and the slight raspy sound of it echoed beguilingly in her sleepy mind. She wanted to wrap herself around that voice, pull it over her like a thick, warm quilt, burrow beneath it and hug it to herself. If she'd had the energy she would have preened against the strong, hard hand that was gently brushing her hair away from her face, but she didn't want to move. Only the slight rocking of the boat was enough, lulling her ever deeper into security....

"Wake up, missy!" Enoch bellowed from directly in front of her, and she jerked awake, slamming her head against the chin beside her, pulling away before she could even assimilate where she'd been. Nestled against Matthew Connelly's chest, letting him stroke the side of her face and listening to his deep, soothing voice. Damn.

"Have a good nap?" Matthew inquired politely as she moved away.

"You must enjoy putting me at a disadvantage," she

grumbled, never at her best when she first woke up. "You've smiled more today than I've ever seen you do."

"I don't think I've been putting you at a disadvantage. After all, I didn't offer my shoulder for you to sleep on. You took it," he pointed out. "By the way, who's Frank?"

"Frank?" she echoed blankly.

"You murmured his name in your sleep. Maybe your saintly reputation is undeserved." His voice was smooth, unconcerned, but she could sense the curiosity beneath it.

"I don't know any Frank..." she began, and then remembered her dream as she'd nestled against her nemesis. "Oh, Frank Furillo."

"Frank Furillo? Who's he?"

"Who's he?" She was outraged. "Where have you been living, on a desert island? Frank Furillo is the police captain on 'Hill Street Blues' and one of the sexiest men in the world."

"I don't think he's my type," Matthew said, but the light of humor had left his gray eyes, and he rose abruptly, turning away from her. "See you later."

Jeannie watched him move away, her mouth open in astonishment. He was barely limping, and he moved quickly, as if eager to get away from her. As doubtless he was.

"You'd better be back here by four-fifteen, unless you're planning to stay till Thursday. Tide and Enoch wait for no man," she called after him. If he heard he made no sign, but bounded off the side of the boat with surprising ease, considering the state of his body.

She didn't need to be considering the state of his body, she reminded herself, pulling her belongings together. Enoch was watching her out of his beady little eyes, and she looked up defiantly.

"Don't say a word," she warned him.

"Wouldn't think of it," he said mildly. "But you might want a bit of friendly advice."

Here it comes, she thought grimly. "No, I don't."

He continued, undaunted. "You'd best watch your step with that man. He's not your usual sort, missy. You'd best keep clear of him."

"But—"

"We had a good long talk before you showed up this morning. There's no harm in the man, but he needs to be left alone. He doesn't need the likes of you bustling around him."

If anyone understood the needs of a hermit, it was a misanthrope like Enoch. "Do you trust him, Enoch?"

"Ayuh, I do."

"Are the police really looking for him?" Enoch might very well not answer, but she had to try.

He considered it for a moment. "Seem to be," he agreed. "I told him as much, and he didn't seem surprised."

A shiver ran across Jeannie's backbone. "Did he tell you what they wanted him for?"

"Nope. But then, I didn't ask. I'm not nosy." It was clear from the tone of his voice who *was* nosy. "Leave the man alone, missy. Everyone's entitled to some peace and privacy."

She squinted her eyes, looking out over the busy morning wharf. Matthew Connelly had already disappeared from sight. "I suppose so," she said dispiritedly.

"And I won't wait a moment longer for you, neither," he announced, stomping away. "So be back on time, missy, or you'll be sleeping on the dock."

"Aye, aye, cap'n," she said. She headed out after Matthew Connelly.

Bellingham was a busy little coastal town with the usual mix of odd Maine bedfellows. Fish-packing plants and art

galleries, boat works and boutiques, foundries and little the-
ater groups abounded. Matthew would have no difficulty
finding Tom and Jeannie's Ice Cream in the trendier parts
of town. If he stayed down among the working man's docks
instead of the yacht marina, he'd have to settle for something a little more prosaic.

Jeannie had no intention of staying in the working part
of town. Her first task was to find a telephone and talk with
Sally Riccetti. Once she'd set her mind at ease, she planned
to spend at least a respectable portion of the large check
that came monthly from Vermont. She still wasn't quite sure
what she wanted to spend it on, but she counted on having
inspiration strike as she wandered around the deliberately
quaint streets in the Old Town section of Bellingham.

It was not her most successful day. They landed in Bellingham just after nine. She found a public telephone in no
time at all, but from then on everything was downhill. Every
half hour she called the number information had given her,
and every half hour she heard the phone ring endlessly at
the other end of the line. She went from mild irritation to
anxiety to a state of advanced obsession, and she was completely unable to concentrate on spending any of her lovely
money in between the vain attempts at calling. She wandered through the fish market, the boutiques, the cooking
stores and art galleries with her mind firmly fixed on the
unanswered telephone of Sally Riccetti and the enigma of
Matthew Connelly. Only the bookstore was enough to rouse
her from her torpor.

They were reissuing some of the old Dorothy L. Sayers
mysteries, and Jeannie was in the mood for Lord Peter's
charm. Ed McBain, bless his heart, had a new hardcover
Eighty-seventh Precinct, and there was a promising raft of
new writers out since Jeannie's last mainland visit. It was
quarter to four when Jeannie finally left the bookstore,

loaded down with enough reading material to get her through the next month, if she rationed herself carefully.

Quarter to four, she thought. She'd just have enough time to try Sally Riccetti's number one more time before she was due back at the wharf. Enoch's bark was far worse than his bite, and in the best of times he'd have waited for her, but Matthew complicated matters. An old misogynist like Enoch wouldn't like having a witness if he waited for her as he had on other occasions. Jeannie had little doubt that if she were late, this time he'd be long gone.

She had long ago given up expecting an answer to the infuriating double ring, and the breathless female voice that said "Yeah?" took her aback.

"Sally?" The books spilled out of her bags, landing on her feet, and she swore lightly, ignoring them.

"Not here," the voice answered unhelpfully.

"Uh...could you tell me where I could get in touch with her?" Jeannie tried to kick the hardcovers away from the puddle of water beneath the phone.

"Nope."

Jeannie's temper snapped. "Listen, I've been trying to get in touch with Sally all day. This happens to be a matter of life and death," she lied. "You have to tell me where I can find her."

"Life and death, eh?" The voice was still patently unhelpful. "Who's dying?"

Jeannie didn't hesitate. "Her brother Matthew."

"Didn't know she had a brother."

Jeannie willed herself to be patient. The teenage voice at the other end of the line wouldn't respond well to being screamed at. "She does," she said with deceptive calm. "Do you suppose you could tell me how to get a message to her?"

"Oh, you can give it to me." There was a snapping at

the other end of the line, one that Jeannie belatedly recognized as chewing gum. "She'll check in with me sooner or later."

"And who are you?" Jeannie inquired sweetly, clenching her fists.

"Mary O'Sullivan. I'm feeding the cats for them while they're away."

Cats, Jeannie thought. *They can't be heinous criminals if they have cats.* "Where have they gone to, Mary?" she inquired in a soft tone designed to lull the girl.

"Camping."

"Camping?" Jeannie shrieked.

"In the Rocky Mountains. They flew out a couple of days ago and won't be back for three weeks. Mrs. Riccetti said she might check in sometime next week, but she wasn't certain." Suddenly Mary was a fountain of information. "You want me to tell her that her brother's dying?"

"No," Jeannie said with a sigh. "Just tell her Jeannie MacPherson called and...Never mind." She looked down at her watch. Ten past four, but the *Morning Star* was in sight at the crowded wharf. "Never mind," she said again.

"But what about her brother?" Mary O'Sullivan was getting positively loquacious.

"He'll just have to fend for himself. 'Bye." She slammed down the phone and whirled around to grab her books when she found herself looking directly up into Matthew Connelly's stormy gray eyes.

She could feel the bright red of guilt and embarrassment flood her face, and she stared up at him wordlessly, searching through her brain for some sort of excuse.

"Tide and Enoch wait for no man," he reminded her in a mild enough voice. "He sent me to look for you. Better hurry."

It took her a moment to gather the tumbled books, and

then she was running along the docks after his long-legged stride, her high-heeled shoes precarious beneath her. As she trailed him, her arms filled with books, she consoled herself with the probability that he had heard nothing damning on her side of the conversation. How could he know whom she was calling? He couldn't have been standing there that long; she had always been acutely aware of his presence.

He made it back to the *Morning Star* well ahead of her, and he was helping Enoch cast off when she jumped aboard, the books dropping at her feet as she tripped. Enoch didn't even look up as he headed out into the bay, and it was up to Matthew to help her gather up her reading material."

"*Murder in Bed*?" he read, then picked up another. "*Murder in the Tropics*? Is this recreation or research?" He piled them back into her arms, and his face was unreadable in the early-afternoon light.

"Recreation." She was still breathless from her chase across the docks. If only there was some way she could tell whether he knew she'd been vainly trying to check up on him. If he really was a hardened criminal, and if he knew she'd been her usual nosy self, she might be in very deep trouble. "Did you find your ice cream?"

There was a hint of something in those distant gray eyes that might just possibly be amusement. "Heath Bar Crunch," he said. "As Enoch would say, finest kind."

"I always liked Rocky Road the best."

"Did you, now? I would have thought you'd go for Heavenly Hash—given your saintlike tendencies," he drawled.

"And I would have thought you'd go for Dastardly Mash," she shot back.

The lines around his eyes crinkled in sudden amusement. "Why?"

The color flooded her face again, but this time Enoch or fate came to the rescue. The *Morning Star* hit a rough patch of water and she lost her balance, tumbling back against the bulkhead, the books landing at her feet once more.

"For God's sake, get below," Enoch bellowed. "Can't have a fool woman falling all over the place when the day's stormy."

"Stormy?" Jeannie echoed in a tiny squeak, looking around her in sudden panic. The bright day had darkened ominously, with threatening clouds scudding overhead.

"Ayuh. It'll be a rough ride home." Enoch came close to a ghoulish smile at that point, and Jeannie let out a low moan.

"Maybe I'll stay on shore."

"And maybe you'll go below and get out of the way, missy," Enoch said. "I'm not turning around at this point. I won't drown you. It'll take more than a little squall like the one we're heading into to get the better of old Enoch."

"Squall?" she shrieked. The wind had already picked up, whipping her russet hair against her pale face, and the boat was slicing through the waves like a lumbering elephant.

"Do you get seasick?" Matthew's husky voice had a curious mixture of dread and sympathy.

"No, I have a cast-iron stomach," she said, pulling herself together as she once more gathered her battered books. "I'll just go below and wait it out." She made her exit with commendable dignity.

Enoch's cabin was a mess of boxes, crates, piles of lobster traps, herring nets, coils of rope, smelly foul-weather gear and assorted flotsam and jetsam. Except, thought Jeannie, that flotsam and jetsam were the debris left floating after a boat sank. With a low moan she crossed the cabin, dumping her books in a pile, and sank down beside them, burying her head in her arms as she felt the sturdy old boat lumber through the ever-increasing waves.

It was dark in the cabin, and getting darker. The boat was

pitching wildly in the waves, and overhead Jeannie heard the crack of thunder.

"I'm not going to drown, I'm not going to drown," she muttered under her breath. "Enoch's a great sailor; he's not going to let us drown." Her voice sounded hollow, forlorn and lost, in the empty cabin.

It was only going to get worse. The boat was pitching wildly, boxes were sliding back and forth, and Jeannie peered through the murky gloom for the doubtful solace of a life preserver. Enoch probably didn't believe in such things, she thought gloomily. The wind was howling like a banshee around the small cabin, the rocking and rolling of the boat tossed her against the bulkhead, and she wrapped her arms around her shivering body in a vain attempt at comfort.

"I'm not going to drown, I'm not going to drown," she muttered. "Oh, the hell with it, of course I'm going to drown. Enoch's going to crash off Moosehead Point and we'll all be lost at sea."

The slamming open of the cabin door broke through the howl of the storm, and Jeannie raised her head from the cradle of her arms. Matthew was standing there, huge, wet, filling the cabin with his solid presence.

"Are we about to abandon ship?" she managed to ask in a low croak.

He shut the door and the storm behind him, moving toward her with surprising balance across the heaving floor until he stood directly in front of her, towering over her like a monolith. He was large and strong and reassuring in the stormlit cabin, and she watched with mournful eyes as he shrugged out of the bright yellow rain gear and dropped down on the floor beside her.

"Not immediately," he said. "Enoch told me I was getting in the way and told me to distract you. Are you sure you don't get seasick?''

She could feel his body warmth through the sweatered shoulder beside her, smell the fresh scent of rain on his skin. The boat lurched again, throwing her against him, and a small moan escaped her.

"Positive," she said through clenched teeth. "I never get seasick."

"Then what's your problem?"

She leaned back against the bulkhead and shut her eyes. "My problem, Matthew Connelly, is that I'm scared spitless."

His immediate response was a disbelieving snort. "You're not afraid of anything, MacPherson. Don't give me that."

She opened her eyes and managed to glare at him through the shadows. He was close, and warm and solid, and suddenly she wasn't nearly as frightened. But that was an illusion, she reminded herself sharply. She was in a lot more danger from Matthew Connelly than she was from the vagaries of the sea. "I'm afraid of storms," she said through chattering teeth, "and rickety old boats sailed by grumpy old sailors, and I'm afraid of the ocean."

"You swim in it every day."

"Then I'm in control. Just me and the elements, with nothing as unreliable as a boat in between."

"Then why do you live on an island?"

It was a reasonable enough question, and Jeannie paused long enough to consider it. "Because I like the isolation. I also happen to be the only person on Muscatoon without even so much as a dinghy. I get in a boat only out of sheer necessity."

"And what was the necessity today? Something to do

with your phone call?'' His voice was silky smooth in all its harshness, and all Jeannie's nerve endings came alive.

"I had to spend my dividend checks."

"On books?"

"On books," she agreed defiantly. "What else would you expect?"

"Oh, some sexy lingerie, maybe."

"Not for the nun of Muscatoon Island. I only wear chaste cotton next to my skin, and...oooh." Her voice trailed off in a wail of panic as the boat chugged up a wave, hovered there for a breathless moment, and then dove downward at a sickening pace.

She shut her eyes in horror, convinced that death was imminent, when strong hands caught her arms, and she felt her small body hauled unceremoniously onto his lap. Instead of struggling, she clutched the thick wool of his ragg sweater, leaning against him with a shuddering sigh of relief as his arms came around her, holding her close.

"You're sure you don't get seasick?" His voice rumbled beneath her ear.

"I won't throw up on you, Connelly," she said in a quiet voice.

"I guess I'll have to trust you." His arm left its comforting circle as his hand reached up to cup her chin. "Maybe I can manage to distract you."

Her eyes met his in sudden dazed wonder, blue eyes into gray, and she watched him wordlessly, as that usually grim, unsmiling mouth reached down to capture hers.

Chapter Nine

He tasted of the ocean, the cold wet wind and the lingering taste of brandy. He tasted of warmth and strength and a haven from the storm, and a temptation far too overwhelming to resist. It was a tentative kiss at first, his lips hard on her soft, surprised ones, and as she felt the strands of seduction wrap tight around her she quickly batted free, pulling away from him the few inches his deceptively relaxed grip would let her.

"What are you doing?" she demanded in an inane, breathy voice.

He grinned. "If you don't know I must not be doing it right. It's called kissing. Let me try it again." Before she could duck his mouth caught hers once more, and there was nothing tentative about it. She opened her lips beneath his, and he took immediate possession, his tongue hot, rough-textured and demanding. He kissed her thoroughly, deeply, nibbling on her lower lip, teasing her tongue, filling her mouth with a passionate desire that shook her to the depths of her soul.

For a moment she forgot everything, forgot her doubts, her better judgment, her sense of self-preservation, and she twined her arms around his neck to kiss him back.

She was lost in the wonder of his mouth. In the dimness

of the rocking cabin there was only the scent of his skin, the feel of his mouth, and the warm, wet, seeking pleasure of the mouth on hers. She wanted to get closer, closer to him; she wanted to climb inside his skin and kiss him from the inside out; she wanted to rip off her clothes and climb on top of him, to blot out the storm and her fears and her doubts and her loneliness that she never admitted existed. She wanted nothing but Matthew Connelly, and the demanding mouth on hers, the strong hands that were threading underneath her sweater to slide up her hot skin told her that he wanted her, too.

His hands were cool on her skin, cool and calloused and deft as they unclasped the bra she didn't really need and caught the small, firm peak of her breast. She moaned into his mouth, moving closer, and she could feel his arousal beneath her, hard and strong and powerful enough to melt the last ounce of common sense left her. The erotic suggestion of his tongue in her mouth, the hands on her breasts, the strong, hot power of his body beneath her were the only reality she knew, and a distant part of her brain recognized that fact and deplored it.

But it was too distant to do any good. His hand slid down the smooth, warm skin of her stomach to the waistband of her skirt, and his long fingers were fumbling with the button clasp when the stormswept boat lurched violently, flinging them both against the wall.

His grip never left her, his body cushioned the blow, but it was just enough to knock some sense into her addled brain. She wrenched her mouth away from his, pulled her arms down to push against his shoulders. It was a useless effort; he allowed her six inches of space and no more, and in the dimly lit cabin there was only the sound of their heavy breathing, rapid, staggered, and she felt her fingers begin to curl around his shoulders.

"Are you out of your mind?" Her voice came out in a husky whisper, barely audible over the rush of wind and the slap of waves against the old wooden boat, but his reply wasn't much louder.

"I suppose so." The hand that was gripping her elbow slid up to gently brush her cheek, and she just sat there in his lap, not jerking away as she knew she should, not leaning into him as she knew she wanted to. "I can't say much for your sanity, either," he added in a husky murmur.

"What did you think you were doing? And don't say 'kissing' again," she snapped, her voice shaky in the aftermath of a passion that was still more of a reality than a memory.

"I thought it would be a little harmless distraction. After all, there wasn't much we could do with Enoch stomping around keeping the elements at bay."

"Wasn't there?" Her skin still tingled with the feel of his cool hands on her flesh, and the feel of his arousal was still strong beneath her. "I don't think this was a good idea."

"I suppose not," he replied, unconcerned, but she could hear a sudden thread of pain through his voice, and belatedly she remembered his hip.

"You idiot, you're in pain," she said, concern and frustration snapping what was left of her temper.

"Yes." His hands were still an effective restraint, albeit a gentle one.

"Then let me get off you. Your hip must be killing you."

"Lady," he drawled, "it's not my hip. And right now I can do with all the discomfort I can get. Stay put."

She was struggling ineffectually, trying to scramble off his lap, and his fingers tightened painfully for a moment. "I said stay put," he growled. "The nun of Muscatoon Island is safe from the sex-crazed hermit."

She did stop struggling, knowing full well that the more she squirmed the more she'd hurt him. "I know that."

"For the time being," he added, and the devilish grin that lit his usually dour face penetrated the twilit gloom of the storm-darkened cabin. "We can finish this in more comfortable surroundings."

She sat unmoving. "Do you want to finish it?" Her voice was quiet in the sudden stillness.

He leaned back against the rough wooden wall; she heard him sigh. "I want to. But I expect I'll think better of it once we're on dry land."

She didn't know whether to be relieved, infuriated or hurt. Relief was the logical reaction, and it was the one emotion she could rule out. She sat there for a long moment, staring at him in the murky light. She opened her mouth to tell Matthew Connelly what he could do once he got on dry land, when the door to the cabin opened, and Enoch stood there, peering down at them from under his beetled brows.

"So that's what you've been doing while I've been up here saving your worthless hides," he grumbled. "I should have known. Damned flatlanders."

Surprise had loosened Matthew's grip, and Jeannie bounded out of his arms, staggering slightly as she got to her feet but none the worse for the last tumultuous hour. "Look at it this way, Enoch. We had enough faith in your seamanship to think of other things." She reached down to gather her books and her long-discarded high heels, being very careful not to look at Matthew's still-lounging figure. "And we were right, of course. You brought us safely home."

"In record time," he said grumpily. "With the wind behind us, it pushed us right along."

Jeannie paused beside him long enough to raise herself up on tiptoes to kiss his salty cheek. "Thanks, cap'n."

"Get along with you," he snarled, not the slightest bit softened by her futile attempt at gratitude.

"That's what I love about you, Enoch," she said with a grin. "You're so consistent." And she headed out of the cabin, her feet more stable on the rocking deck without shoes.

Matthew looked up from his spot on the floor. "You're a wonder, Enoch," he said, pulling himself to his feet with a faint grimace of pain.

"Why? Because I brought you through a squall? Any sailor worth his salt could do it," Enoch grumbled.

"No. Because you can resist Jeannie MacPherson. It's more than I seem to be able to do." With a wondering shake of his head, he followed Jeannie out of the darkened cabin, with the sound of Enoch's disbelieving snort trailing him.

The squall that had taken ten years off Jeannie's life had passed over the island, leaving it wet and shining in its wake, smelling of fresh rain and late spring and a thousand other things, all sensuous and distracting. The crowds of early-season tourists were just beginning to head toward the ferry, and Jeannie passed them with a vague smile on her face, loaded down with her books and her shoes, her stockinged feet moving along the rough roadway toward the hotel with a mindless determination. It took all her strength of will not to turn around to see whether Matthew was following her.

The wide veranda of the Muscatoon Inn looked deserted at first glance. Jeannie dumped the heavy armload of books on the bottom step and climbed upward, grimacing at the shredded stockings on her feet. She should have known better than to dress up. Life on a Maine island was not conducive to high heels and stockings.

Hal was lounging at the far end, deep in conversation with

a willowy blonde of indeterminate years, and Jeannie paused there long enough to admire the picture he made.

There was no question about it, Hal Vreeland was an astonishingly attractive man. His golden-blond hair was lit by the late-afternoon sun, the perfect preppy clothes set off his tall, tanned body, and his handsome face with its rugged, devil-may-care smile was having its predictable effect on the woman beside him. He was much, much better-looking than Matthew Connelly. So why couldn't she even summon up a quarter of the interest in him? Hal couldn't even begin to make her blood race, her heart pound, her pulses leap. He left her completely unmoved. The only man she wanted was Matthew Connelly.

"You look like you lost your best friend." Karen's voice broke through her abstraction, and Jeannie looked up with a wry grin.

"Not especially. I was just trying to decide whether to give in to Hal," she admitted, grabbing the wicker rocking chair beside her friend. They were at opposite ends of the porch, and Hal wasn't even aware of their presence.

Karen leaned back in the chair, eyeing Jeannie dispassionately. "Well, from a performance aspect I can recommend him highly. He was very good two years ago, and he's had a lot more practice in the ensuing years. From an emotional standpoint it might not be such a good idea. But then, your emotions aren't involved, are they?"

Jeannie flushed with guilt. "I'm sorry, Karen. I forgot— yours are."

Karen shrugged. "I'm used to it, Jeannie. Hal Vreeland doesn't spend the night alone if he can help it, and I've watched women come and go. After all, I was only a five-night stand between his second and third marriages. I think he's even forgotten it ever happened."

Jeannie looked from Karen's tanned, pretty face, with the

graceful lines of thirty-eight years of living only enhancing the fine blue eyes, and then turned to eye Hal's boyish charm. "I don't think he's forgotten," she said.

"Why do you say that?"

"He's kept strictly away from you ever since the last wife left. What was her name—Madge? She wasn't around long enough to make much of an impression." Jeannie yawned. "Hal goes after every single woman on the island, and you're one of the best-looking ones here. Yet he's very careful to keep you at arm's distance. Why?"

"Because he's only interested in conquests, not repeats?" Karen offered.

"Nope. He has plenty of reruns, and you know it. What happened after those blissful five days?" She was being impossibly nosy, and she knew it, but Karen seemed in the mood to confide, and Jeannie was by nature overwhelmingly curious.

Karen sighed, and the wry smile on her pale mouth did nothing to obscure the sorrow in her eyes. "He told me he valued me more as a friend than a lover."

"Tactful."

"Not very. As a matter of fact, Hal was surprisingly inept around me. Oh, not in bed. I doubt Hal Vreeland could be inept in bed. But he always seemed to be saying the wrong thing. The first night was more of an accident than anything else. We were working late, we'd both been drinking too much and lamenting our failed marriages, and it just sort of happened. For the next four nights he told me it wasn't going to happen again, and then he'd show up at my place around midnight and spend the night. Until he said it was no good for both of us."

"And that time he didn't change his mind?"

Karen laughed, a short, bitter laugh. "He didn't have the chance. He left for the mainland that day and when he returned two months later he brought the forgettable Madge with him. Except that her name was Midge.''

"Like a black fly," Jeannie grumbled. "So don't you think it's interesting that he's never come on to you again? He does with Blanche Marten every summer when she arrives.''

"Are you suggesting he's still carrying a grand passion for me these last few years? It's a lovely thought, but I doubt it. I imagine he meant what he said, that I'm a lot more use to him out of bed than in it.''

"I guess I won't take him up on his offer after all. It was a dumb idea," Jeannie said in a morose tone of voice.

"For God's sake, Jeannie, don't change your mind on my account. It's past history. As long as you aren't expecting love forever after, go right ahead. I have no claim on him.''

"You have a claim on me," Jeannie said quietly. "We're friends; I'm not about to do anything that will hurt you if I can help it.''

"Sleeping with Hal Vreeland will only hurt me if it hurts you. If it gets something out of your system, be my guest. But are you sure it's Hal you want to be with?''

"Meaning what?''

"Meaning, aren't you using him as a surrogate for your brooding artist?''

A reluctant grin lit Jeannie's pale face. "Guilty. Rotten to the core, in fact. The problem is, I don't trust him.''

Karen hesitated for a moment. "You're probably right not to. I promised I wouldn't repeat this, but the hell with it. The police were out here today, looking for your Mr. Connelly.''

Jeannie knew a sudden sinking feeling in the pit of her stomach, one that was getting far too familiar. "What did they want with him?''

"They wouldn't tell me. They talked with Hal, with me

and with Ernie down at the store. I don't know what they told the others, but they left me with a very uncomfortable feeling. I think you'd be far safer with Hal than with someone like Matthew Connelly. I don't even like you alone on that end of the island with him.''

Jeannie sat there for a moment longer. "This is completely ridiculous,'' she said finally, jumping out of her chair. "Here I've been skulking around, imagining all sorts of things. I'm going to do something incredibly obvious.''

"What?''

"Ask him. Ask him why the police want him, ask him what he's doing on Muscatoon Island, ask him how he got a gunshot wound in the groin.''

"What?'' Karen shrieked.

"You're getting redundant,'' Jeannie said. "I'm simply going to confront him and find out what the hell is going on.''

"And what if he's a major criminal? What if he's a dangerous murderer, drug dealer or something? Once you let him know you suspect him, you'd be putting yourself in danger. Why don't you just wait? I told the police that he'd gone to the mainland. They left on the afternoon ferry, and they won't be back any sooner than the Thursday ferry, if they come at all. Why don't you wait till then? Let them confront him? Or talk to them yourself? You could be putting yourself in danger if he's wanted by the police.''

"And I could clear up a simple misunderstanding instead of worrying for the next few days. I'm doing it, Karen. Who knows, he might be a crusading reporter with crucial testimony in some big murder case.''

"Sounds nice, Jeannie. It also sounds like you've been reading too many mysteries. You sure you want to do this?'' The worry was unmistakable in Karen's voice, but Jeannie was undaunted.

"I'm sure." She headed across the wide pine porch, pausing by the steps for a moment. Hal was still lost in his current seduction, and Jeannie looked back to Karen's solitary figure. "You know where to send the body, don't you?"

"Jeannie!" Karen shrieked. "You damned well better check in with me tomorrow and let me know what he said. Or I'll show up at your doorstep at the most inconvenient time I can think of."

"I'll let you know tomorrow morning. I'm cooking breakfast, and it looks as if 'mine host' is going to be sleeping in." She nodded toward Hal's preoccupied figure.

"Looks like," Karen agreed. "You'll be careful, Jeannie? Don't ask him if it looks like you'll get the wrong sort of answer. Promise me? If it seems dangerous, leave it up to the professionals."

"I promise. Besides, I'm looking forward to meeting real live detectives."

"I don't know if they're detectives, I only know that they're cops. And Frank Furillo they're not. Nor Dirty Harry."

"Who is?" Jeannie said philosophically.

"Matthew Connelly?" Karen suggested.

"Don't I wish?" Jeannie sighed. "Don't I just wish?"

Chapter Ten

He'd stood there for far too long, watching her move across the packed dirt roadway leading toward the Muscatoon Inn. He should have known better, he told himself wearily. Jeannie MacPherson was nothing but trouble, and if he hadn't known it before, this day should have proved it to him.

Still, she did have a delicious walk. Delicious when she was wobbling around on tottery high heels that made her at least a respectable height. Even more enticing in her stockinged feet, as she was now, her arms laden down with books and her shoes and her overstuffed purse. He'd never liked short women, but there was something about her, with that compact, boyish figure that was anything but boyish to the touch, that made him forget that she wasn't his type at all.

Which was his forty-second mistake of the day. His forty-third was standing there, mooning after her, so that he almost didn't notice the telltale figures heading down from the small café that provided early-morning coffee and late-afternoon mug-ups to lobstermen and tourists alike. Some errant whim of a formerly unkind fate caught his attention, and the unmistakable walk of two of Chicago's finest alerted him long before they looked in his direction. When they did, he was gone, into the cloudy afternoon sunshine.

She'd gone to the inn, he thought as he climbed the front

steps of his cottage. Probably to see that jerk Vreeland. Not that Hal Vreeland actually was a jerk, Matthew thought fairly. He seemed like a decent enough sort. As long as he kept his hands off Jeannie MacPherson.

Was he out of his mind? What the hell right did he have to be jealous when he was doing everything he could to keep the woman at arm's length? Hal Vreeland would be just the ticket, the right sort of preppy prince to distract Jeannie from her headlong pursuit of him. He should do everything in his power to matchmake. So why was rage gnawing at his gut at the memory of her slender back disappearing toward the inn?

There was no room in his life for an ice-cream lady. Never had two people been more mismatched, and every ounce of his being told him so. Well, not every ounce. There were scattered patches that kept denying the inevitable. Like the part of his brain that kept remembering that clear, astonishingly warm look in those incredible blue eyes of hers. Like his mouth, that could feel only too well the softness of her lips beneath his. Like the current ache in his groin that had nothing to do with the four-month-old bullet wound.

He could try and walk it off. The long walks by the cliffs were strengthening his hip, soothing his mind, calming his soul. They ought to do wonders for the current uproar in his libido. Why hadn't he listened to reason and left her the hell alone in that dark little cabin?

But he knew very well why he hadn't. No matter what his common sense told him, he found her completely irresistible. In the best of times he could fight it, but that frightened look on her usually indomitable face proved his undoing, and it had almost proved hers as well.

For all that she was clearly attracted to him, he wasn't what she wanted or needed. If ever a woman looked ready to fall in love and settle down, Jeannie MacPherson did. She looked ready to love, honor and cherish at the drop of a hat, and Matthew couldn't rid himself of the uneasy suspicion that he was a likely candidate. Nor the even worse suspicion that made that ridiculous idea inexplicably attractive. Some weird, demented part of his brain could see him with Jeannie MacPherson by his side, a baby in her arms.

It must be a mid-life crisis, he thought in disgust as he headed out onto the cliffs. Brain damage, but he could walk it off. And he could keep his mind a perfect blank, not thinking about the house that shared this lonely spit of land and the woman who'd be sleeping there, alone in her bed. Or even worse, who wouldn't be there at all, but at the Muscatoon Inn.

"Damnation," he swore, but the swirling wind carried the sound off into the misty afternoon, swallowing it up in the rush of the ocean. With a grim expression, Matthew strode onward, ignoring the ache in his hip.

"Matthew?" Jeannie stood at the open door, peering into the darkened interior of the inaptly named Sunshine Cottage. She'd stopped off at her house just long enough to drop her parcels and change into an old pair of jeans and a loose sweater, all the time itching for the confrontation that had been too long in coming. What a complete and utter fool she had been, not to come right out and simply ask him.

Granted, Matthew Connelly could be somewhat intimidating, but Jeannie MacPherson was not the sort to be intimidated. The sooner she tracked down her reluctant neighbor and forced some answers out of him, the better.

"Matthew?" she called again, pitching her voice a little louder. Still no answer from the silent cottage. It was getting on toward dinnertime, and the evening mist was growing heavier. For a moment Jeannie allowed herself to experiment with worry, like checking a sore tooth to see if it still ached. Was Matthew fallen on the rocks somewhere again, lying in agony, unable to move? There was no answering twinge, no sudden upsurge of panic. No, this time she'd go with her instincts. Matthew was perfectly safe, perfectly fine. He just wasn't there.

There would be no way she could find him in the mist. Indeed, the wisest thing she could do would be to head homeward, now, before the fog got too thick to see. She knew her way along the cliffs and beaches very well, even in pea-soup fog, but it was silly to tempt fate, with the late-afternoon sun setting rapidly behind her. She turned to leave, when something in the shabby living room caught her eye through the ripped screen door that let in more than its share of black flies.

Sometime during the last few days he'd set up his easel in the living room. And mounted on that easel was a canvas, its braced back to Jeannie.

"Don't you dare, Jeannie MacPherson," she said out loud, her voice quiet and determined in the stillness. "The man's entitled to some privacy. You turn around and head homeward. If he wanted you to see his paintings he'd show them to you."

But her feet remained glued to the splintered deck, and all her good intentions were melting fast in the face of her overwhelming curiosity. She reached for the door knob, let her hand drop back to her side, and then reached again. Without another moment's hesitation she walked into the silent cottage, directly over to the easel.

She stared at it in shock. It was a landscape, one that might just possibly resemble the spit of land where Matthew had been painting during the last week. It was also the worst thing she'd ever seen in her entire life, the work of someone who had clearly never held a paintbrush before in his life and who ought to be forcibly restrained from doing so in the future. She was so astonished she just stood there, staring, not even hearing the sound of uneven footsteps on the front porch.

"Enjoying yourself?" Matthew's gruff voice came from a few feet away. "I didn't realize you were an art lover."

Jeannie jumped, guilt and sudden nervousness flushing, then paling, her face. "I didn't hear you coming."

"Obviously. What are you doing here?"

Jeannie looked at the dreadful painting for a moment, then back to Matthew's dark, still face. *You're crazy,* she told herself. *This man is clearly here under false pretenses, he's wanted by the police, and you think you can just come right out and ask him? You're out of your mind.*

Matthew moved closer. His limp was almost imperceptible, and the glint in his eye looked nothing short of dangerous. Was it dangerous for her safety, or merely her current state of chastity?

"You didn't answer my question."

Here goes nothing, Jeannie thought. She raised her head, meeting his stony gaze with deceptive boldness. "I had a few questions of my own." Her voice came out slightly hoarse.

"Did you now? Ask away," he said with mock generosity. "Would you like a drink?"

"No. At least, not until you answer my questions."

"I didn't say I'd answer them. I just said you could ask them," he pointed out. "And I need a drink." He walked past her into the kitchen, and she trailed after him, determined not to lose her nerve.

"Why are you here?" she asked as he pulled a dark beer from the gas refrigerator.

He shot her a glance from those distant gray eyes of his before he took a deep swig of beer. She watched as he let it travel down his throat with a flash of absent longing. Longing for a beer, or longing for him, she wondered, knowing the answer.

"I'm here to paint," he said, leaning against the ancient porcelain sink. "And to recover from surgery. But you know that already."

She plowed onward valiantly. "What do you do for a living?"

"Would you believe I'm a painter?"

"Not after seeing your landscape."

"I didn't think so." He sighed, taking another long drink of the beer.

"So what do you do?" she persisted.

"Oh, this and that."

"Is that a gunshot wound on your hip?"

He was suddenly very still, and she could feel the tension radiate through the low-ceilinged kitchen. "It's in my groin," he corrected flatly. "Yes, it's a gunshot wound." He offered no more information.

Not that she expected it. Getting anything out of him was like pulling teeth. "Are you wanted by the police?"

It must have been a trick of the foggy, early-evening light. He hadn't lit any kerosene lamps yet, and the light was diffused and eerie in the room. The look on Matthew Connelly's usually wary face seemed curiously akin to amusement.

"What makes you ask that?" he parried.

"They've been looking for you."

He shrugged. "Then I can't very well deny it."

Jeannie let out a small gasp of dismay. "Who's been looking for you?"

"Oh, I rather think I'm wanted in several states," he said blandly.

"What for?"

He smiled, a sinister smile, she thought dazedly. "None of your damned business, Jeannie MacPherson."

He was still leaning against the sink, completely at ease, and Jeannie stared at him for a long, distracted moment. Never had he looked more attractive. The chambray shirt he was wearing was open halfway down his chest, and the dampness of the fog clung to his sandy-colored hair, his eyebrows, his cheeks, his mouth. His long legs were stretched out in front of him, his arms crossed on his chest, one long-fingered hand cradling the dark beer as he watched her, that peculiar amusement now unmistakable in his face. She stared at him, knowing the danger was out in the open now, knowing that he was even more trouble than she had first suspected, and knowing that it wasn't going to help. She was drawn to him, irresistibly, uncontrollably drawn to him, and it didn't make the slightest bit of difference to her if he was a felon on the run. She still wanted him with a longing that was new and frightening to her.

So frightening that she whirled around. "See you," she said breathlessly, over her shoulder, as she headed for the door.

The hand that clamped down on her arm was strong, unshakable, yet surprisingly gentle for all its immovable force. She came to an abrupt stop as he pulled her around to face him. "Are you going to turn me in?" he questioned lightly.

It was even darker in the living room, and she could hear the rushing sound of the waves on the beach below them. The sound, the smell of the sea mixed with her sudden panic, entwining with it, and she stared up at him wordlessly for a moment. She knew without question that she wasn't afraid of violence from him. Not that he was a man incapable of violence; clearly his life had had more than a run-in with it. But that violence wouldn't be directed at her.

"I don't know," she said, wetting her lips nervously.

He didn't release her, and she could feel the slight knead-ing pressure of his long fingers on the tender flesh of her upper arm. The pressure was driving her senses into an up-roar. "But you're going to run away." It was a statement, not a question, but she felt obliged to answer anyway.

"It seems wisest."

"Would you have run if I'd given you a different an-swer?" The question was almost casual, but his hand still kneaded her arm, gently, sensuously, and she could feel her body drifting toward his, pulled by some magnetic force as mysterious and ungovernable as the tides.

"Probably." It came out as a whisper. Her mouth was inches from his, and her hand had come up to rest lightly against his chest, her fingertips softly caressing the soft faded cotton and the firm, warm flesh beneath it.

"Should I let you go?" His words came out on the breath of a sigh, and he was warm and strong and so very near.

"Yes," she whispered, and raised her mouth to his, no longer able to fight it.

He wrapped her in his arms, pulling her into the haven of his body, and she went gladly, mindlessly, sinking against him with a sigh of pure delight. There was no question that this was dangerous and very wrong, no question that she was a fool. And no question that it no longer mattered. She kissed him, reaching up to him, and it was long and slow and deep, and finished the last shreds of common sense left to her. His tongue was hot and rough and wet in her mouth, bold and demanding, allowing her no pretensions. She couldn't be kissed like that, return a kiss like that, and still pretend they weren't headed directly for bed.

Darkness closed about them in the tumbledown cottage—thick, soft, enveloping. There was only the sound of their labored breathing, the rustle of clothing, the distant rush of the ocean. For all the disparity in their heights, Jeannie felt her body match his contours perfectly, softness to hardness, strength to gentleness, his heat warming a chill that had seemed to reach to her very soul. She could feel the hardness of his arousal against her body, the rapid pounding of his heart in counterpoint to hers, the tension in the strongly muscled arms that held her prisoner. He finally broke off the kiss, moving his mouth a fraction of an inch away, and she could feel those gray eyes of his staring down at her in the murky darkness.

"This is crazy." The words were flat, his tone ragged.

"Yes."

"I should never have started this on the boat today."

"Yes."

He continued to look down at her, and the silence filled the room. "You should go home right now. Before this gets any more complicated."

"Yes."

His mouth brushed hers, softly, tantalizingly, and she could taste the regret and longing that mingled with hers.

"Will you go upstairs with me?"

"Yes."

The one flight of stairs in Sunshine Cottage was narrow and rickety. The bedroom at the top was lit by the last trace of the late-setting June sun, filtered through the thick sea mist, and a white curtain fluttered in the soft breeze. There was an iron double bed against the wall, almost the twin of her own, with an old patchwork quilt across it. She stopped just inside the threshold, as Matthew came up behind her, and again she reveled in the feel of solidity and strength his tall body radiated, the sense of power and security. A feeling totally false, she realized. She was about to go to bed with only the second man in her thirty-three years, and he was an admitted felon. And she didn't even care.

"Second thoughts?" The question was almost casual in his husky voice.

She turned then, looking up at him quite fearlessly out of her blue, blue eyes. "No," she said.

The smile that lit his face was a revelation, lighting his winter-gray eyes, banishing the grim lines of anger and pain that usually bracketed his mouth. "I wish I could say you won't regret this," he murmured, pulling her back into his arms, "but you probably will."

"Yes," she said.

A faint tremor of laughter and something more basic ran through his body. "Is that all you ever say?" he whispered against her russet-colored hair. "Yes, no. What happened to that motor mouth of yours?"

"You're the one with the motor mouth, Connelly," she murmured against the heavy thudding of his heartbeat. "Why don't you just shut up and take me to bed?"

"I thought you were taking me to bed," he said lazily.

Before she could open her mouth to protest she felt her body swung abruptly up into his arms. He crossed the room in two strides, dropping her down on the bed and following her down, covering her small body with his.

"But your hip..." she began.

"Let me worry about my hip," he whispered in her ear. "You'll have enough on your mind." His mouth caught hers before she could protest, and she gave herself up to the wonder of it, ignoring her last worry. Then there was no more room for thought, only sensation.

First there was his body, covering hers, heavy denim pressing against her, and then it was hot, smooth skin to skin, with mouth, hands, limbs touching, caressing, entwined, enmeshed, with the heavy old quilt beneath her on the sagging bed and his warm, strong body on top of her, around her, within her, invading, conquering, giving, releasing, with his sweat-slippery shoulders beneath her clutching hands as she began suddenly, helplessly, to convulse around him, and her nails dug into his flesh, and her voice was sobbing, sobbing.

He was with her, the force of his thrusts pounding her into the bed, and the ancient springs creaked in protest, a protest they both ignored as she reached for him, with her arms, her hips, her heart and soul, dissolving against him in a damp tangle of arms and limbs and love.

Slowly, slowly reality returned. The uneven rise and fall of his breathing, the distant sound of the surf, the cool dampness of the night fog coming in the open window, filtered into her consciousness. She had just made love with a man she scarcely knew, wasn't even sure if she liked. A man wanted by the police, with more secrets than a man had a right to. And she didn't have a single regret.

He murmured something unintelligible in her ear, something lazy and sexy, loving and definitely complimentary. She smiled in the darkness, too exhausted to respond more enthusiastically. A moment later she was asleep, still trapped in the shelter of his body.

Chapter Eleven

It was cold in the upstairs bedroom of Sunshine Cottage, and Jeannie nestled closer to the big, warm body next to hers, seeking some morsel of body heat. Dawn was just filtering into the room, sending gray tendrils of light into the corners, and she lay there, trying to control the shivers, as she looked about her for the first time.

The eaves were low-hanging, so low that Matthew probably bumped his head if he got up in the middle of the night. The wallpaper featured huge, faded cabbage roses, peeling in places, and the gray painted window trim had originally been white. The window was still open, letting in the chilly morning breeze off the ocean, and the white curtain flapped limply.

Jeannie lay there, in some sort of limbo between waking and sleeping, and dreamed of the night before. Matthew was real and solid beside her; his breathing followed the slow and even rhythm of sleep. He ought to be asleep, she thought muzzily. He'd had enough exercise during the night to ensure hours of rest.

She smiled against the smooth, warm flesh of his shoulder. She was just as exhausted, and rightly so. But unlike Matthew, she had duties to perform, one of which was the breakfast shift at the Muscatoon Inn. She would have given ten years of her life to be able to shut her eyes, snuggle closer to the man beside her, and forget all about it. But thirty-three years of responsibility were hard to break. If she didn't show up, Karen would bear the brunt of it, and Jeannie couldn't do that to her. With infinite regret she began to slide away from him.

It was a difficult feat to manage gracefully, given the sagging, concave nature of the old iron bed. She'd barely gotten to the edge of the mattress when a strong hand reached out and caught her wrist, dragging her back down.

She sprawled across him, her red hair a tangle in her eyes, and for a moment she lay there against him, content. Until she remembered Karen, and began to struggle.

"Where the hell do you think you're going?" Matthew growled in her ear.

"I've got to work." She allowed herself the liberty of kissing him, lingeringly, on his sleepy mouth. "I promised Hal."

"Screw Hal."

"Sorry, I'm only interested in you," she said with a shaky little laugh. "And I can't leave Karen alone there." She pulled away again, and this time he let her go.

If it had been cold in bed, it was icy out of it. Her clothes were scattered around the rough pine floor. She dressed quickly, her fingers shaking, all the time aware of those winter-gray eyes, watching her. She only wished she could tell what he was thinking.

"We have to talk," he said abruptly, just as she was pulling on her Nikes.

She looked up, startled. She'd sat on a spindly chair by the open window, rather than risk the temptation of the bed again, and Matthew's tone of voice only increased her nervousness. "About what?"

"About last night."

She grimaced. "I don't know if I want to hear this."

He hesitated, a fleeting expression crossing his face as he lay stretched out under the old patchwork quilt, and Jeannie recognized that look. It was guilt, pure and simple. *Damn,* she thought. *I know I don't want to hear this.*

Matthew apparently wasn't wild about the idea, either. "We'll talk later. Come back here when you're finished at the inn."

"Okay." She rose, feeling awkward and lanky, all arms and legs, which was a novel sensation for someone only five foot one and three-quarters. At least it wasn't going to be a one-night stand. Was it? She headed for the door. "See ya."

"You forgot something." That husky voice could still send shivers down her spine, even more so since the deliciously long night. She turned back to him, noting with absent longing how beautiful he looked, lying in that bed, his blond hair rumpled around his face, an unreadable light in his eyes.

"What?"

"Come here." It was a command, an entreaty, a teasing whisper, and she was helpless to resist. She moved slowly, over to the side of the bed and his outstretched hand, placing her own in it.

He pulled her down, gently, inexorably, his mouth catching hers, kissing her with a surprising tenderness that was at odds with the fierce passion of the night before. She opened her mouth to him with a shuddering sigh of longing and love, putting her heart and soul into it, and started to climb back onto the bed when he broke it off.

"Are you going to work?" he whispered huskily against her mouth.

Slowly, regretfully, she pulled back. "I have to."

"Then go now, MacPherson," he said. "Or in another minute I won't let you."

"Yes, sir. I probably won't be finished till late afternoon. I have to do lunch and the desserts for dinner. I'll be back as soon as I can."

"Okay."

"Matthew..."

"Yes."

"Will I want to hear what you have to say?" Her voice sounded forlorn in the early-morning stillness, and there was nothing she could do about it.

He watched her for a long moment, a distant look in his eyes, and then a small, wry smile twisted his mouth. "Maybe. Maybe not."

"You want to give me a hint?"

"I thought I'd tell you more about my profession," he said carefully.

She had tried to forget. She had tried to ignore the fact that she'd gone to bed, wholeheartedly and enthusiastically, with a self-confessed criminal. "That would probably be a wise idea," she said numbly.

"Probably." He didn't sound any more excited about the idea than she did. "Come straight back here. Okay?"

She only hesitated a moment. "Okay."

He watched her run out of the room as if pursued by devils. He lay back against the lumpy pillow as he listened to the sound of her sneaker-clad feet clatter down the narrow staircase, the muffled sound of the screen door slamming behind her, and then her footsteps were lost in the sand and the distant sound of the early-morning surf.

"Stupid," he said softly, out loud to the empty room. "Stupid, stupid, stupid. Why couldn't you keep your damned hands off her?"

There was a rush of wind through the open window, and

Matthew slid lower under the threadbare quilt, swearing. "Or at least, couldn't you have waited long enough to tell her the truth? She's not going to like being made to feel like a fool."

But then, he hadn't expected last night to happen. Or had he? Maybe, just maybe, the whole thing had been inevitable from the moment he took a good look at her, standing in the middle of his kitchen with a smashed casserole around her bare feet. There was something undeniably appealing about the fact that she went to bed with him thinking he was a criminal. She should be happy and relieved to find out that instead of a wanted felon he was exactly what fascinated her most—a cop.

Albeit a retired one, he reminded himself, *and not if Fred and Tony had their way.* It had to be the two of them hunting him down. No one else would care enough; the search committees from cities as diverse as Schooner Springs, Colorado, and Gary, Indiana, had mainly contented themselves with importuning letters. No, Fred and Tony wanted him back with them, in the Chicago Homicide Department. And that was the one place he had no intention of going.

They hadn't taken no for an answer, and that was partly his fault. Sooner or later he was going to have to face them, put it to them as gently and firmly as possible, that after seventeen years and a closer relationship with them than most husbands and wives had, he was never going to work with them again.

Right now he had other things to worry about. Mainly a boyish little flat-chested redhead who'd proved she was neither flat-chested nor boyish at all last night. Who'd been hot and damp and clinging and more woman than any blond, buxom Amazon he'd happened to take to bed during the last twenty-five years or however long it had been since he'd been initiated by Mrs. Payne in the backseat of her station wagon.

Jeannie MacPherson was just another in a long line of women, he reminded himself. Granted, she didn't look like the others. And granted, she didn't act like the others. She had an annoying way of insinuating herself into every part of his life. Even when she wasn't around he found himself thinking about, fantasizing about her, torn between irritation and a reluctant tenderness that might possibly be edging toward something very dangerous indeed.

"Enough, Connelly," he ordered himself sternly. "She's not going to be your problem for much longer. The moment you tell her you're a cop she's going to be so pissed off she won't come near you. And you won't have to worry about whether you're going through a mid-life crisis or falling in..."

He swore then, furious with the word that had almost slipped out. Using every ounce of his formidable determination, he shut his eyes, he shut off his mind, and slid lower in the damnably uncomfortable bed, which had proved very comfortable indeed during the night before. With the faint, flowery scent of her lingering in his nostrils, he fell back into a deep, dreamless sleep.

JEANNIE SET DOWN her hundredth cup of coffee for the day on the butcher block countertop, wiped a weary hand across her forehead, leaving a trail of flour in its wake, and surveyed the piecrust in front of her. It was four-thirty in the afternoon, and never had a day seemed so long.

She'd been late, of course, and Hal had been furious. She'd rushed through twenty-three breakfasts, borrowed Hal's sybaritic shower, cooked lunch, supervised the cleanup and began the pies, fortified by cup after cup of coffee. At least it was blueberry pie tonight, and not apple.

She simply didn't have the energy to pare and slice enough apples for three pies.

Of course, she was going to need some energy when she got back to Sunshine Cottage. At least she hoped so. Memories of last night had tumbled around and around in her brain all day long, staining her cheeks red, making her eyes sparkle, sending her attention on a tailspin that forced Karen to repeat everything three times. Regrets and a defiant pleasure warred for control, and by late afternoon Jeannie couldn't tell which had won. She was too exhausted even to guess.

"Jeannie!" Karen's voice was a hissing whisper from the back doorway. "Psst, Jeannie."

Jeannie looked up, shoving an errant strand of russet hair under her bandana. "For heaven's sake, what?" she snapped with uncharacteristic bad temper.

"They're back."

"Who's back?"

"The police."

The last of Jeannie's exhaustion and irritation vanished, leaving panic and disbelief in their place. "They couldn't be. The ferry doesn't run today; Enoch goes out to haul lobsters on Tuesdays."

"They hired a boat. They're here, all right, and asking all sorts of questions."

"Damn," said Jeannie, dusting her hands on her hips and dumping the apron on top of the half-finished blueberry pie. "Who are they talking to?"

"Hal," Karen said. "He's not telling them much, mainly because he doesn't know that much. He was telling them they ought to talk to you."

"Great. Listen, Karen, you'll have to distract them while I go warn Matthew...."

"Forget it, Jeannie. You must be out of your mind. *You*

may want to aid and abet a fugitive, but I have no intention of being an accessory. If you want to distract them you'll have to do it yourself.''

"But Karen!" she wailed.

"If you had any sense, you'd tell them where they can find him and then stay right here until it's all over," Karen said sternly. "You're old enough to know better than to get involved with someone like that. I never figured you for someone with a death wish."

"Karen, I know him. He couldn't have done anything so terrible," she said in a pleading voice. "It must be something silly, like computer crime or phony credit cards. He's not violent." She remembered the gunshot wound that hadn't slowed him down at all last night, and determinedly wiped the memory from her mind.

"Jeannie, you can defend him all you want," Karen said in a ruthless tone of voice, "but you know and I know that this is crazy. You've been on Muscatoon too long; the fog has addled your brain. If you had any sense at all you'd—"

"Jeannie?" Hal's beautifully modulated voice carried from the deserted dining room. "Are you still there?"

Jeannie stood motionless, looking about her for a quick escape. Karen was standing at the back door, blocking it, and Hal was just outside the only other exit. She could always hide under the table.

"She's here," Karen called out.

"Damn you, Karen."

"I'm doing it for your own good, sweetie," Karen murmured. "Go face the music."

Hal ambled into the kitchen, trailed by two men who could be nothing other than policemen. If he was the slightest bit flustered, only the unwonted grimness of his noble jaw and the slight twitch in his left eye gave him away. "Jeannie, meet Fred Mechewski and Tony Tonetti, both of the Chicago Police Department. They're looking for someone and think you might be able to help them out.''

A small, desperate shudder passed over Jeannie's slight frame, and then she looked up, smiling with false brilliance. "I'll do anything I can to help you," she lied sweetly. "Why don't we go someplace where we can talk?"

Hal began backing out of the room with more relief than grace. "Why don't you come with me, Karen?" he called. "We can go over the...the seating arrangements for tonight."

Karen hesitated, her blue eyes clearly distrusting. Jeannie only gave her a dulcet smile, and Karen had no choice. She glowered at Jeannie as she passed her, and followed Hal into the dining room, her straight back radiating distrust and disapproval.

Once they were out of earshot Jeannie turned her bright smile on the two policemen, carefully dimming the wattage to one of casual concern. "Who are you looking for?"

"A man named Matthew Connelly. He's forty, six feet tall, blond hair cut short, walks with a limp," the one named Fred said in a flat, Midwestern accent.

"Forty?" Jeannie echoed, startled out of her act for a moment. "I thought he was older."

Tony pounced. "That's the man. Vreeland said he thought he was living out on your end of the island. Can you give us directions?"

Jeannie smiled again, careful to keep it believable. "Of course, I'd be more than happy to help you. What's he done?"

It was casually asked, but Fred looked at Tony, who returned the expression. "I'm afraid I can't say, miss. Don't you worry about it, though. We just want to talk to him."

"But if he's dangerous..."

Another shared expression, and this time Tony jumped

in. "Not to worry, miss. We just want a chance to talk to him without anyone around. If you'll just tell us how to get there..."

"It might be best if you stayed around here while we do it," Fred added. "It'll be better without interruptions."

Jeannie looked at the two men, searching their bulky jackets for the suspicious bulge of a gun, searching their tired, middle-aged faces for the tension of an imminent shoot-out. They didn't look strung out, tense; they just looked tired. As tired as she suddenly was.

Once more she plastered the smile on her face. "Of course. I'll draw you a little map."

Five minutes later the two Chicago policemen were optimistically heading toward the western tip of the island, a route that would take them through a cranberry bog, an abandoned granite quarry, a junkyard, an ancient boatworks and the thickest pine forest on the island, a pine forest that still managed to confound long-time residents. All culminating in a deserted spit of land at the opposite end of the island to the location of Sunshine Cottage.

Ten minutes later Jeannie bid a sunny goodbye to the suspicious Hal and Karen. Fifteen minutes later she was racing across the sand dunes, her Nikes filling with sand, her heart racing and her lungs gasping for breath. She fell once, sliding down and cutting her palms on crushed seashells, but still she ran, determined to warn Matthew.

He wasn't there. The cottage was deserted; the horrible painting, the easel and his painting supplies were gone with him. She slammed into the living room, calling out for him, but there was no answer. Her voice echoed through the empty rooms, filled with panic and despair, and she raced back out onto the porch, searching the horizon for him. There was no one in sight.

There was always the unpleasant suspicion that he might

have decamped. Last night might have been a farewell gesture, she thought dismally, moving slowly back into the house. But no, his faded denim jacket still hung on a peg by the door. With a desultory gesture she pulled open a drawer in the table by the window, then slammed it shut again with a horrified gasp. There was a very large, very deadly looking gun in there, and she knew it certainly didn't belong to the eighty-year-old landlord of Sunshine Cottage.

So he hadn't gone. He wouldn't have left without his piece, she thought, remembering the slang with a note of pride. He had just gone off painting for the day, God knew why, and sooner or later he would show up at the cottage to meet her and tell her all about his nefarious career. After all her work in distracting the police and sending them off on a wild-goose chase, his arrival would probably coincide with theirs.

The sun was sinking lower when she finally heard his uneven footsteps on the front porch. She had given up watching. Her eyes felt blistered from the strain, her stomach was jumping, and every muscle in her body was clenched tight.

"Where the hell have you been?" she shrieked as he walked in the door.

He raised his head to look at her mildly. "I was painting. You been waiting long?"

"I've been waiting for hours!" she wailed. "They've found you."

He set the easel down with maddening calm. "Who's found me?"

"The police, you idiot!"

"Which police?" He might have been asking the time, he was so cool. He headed toward the kitchen, opened the refrigerator and pulled out a beer. "Want one?"

"You don't have time for that! For God's sake, Matthew,

haven't you listened to a word I've said? The police are here; they're after you! You've got to get away; you can't stand around drinking beer and acting like nothing's wrong."

"Which police?" he queried again, leaning against the door jamb.

With a great effort Jeannie controlled her panic. "Two men from the Chicago police force. Tony and Fred something, I forget."

He nodded. "I know them."

"For God's sake, Matthew..."

"Hush, Jeannie. I can take care of them."

She remembered the gun. "No, you won't. I won't let you shoot them, Matthew. Whatever you've done, it can't be so bad that killing won't make it worse. If you won't turn yourself in, at least let me hide you. I've got it all figured out. Hal's yacht is practically deserted—we could swim out there...."

He was looking at her with a mixture of amusement and astonishment. "Jeannie..." he began patiently, when the sound of voices filtered up from the beach.

"Connelly?" a rough, Midwestern voice shouted. "You in there?"

Jeannie went into action. Racing across the room, she slammed shut the front door, leaning against it. "Run, Matthew, for pity's sake," she hissed. "I'll stall 'em for you."

"Connelly, cut the crap," the other voice called out, and Jeannie could feel the thudding of their flat feet on the deck. "Will you open the damned door? We've been on a wild-goose chase all over this island, and we're getting sick and tired of it."

"Run," Jeannie whispered.

They were pounding at the door, temper and frustration

battering at it, and Jeannie knew she couldn't hold out for long.

"Connelly, if you don't let us in I'm going to break the damned door in," one of them snarled. "We know you're in there."

"Get out," Jeannie pleaded, tears in her eyes.

Matthew just looked at her, a rueful expression in his winter-gray eyes. The pounding and shouting increased, and he shrugged. "You'll never take me alive, copper," he shouted.

The pounding ceased abruptly. "Connelly," Fred's voice came back, plaintive, irritated and confused. "What the hell is going on here? If you don't want your job back as chief of detectives, all you have to do is tell us." There was a dead silence on either side of the door, as Jeannie raised frozen eyes to Matthew's face. "But at least let us in and give us a beer. We've been through hell and back, and after working together for close to twenty years, you owe us that much."

"You—you—" Jeannie said, words disappearing in her rage.

"Cop?" he supplied helpfully. "Heat, fuzz, whatever..."

"Pig will do nicely," she spat out and yanked open the door.

Chapter Twelve

He figured he'd give her a couple of days to calm down. Redheads were known for their temper, and the look she'd given him out of her steely blue eyes before she took off into the Muscatoon night would have melted a lesser man. But Matthew Connelly had stood up to bullets, marauding street gangs, his ex-wife and the Springside Strangler. One pint-sized, red-haired tomboy wasn't going to prove his undoing.

Fred and Tony had taken their leave the next day, reluctantly accepting Connelly's final decision. If the number of beers the three of them had downed for old times' sake hadn't quite managed to erase Jeannie's shocked expression from his mind, well, there were plenty of other memories that had haunted him over the years. He could just add that to the others.

Except that he hadn't been to blame for the other nightmares, and he was clearly to blame for disillusioning Jeannie MacPherson. Granted, she'd jumped to ridiculous conclusions. But he'd done nothing to erase those suspicions; had even, if he were honest with himself, done his mischievous best to foster some of them.

What he really needed to do was pick one of those many offers that had come his way and get back to work, instead of wasting his time painting lousy paintings and getting involved with just the wrong sort of woman. And that was what he was going to do, right after he had it out with her.

Once she'd cooled off, that is. He had no doubt at all that if he showed up at her doorstep one minute too soon she'd send a cat hurtling at his head. No, two days was just the right amount of time. One day she'd still be too angry, three days and she'd be gone beyond anger to fury. In the meantime he'd put the finishing touches on his lugubrious seascape and try to figure out where he wanted to spend the rest of his life. And try to keep his mind off the ever-present memory of two short nights ago.

JEANNIE COULD HAVE cheerfully come up with a few suggestions as to where Matthew Connelly could spend the rest of his life—most of them places cold and uncomfortable, with the possible alternative of someplace exceedingly hot indeed.

If he'd come around immediately he might have had some chance, she told herself. If he'd have followed her headlong dash back to her house, given her a chance to rant and rave and scream at him, then she would have been able to release her rage and turn all that bottled-up energy into some more constructive use.

But he hadn't followed, he'd left her to spend the night and the next day and a half pacing the suddenly empty-feeling rooms of her house. As the hours and days passed, her temper only increased.

The evening of the second day she made her way slowly across the sand dunes, back to her solitary house, depression, rage and a slow-burning sense of revenge racketing through her uncertain state of mind. A row of cats were lined up on her front porch, clamoring for the fish scraps she'd brought back from the inn, and for a brief moment her spirits lightened. Until she spied the figure lounging with deceptive ease on her porch, his feet propped up, a pair of dark glasses perched on the tip of his nose, shielding his eyes from the glare of the sinking sun, shielding his eyes from the glare of Jeannie MacPherson's formidable temper.

She stopped, staring up at the central figure in her vengeful fantasies, and a slow, ominous smile lit her face. "Hello, Matthew," she said, continuing up the steps. "Fancy seeing you here." It wasn't a great opening, she thought, but it would do in the circumstances. Her delivery was perfect, cool, even friendly in a distant sort of way.

Connelly didn't look fooled by her lack of hostility. Some of his spurious calm vanished as he dropped his feet to the porch floorboards and took off the sunglasses to squint at her. Those winter-gray eyes of his were unreadable as always, and she did her level best to keep hers equally opaque.

"I thought it was time we talked," he said slowly, his husky voice beginning to work its peculiar magic on her weakening backbone.

Quickly she stiffened it. "That would be charming," she said brightly, "but now isn't a good time for me. You should have come by earlier." Her affable voice descended into snappishness, and she pulled it back. "As a matter of fact, I was going to stop by your place tonight."

"You were?"

She smiled with genuine goodwill at this point. Vengeance was waiting to pounce. "I wondered if you'd check on my cats for me. I'm not planning on coming home tonight, and I have to work all day tomorrow, and they'll be starving, poor things. So if you'd feel like being neighborly..."

Matthew didn't blink, not a muscle moved in his face, and yet Jeannie could feel the slow fire of rage begin to build. "Where are you planning on staying?"

"With Hal," she said blithely. "On his yacht. He's promised to help me get over my nervousness on boats."

"And how's he planning to do that?"

Jeannie smiled. "I believe he's planning to distract me. Somewhat like you did."

He exploded. "Don't be childish, Jeannie. If you think you're going to make me jealous by going off with that—that—"

"That handsome, charming man?" Jeannie supplied helpfully. "Oh, I do expect to make you a little bit jealous. But to be perfectly honest, I've discovered that I enjoy making love, and Hal's reputation in that area is certainly impressive. So I thought I'd try him out." She reached out and placed a carefully gentle hand on his arm, controlling the impulse to dig her nails into him. "I'm sorry if that hurts your feelings, Matthew, but I thought we agreed that we had no strings. We certainly weren't planning more than a one-night stand, were we? You weren't about to offer me anything more, like commitment, or even a long-term affair, were you?"

Matthew just glared at her. "Are you seriously trying to tell me you aren't sleeping with Hal Vreeland to get back at me for not telling you what I did for a living?"

"That would be childish, wouldn't it? Though I think it went a little bit further than simply not telling me, don't you agree?"

"You jumped to a conclusion—"

"And you pushed me the rest of the way," Jeannie broke in. "I admit I was irritated, but not for long." She removed her hand, smiling up at him gently. "The problem is, dear Matthew, that a cop simply isn't as interesting as a criminal. Not nearly as exciting. I'm sorry."

She couldn't tell whether he believed her or not, but it wasn't important. He was furious, and that was what mattered most. "And you think you'll find an innkeeper more exciting?"

"I'm willing to try. Will you feed my cats?"

"Your cats," he said softly, "and you can go straight to hell." He bounded off the porch without a backward glance.

"We'll be anchored down by the cove," she called after him, a lilt of laughter in her voice. "You might take your walk in another direction."

He made no sign that he heard her, and she watched him go, the smile vanishing from her face, the gleeful humor fading quickly. She was due back at the dock in an hour and a half, giving her just long enough to bathe, change and fix her hair. And try to avoid the wretched thought...what had she gotten herself into?

THE WITCH, HE THOUGHT, stomping over the uneven terrain with a careless disregard for his throbbing leg. The unmitigated, heartless, soulless witch. So much for her sweetness and light, her neighborliness and concern. She was just like all the rest, waiting to get him entangled in her snares and then pulling the ropes tighter and tighter until they strangled him. Coming around with her casseroles and her coffee and that seductive little body of hers, smiling at him, flirting with him, making herself indispensable to him so that he could hardly think straight and wanted nothing more than to wrap his hands around her throat and—

Kiss her. That's what he wanted to do, damn it. He wanted to shake some sense into her, and then carry her up to bed, where the two of them belonged. And despite that cool, to-hell-with-you expression on her pale face, he knew that that was what she wanted, too.

He stopped short, looking at the sea cliffs around him with unseeing eyes. He could go back, of course. He could drag her out of the house, tell her she wasn't going anywhere with Hal Vreeland, and if she wanted to learn how to conquer her nervousness on boats, he'd be the man to do it. Vreeland wasn't going to offer her any more long-term commitment than he was. Why didn't he just go for it and let the chips fall where they may?

But they'd fall on Jeannie MacPherson's head, like coals, and she didn't deserve it. Hal's fleeting attentions wouldn't break her heart—she didn't want forever-after love from him. She wanted it from a broken-down detective who was too haunted by the Springside Strangler to give it to her, and the sooner she accepted it was hopeless, the better for her. If not for him.

She was on her way to forgetting about him. When it came right down to it, Matthew thought as he moved slowly back toward Sunshine Cottage, Vreeland would probably provide a perfect distraction. What was the saying—all cats are gray in the dark? One body was pretty the same as the next, and within a couple of days—hell, a couple of hours—she'd have forgotten all about him. Now, why didn't that thought reassure him?

If all cats were gray in the dark, why didn't he go distract himself with one of Hal Vreeland's leftovers? The waitress at the inn—Karen, wasn't it?—was warm and pretty and looked undemanding. So why didn't he turn around and head back toward the tiny village?

He moved slowly up the steps, his pace measured and calm. He had no need to distract his mind, he told himself righteously. Jeannie was doing the right thing, and he was mature enough and uninvolved enough not to mind in the slightest. He calmly put his fist through the screen door.

"ALL RIGHT, MACPHERSON," Jeannie said in a wry, drawling voice as she surveyed her reflection, "so you look like a Victorian virgin. Are you sure that's the message you have in mind?'' She plucked at the white eyelet ruffles of what resembled an antique nightdress, and frowned. Her tawny russet hair was clean and shining around her narrow face; the blue eyes were troubled but fearless; her long, slender fingers were nervous on the white cotton.

With a resigned sigh she turned away from the revealing reflection. ''You look more like a virgin sacrifice than a woman bent on hot passion,'' she muttered as she headed out the door. ''Are you sure it's the inn you're wanting to head toward, and not Sunshine Cottage? Sunshine Cottage, ha! More like Gloom-and-Doom Cottage. A fitting place for someone like...like him.''

The sound of her voice with its heavy contempt helped stiffen her resolve. It got her across the headlands, through the pine forest and onto the front porch of the Muscatoon Inn with only the faintest of misgivings pricking at her. If the sight of Hal Vreeland in all his masculine glory didn't banish her doubts, at least it assuaged them a bit. If anyone could help her forget Matthew Connelly, then Hal Vreeland ought to be that one. And thank God, Karen was nowhere to be seen.

''You look ravishing, Jeannie,'' said Hal, his blue eyes alight with pleasure and something more. ''Or should I say ravishable? Good enough to eat.''

Jeannie managed a smile. Hal would be wearing an ascot, she thought miserably. How could you take a man seriously who wore an ascot? A yellow one at that. Despite the warmth of the night she was beginning to suffer an advanced case of cold feet. ''Uh, Hal...''

He was miles ahead of her. Before she could even form the words that would tactfully extricate her from a situation she now recognized as unforgivably stupid, her arm was caught in his, and he was gently, inexorably leading her down to the dock, a wicker basket full of goodies on his other arm, his mouth going a mile a minute, determined not to let her speak a discouraging word.

"It's a perfect night, Jeannie," he murmured, and she had to admit the strength of his arm beneath her unresisting hand was pleasant. "We'll anchor out by the cove, have a marvelous dinner, the best bottle of wine in existence on the island, and Cognac that's at least fifty years old. By the time I've finished with you the boat will feel like a second home."

"By the time you've finished with me it sounds like I'll be drunk," she said. "Hal, are you sure...?"

They'd reached the dock, and the choice was suddenly upon her. She could pull back or give in to Hal's gentle, inexorable tug upon her arm. The moon was rising, silvering his blond hair so far above her own diminutive height, there was a soft sea breeze on the air, and Jeannie felt longings she couldn't even begin to express.

"I'm sure," Hal said. "Watch your step."

She followed him, lifting her ruffled white skirts high and stepping carefully in her thin-strapped, high-heeled sandals.

Well, there was one thing to be said for the debacle of the evening, she thought three hours later. She no longer gave a damn about being on a boat. She'd sat through Chef Bernard's most inspired creations, dutifully swallowed three glasses of an admittedly superb Cabernet, listened to Hal's semiteasing come-ons with amusement, appreciation and panic, and now sat curled up on the duck-covered seat on deck, sipping at the ancient Cognac and watching Hal's technique.

Part of its power, she thought as she listened to his warm voice with only half an ear, was that it seemed so effortless, so sincere, so utterly charming. If she hadn't seen him practice those same wiles a dozen—no, a hundred—times she would have gladly succumbed. She'd spent the first two and a half hours trying to convince herself that she should abandon all her doubts and simply enjoy herself anyway. By the time three hours had passed she knew it was out of the question. She'd spent thirty-three years trying not to be self-destructive; now was no time to start.

He'd been edging closer during the last half hour, and his voice had dropped to a low, caressing murmur. Within ten minutes he was bound to pounce, gracefully of course, and at a time when he thought she was offguard. Those sensuous eyes of his were half-closed with lazy promise, and the long fingers that twirled the brandy snifter were no doubt extremely deft.

"I think we'd better head home," Jeannie said abruptly, interrupting Hal in the midst of one of his more amusing anecdotes.

He stared at her, flustered, for the first time no longer sure of himself. "I beg your pardon." The lazy, seductive tone had slipped into a high-pitched one of surprise, and it was with great difficulty that Jeannie controlled a smile.

"I've got a long day ahead of me," she said. "It's time we called it a night."

Hal made a noble effort and regained some of his former suavity. "Jeannie, there's no need to be nervous. It's taken you two years to get to this point; I'm certainly not going to let you back out now."

Jeannie smiled then, a dangerous smile that Matthew Connelly would have recognized. "You're not going to let me back out now?" she echoed sweetly. "What exactly does that mean?"

Hal had the grace to flush slightly, but his jaw stuck out like a stubborn little boy's. "I'm not going to rape you, if that's what you're afraid of," he muttered. "But I think you're being ridiculous, and I have no intention of showing up back at the dock with an audience of half the people in town. I have my reputation to think of.''

"Hal, your reputation is firmly established. So is mine. If we get back before eleven they'll just think you're a fast worker.''

"That's not part of my image. Besides, Karen will be at the inn.''

"Aha," said Jeannie, "the light is beginning to dawn. So Karen is watching the inn for you, is she? Why don't you want her to think we didn't go to bed together?''

"Because I don't.''

"Why don't you go back and go to bed with her? I promise you, you'll have a much better time," she said persuasively.

"I'm sure I will. Which is exactly why we're staying on this boat all night. So I'm not tempted.'' Hal was sounding more and more like a petulant schoolboy, all trace of the great lover having vanished, and Jeannie leaned forward on the bench seat, tucking her bare feet underneath her.

"I've never known you not to give in to temptation before, Hal. Why does Karen scare you?''

"She doesn't scare me.''

"Are you going to tell me she doesn't attract you, either? I wouldn't believe that.''

Hal flushed, drained his Cognac, and then leaned forward and refilled his glass. "She attracts me," he muttered. "She attracts me too damned much. If you must know, she scares the life out of me. We spent less than a week together once and I couldn't call my soul my own. I couldn't eat, sleep, walk or talk without thinking of her. There was only one thing I could do, and that was run like hell. I'm not the type who can make those sorts of commitments.''

"But, Hal, you ran off and got married!'' Jeannie said in exasperation.

"You should know that for me marriage has nothing to do with commitment. Hell, I've done it three times already, and I'm probably not finished."

She stared at him in confused fascination. "Well, why don't you marry Karen next time?"

"Look, Karen got over me. It was nothing more than a brief affair for her. Just because I haven't quite gotten it out of mind is no reason to suppose she even remembers it happened."

Jeannie shook her head. "I don't know how you got the reputation for being good with women. You don't know diddly-squat. Karen's in love with you, always has been, always will be. God knows why."

Hal managed a wry smile. "Maybe she's got good taste?"

"Maybe she's masochistic," Jeannie snapped. "Okay, Hal, enough of this. You can screw up your life if you want, but you can't screw up mine. Start the engines on this thing and head back."

"Nope."

"Hal..."

"I promised you I'd help you get over your fear of boats. You're going to spend the night here, whether you like it or not. I promise I won't touch you unless you want me to."

"Unless I want you to," Jeannie echoed in an outraged shriek. "Hal, you have, without a doubt, the most overweening ego!"

"Unless you want me to," he said again in a firm voice. "And I think I know what I'm doing in regard to Karen. In the meantime, just relax, and I'll get us some more Cognac."

Jeannie watched him disappear down into the cabin, watched him go with a calm smile. She shook her head in amazement over the foolishness of mortals, herself included. Who was she to pass judgment on Hal's stupidity, when she considered the mess she was currently in?

She sat and waited. The moment his broad shoulders disappeared in the companionway she rose from her comfortable perch, crossed to the stern and dove overboard into the icy, inky dark sea.

Chapter Thirteen

The water hit her body with a shock of icy coldness that momentarily knocked the breath out of her. She sank beneath the waves, allowed herself a brief flirtation with panic, and then kicked upward again, into the blessedly pure night air.

She flung her wet hair out of her face, checked out the distance to the shore and headed out, with the long, easy strokes that were second nature to her. Behind her head she could hear Hal shouting at her, a mixture of exasperation and obscenity, but she paid him no mind. He knew as well as she did how good a swimmer she was, and he wouldn't worry unduly. She knew the currents, the reefs, the submerged rocks in this cove as well as she knew her own bedroom, and nothing would interfere with her speedy transit to the small semicircle of sandy beach.

The long white dress was doing its damnedest to wrap itself around her ankles. She considered treading water long enough to slip out of it, then thought better of it. It was her most expensive dress, and she had no intention of abandoning it to the ocean floor, and it would be even more difficult to swim with it draped over an arm. Besides, the water was surprisingly cold, and the sooner she got to the shore the happier her cramped, chilled muscles would be.

For some reason it seemed to take twice as long as it usually took her to swim from the point back to shore. When she finally felt the gritty ocean floor beneath her feet she allowed herself a shiver of reminiscent fear, a brief moment to consider the possibility that she might not have made it after all. For a woman not self-destructive she seemed to be doing a good impersonation of one these past few days.

The white dress dragged around her as she stumbled from the sea. Reaching down, she caught the hem in her strong hands and began to wring the sea water out of it. Then she stopped, motionless, the soaking dress pulled up to her thighs, and raised her head.

Matthew was standing there in the shadows, a silent, waiting figure. "You're crazy, you know it?" he said finally, his voice a husking rasp in the chill night air.

She managed a watery smile. "A little bit, I suppose," she admitted. "What are you doing here?"

"I was watching you from the cliffs. You were very clearly illuminated when you jumped overboard. What did Vreeland do to make you take such a drastic step?" He spoke casually, his voice almost a drawl, but Jeannie didn't miss the very real threat beneath that deceptive ease, and she shivered again.

"If you mean did he try to rape me, you can relax," she said. "I think he planned to make me sleep on deck. He just didn't want his reputation as a ladies' man tarnished by taking me home sooner."

"What made you decide to go home? Couldn't get used to the boat?"

Jeannie shrugged. Her lips were probably blue right now, and her whole body was a mass of shivers. Matthew, damn him, didn't even notice. "Couldn't get used to the company," she said finally.

There was a swift intake of breath from the dark figure

by the path. "Then maybe I won't have to kill him," he said finally. "Just bruise him a bit."

"You don't have to do a damned thing, Connelly," Jeannie said, her teeth chattering quite audibly. "I was able to defend my own honor."

She could see the slash of white as he smiled in the moon-lit darkness. "Apparently you were. So where does that leave us?"

Jeannie was at this point pushed to the limit of her endurance. "Wherever you want it to," she snapped. "It probably leaves me with rampant pneumonia."

"You aren't going to get warm standing there glaring at me," he observed.

Jeannie counted to ten mentally, then managed a smile as chilly as her icy flesh. "What do you suggest I do about it?" she demanded.

"You could come over here and get warm."

She stared at him in amazement. "You think you could warm me up?"

"Oh, I think between the two of us we could manage quite a conflagration," he said, and the rough silk of his voice began to melt the ice around her heart. "Come here, Jeannie."

Pride and common sense would have kept her rooted to her spot in the sand, but pride and common sense were at the bottom of the ocean. Dropping her sodden skirts, she moved across the tiny crescent of beach like one mesmerized.

"You blew your chance, you know," she said in a husky voice, not hurrying. "If you'd brought me a towel I would have loved you forever."

Without a word Matthew reached behind him and tossed her a huge, thick towel. She caught it in numb hands, stopping within a foot of his waiting body and making no effort to drape it around her chilled shoulders. "I guess I have no choice," she whispered. "I never go back on my word."

He reached out, taking the towel from her numbed fingers, and slowly, carefully draped it around her shoulders. He pulled her against him, her cold, wet body pressed up against his warm, dry one, and the towel was around them both. "That's the easiest undying love I ever earned," he whispered, and his mouth met hers, warm and wet and demanding, heating her mouth with his.

She clung to him like a piece of rockweed clinging to a rocky shore, wrapping her arms and her body around him like tendril of kelp. Slowly the heat began to penetrate through her wet clothes, her salty skin, into her very bones, and then she was shivering with something other than cold, and he was shivering, too.

"I feel as if I'm kissing a mermaid," he whispered against her ear.

She laughed against the solid warmth of his chest, a rusty, shaken sound. "You have been. Actually, I'm a siren, here to drown unsuspecting sailors."

"I believe you," he said, his voice somber. "Let's go back to the house, Circe. We have better ways of drowning."

He drew back from her, and before she could cry out he pulled the towel tighter around her chilled body, leaning down to kiss her softly on her protesting lips. "Unless you'd rather I warmed you up right here on the beach?"

Tell him you want to go home, alone, she ordered herself sternly. *Tell him thank you very much, but nothing's changed. Tell him to go away.*

"I...I..." Before she could form the words he kissed her again, his lips soft and warm and damp against hers.

"Your place or mine, kid?" he murmured.

Tell him. "Your place," she said with a sigh of both defeat and triumph. "Your place."

It was a night made for love, Jeannie thought dazedly, hours later, as she lay curled up in the sagging bed, her body warm and sated and exhausted well beyond sleep. The soft night breezes had been calling to her, beckoning her, and she had almost made the worst mistake of her life. They'd been calling her to Matthew, and instead she'd ignored them, intent on her own bloody-minded anger and revenge.

Her temper would be the death of her one day, she thought, snuggling closer against the warm body next to her. Sooner or later she'd let her red hair drive her into an action that she couldn't escape from so easily. Not that diving overboard and swimming to shore in the middle of the night was necessarily an easy escape. But at least reason had intruded in time, and she was exactly where she wanted to be—lying next to Matthew Connelly.

Though perhaps it wasn't exactly where she *should* be. No, there was no "perhaps" about it. Where she ought to be was home alone in her own bed, with Travis McGee or her own personal fantasies of Frank Furillo. At least they were harmless, but not nearly so satisfying. She let out a small, weary sigh, part pleasure, part despair, and his hand came up to cup her head, his long fingers threading through her now dry hair, his thumb tracing a delicate pattern against her willful chin.

"Why the sigh?" His voice rumbled from deep in his chest.

She didn't move from her comfortable spot curled up against him. "I thought you were asleep," she murmured.

"I thought you were. I repeat the question—why the sigh?"

She shifted then, peering up at him through the misty

darkness of predawn light. "I was thinking that this would never work out."

If she expected a denial she expected too much. "I know."

"So why are we doing it?"

He smiled, a weary, resigned, almost tender smile. "Because we can't help ourselves?" he suggested. His other hand had reached over to stroke the gentle swell of her hip, a soft, almost absent touch, soothing rather than arousing.

"I don't believe that," she said. "I think we're both strong enough to resist temptation."

"Maybe we didn't want to resist it."

She considered that for a moment, turning it over in her mind. "Matthew, why can't it work out?" she demanded suddenly. "Why, if we try very hard, can't we—"

"There's no future for Dirty Harry and an ice-cream lady," he said, his voice flat and certain. "You know that as well as I do, even though you're trying to convince yourself otherwise."

"Why?"

He shifted then, so that he was leaning over her as she lay against the pillows, and his face was grim. "Because I've seen too much, done too much, remembered too much ever to be comfortable in your cotton-candy world. I've got too many ghosts haunting me to leave room for anybody else."

"I don't live in a cotton-candy world!" she protested, trying to sit up, but he pushed her back.

"Maybe not. But you don't know a thing about the sordid sleaze that I've lived and breathed for the past seventeen years. At this point I don't think it's something I can ever escape from."

"But what if you can?" she said in a desperate whisper.

"What if you can simply put it all behind you, forget about it?"

"That's what I've been trying to do all summer, and so far I haven't had much success."

"But what if you could?" she persisted.

He looked down at her, lying against the pillows, her russet-colored hair black in the moonlight. "Then I'll find you," he said softly.

"And I'm expected to settle for that? A vague possibility?" Her voice wasn't angry, only resigned and very, very sad.

"It's all I can offer."

She stared up at him. "All right," she said. "And what do we do in the meantime?"

He stared down at her, his shoulders a curtain against the night, and then slowly he lowered his mouth to hers. "This," he said, and kissed her.

If the first time that night had been hurried, fevered, this was slow, languid, with an underlying edge of desperation that made it all the more poignant. His body was strong, hot and slippery above hers, his mouth teasing, arousing, telling her all the things he wouldn't, couldn't put into words.

She kissed him back, clinging to him, her mouth answering that unspoken love, kissing him with desperation and wanting and needing all tied up in a bundle of emotions that left her shaking with arousal and hopelessness. When he covered her she clung tighter, when he entered her she cried out, and when they came she wept against him. There was no more room that night for second doubts.

THERE WAS PLENTY OF ROOM during the next ten days for second, third and forty-seventh doubts. Jeannie did her level best to keep them out of her mind, going through the mornings with a single-minded attention to business, to cooking, to working on her house, to not thinking about the future. The afternoons and evenings were given over to Matthew.

She'd never lived through anything like it, she thought on the fourth day. Given her own disrupted upbringing, the absence of anything resembling a father after she was six years old, she'd promised herself that she wouldn't settle for anything less than a solid promise of security and a future. And here she was, completely, devastatingly in love with a man who offered her no future at all.

It hadn't taken long to realize it was love. She only had to wake up the next morning, know how irrational and impractical this whole affair was, and know that she had no intention of breaking it off, and the conclusion was obvious. Only love would melt the last traces of her common sense. She knew it was crazy. Matthew Connelly certainly wasn't her definition of lovable. He was grouchy, uncommunicative, with a wall of defenses a mile thick around him. But there was something behind those defenses, something that called to her and it was a call she couldn't ignore. Jeannie MacPherson knew herself very well after thirty-three years, and she knew true love when she found it. And whether she liked it or not, whether it made any sense at all, she'd found it with Matthew Connelly.

Once she accepted that she was in love, things were a little easier. Love excused a lot of stupidity. She even found she could shrug off Hal's hurt expression, Karen's concern, her own misgivings. After all, she was a red-blooded American female. Didn't she believe in happy endings?

It didn't seem as if Matthew did. Every day he grew quieter and quieter. Every night their lovemaking grew more and more intense. If she had any doubts about his feelings out of bed, she had no doubts whatsoever about his commitment in bed. He wanted her with a single-minded intensity, needed her with an overwhelming, insatiable need, loved her in a way perhaps only he understood. For the time being Jeannie told herself it was enough.

She was walking slowly back from the village nine days later, the mail tucked in her canvas bag, her sneakered feet slow on the rocky path toward the east end of Muscatoon. She didn't have to work at the inn that day; indeed, she'd done her level best to get out of everything she could. She had the ominous feeling that Matthew Connelly wasn't going to be around for very long, and she wanted to spend every spare moment with him.

That made her current problem even worse. Today's mail had brought a request—no, a demand, a plea—that she come for Tom and Jeannie's annual meeting. There was a question of Western expansion, a question of using some newly developed artificial ingredients that were supposedly superior to their natural predecessors, and Tom and company didn't want to go ahead without her input. The meeting was in two days' time—was there any chance she could give up her current hermitlike existence long enough to talk to them?

She knew she should. She'd avoided her responsibilities for too long as it was, sitting on her island and collecting huge amounts of money for very little work. Granted, she'd done more than her share in the early years, but still, the Protestant ethic was an integral part of her backbone, and she knew she had to go, no matter now much she hated to leave Matthew.

Well, it wouldn't be for long. She'd be gone a week, from one Thursday ferry to the next one. And Matthew had rented Sunshine Cottage for the entire summer. It was only early July; that would still give them most of the summer to come to some sort of understanding.

So why did she dread telling him she was going? Was she afraid he'd make a fuss, demand that she not leave? Or was she really afraid, deep down inside, that he might be glad to see her go?

He wasn't at the house when she got there. It was after five, and the light was no longer good enough for his so-called painting. By that time he was usually sitting on the porch, waiting for her, his winter-gray eyes watching her with a bleak expression that she could only intermittently warm.

Tonight he wasn't there. The painting was tucked in a corner, and Jeannie could see he'd added another layer of greeny-brown to the sky. She shook her head in wonder, then started through the cottage, calling to him.

The wind had come up sometime in the later afternoon, and it whipped her cotton skirts around her bare legs as she came back out on the porch. For a moment she considered the possibility that he'd fallen again, but she knew what good shape he was in. The wound scarcely troubled him, and if it was good enough to support their strenuous night-time activities, then it could support a walk along the head-lands.

But he hadn't walked along the headlands, she realized with sudden certainty. He'd gone to the beach. She paused long enough to change into her bathing suit, and then fol-lowed him down.

He was sitting on his jacket in the gritty sand, his legs stretched out in front of him, his eyes on the distant horizon. He must have heard her scrambling down the path, but he didn't turn, didn't look. He just sat there, staring out to the sea as if it held the answers.

Jeannie stopped to watch him for a long moment, and she felt a peculiar clutching at her heart. He looked so solitary, so determinedly alone, sitting there, as if he had no room in his life for anyone. But it was an illusion, she told herself firmly. Everybody needed somebody.

"Hi, there," she said, wincing at the brightness in her voice. "I thought you might be down here."

He still didn't turn. "I needed some time to think."

Not promising, she thought dismally. "Did you come to any conclusions?" She moved across the sand and sank down beside him.

He did turn to look at her then, and the result wasn't reassuring. His face looked grim, bleak, hopeless. "No," he said.

"You want more time?"

His bleak expression grew wary. "What do you mean?"

"I have to go to the mainland," she said, guarding herself against the pain she was going to feel when she saw the relief in his face. "To Vermont, actually. For Tom and Jeannie's annual meeting. I've been too irresponsible as it is; I really have to go." Her voice sounded almost desperate, pleading.

Matthew shrugged. "If you say so," he said, leaning back against the rock and turning his attention back to the sea. "How long will you be gone?"

It could have been worse, she thought. If he didn't appear brokenhearted, at least he didn't seem happy to see her go. "A week," she said. "I'll take the ferry out tomorrow morning and be back next Thursday. If you don't mind."

"I don't mind." He kept staring at the damned ocean, until she thought she might scream. *I must really be crazy,* she thought, *to be jealous of the damned ocean.*

"Will you be all right?"

"I'll be fine."

She stared at his averted profile, sick with longing and frustration. In a few hours' time that distant expression would vanish, vanish in a white-hot blaze of love and passion that would leave them both scorched and wanting more. But in the daytime he grew more and more distant. "Well,

I guess I'll go pack. Do...do you want to stay at my house tonight?'' She was fully prepared for him to suggest they spend the night apart, but he turned, and for a moment warmth returned to his eyes.

"Sure. You go on ahead. I'll be up in a little while."

There was nothing more she could say. At least he wanted her for one thing. Two, if you counted her cooking. She knelt there in the sand, watching him, and then she started to rise.

His hand shot out unexpectedly, catching her wrist and pulling her off-balance, into his lap. She looked up at him, laughing, expecting to see a lightening in his dark mood, but if anything he looked even grimmer. "Jeannie, I..." He thought better of whatever he planned to say, though, and instead he kissed her, a savage, deep kiss that left her shaken and trembling in his arms.

As quickly as the kiss began it was over, and he released her. If his hands seemed to linger for a moment on her bare arms it was probably just a figment of her imagination. "I'll be up shortly," he said again. And he turned his gaze back to the ocean.

He waited until her footsteps were out of hearing, and he had excellent hearing. Then he looked up, at the pathway she had taken, almost as if he could see her shadow.

Thursday to Thursday, he thought. But he'd be gone by Monday. He leaned back against the rock and called himself the fool that he knew he was. Trading the sweet forgetfulness of Jeannie MacPherson's arms for the inescapable memory of the Springside Strangler. It was a crazy, uneven trade, but one he had no choice but to make. He could only hope it ended up being the right one.

Chapter Fourteen

She really was cured, Jeannie thought as she eyed the choppy ocean about her with a fearless expression. The whitecaps, the thick white thunderheads scudding overhead, the brisk, stinging salt breeze would have driven her below on any previous trip on the *Morning Star*, if she would have even boarded in the first place. A northeaster was due sometime in the next twenty-four hours, with plenty of wind and rain, and the normally chicken Jeannie MacPherson would have stayed on the mainland for another three days rather than risk what would have seemed like certain drowning.

But that was the old Jeannie MacPherson. The new Jeannie MacPherson had done her duty at the board meeting—hurriedly, it must be admitted—and had then driven all night long in order to meet the Monday ferry. She'd vetoed the artificial ingredients, okayed the expansion plans, promised to be more involved in the future, got depressed at the sight of Tom's two babies, and then ran like hell before Tom could think of something else to keep her busy. All she had left to do was pick the site of the Western plant, and there was no hurry on that. She could read all the papers and prospectuses once she was back in Sunshine Cottage.

"Can't you make this old tub go any faster?" she called out to the glowering Enoch. Enoch only sneered, steering into a choppy wave with deliberate malice. Jeannie clung more tightly to the rail and gritted her teeth, willing the boat to hurry.

It had done her good to be away these few days, she had to admit. It had helped her to view Matthew and their tangled affair with a bit more equanimity, and if it hadn't lessened her longing, it had at least helped her determination. She was hurrying back to Matthew Connelly, determined to make him see that he couldn't simply turn his back on love—couldn't turn his back on her. He couldn't let his past, his damned ghosts, win. With any luck the few days' absence would have made him come to a similar conclusion.

She had spent the long night driving the twisting, deserted roads through Vermont and New Hampshire, fantasizing about how she'd surprise him. He wouldn't be expecting her back until the following Thursday. It would be absolutely delicious to sneak up on him while he was painting that horrendous picture. Or, if she could hold off long enough, to sneak into bed with him, a time when he'd be sure to be missing her the most, she thought with a trace of depression.

No, she'd simply kick off her ridiculous high heels and run home, across the rocky paths and over the headlands to the cottage on the eastern point, and when she found him she'd throw herself into his arms and tell him she loved him. Somebody had to say it first, and she might as well be the one. Sooner or later he would realize he felt the same way.

"You been busy, Enoch?" she called out cheerfully, turning away from the churning water. "Lots of visitors?"

"Not since your man got rid of the cops," Enoch said with a malicious sneer. "Just the usual summer complaints."

"That's nice." She refused to rise to the bait. She hadn't

volunteered the information as to Matthew Connelly's real line of work, and no one had dared to ask her. As far as she knew they still thought he was a wanted man, and that she was half-crazy for sleeping with him. On an island the size of Muscatoon everybody knew who was sleeping with whom. Jeannie knew it, and accepted it with equanimity. It didn't help Hal's current state of outrage, and it didn't help Karen's worried expression, but it suited Jeannie Mac-Pherson just fine.

"You planning on staying long, missy?" Enoch grumbled in the modified shout necessary to be heard over the engines.

Jeannie blinked. "Of course. Why shouldn't I?"

"I thought with your man leaving you might be a little lonely out there."

Jeannie shook her head in disgust. "Stop trying to cause trouble, Enoch. I know you too well. My man's not leaving. Not yet, at least."

"Happen he sent word for me to pick up his bags," Enoch drawled, an evil gleam in his rheumy old eyes. "He's leaving you, all right, missy. Going back to the mainland; hire me special for the trip once I finish the usual run. He just didn't bother to tell you."

A wash of panic and pain swept over her for a moment, but resolutely she pushed them away. "You're a nasty, trouble-making old man," she said calmly. "And I'm not going to let you do this to me. I'm going up front where I don't have to listen to you."

"To the bow."

"What?" she shouted, and her voice sounded a little ragged. *Damn, I did let him get to me.*

"I said the bow. You call it the bow, you don't call it up front, you foolish woman," Enoch snapped.

"I'll call it any damned thing I please. And I'll call you

any damned thing I please, one of which is liar. Go to hell, Enoch.'' It was hard to stomp the length of a boat, particularly when said boat was pitching and tossing in the rough sea, aided no doubt by the malicious boatman. Jeannie fell against the bulkhead once, tripped over a coil of rope, but finally managed to make it...to the bow...she thought with a glower, and there she stood, hands clenched on the railing, back tall and straight and turned with patrician disdain on the evil old man piloting the boat.

The harbor on Muscatoon Island looked small and sleepy to Jeannie's eyes, and blissfully deserted. There were only the usual assortment of lobstermen milling around, a few plump tourists thrown in for color, and one or two seedy-looking artists. Jeannie let out a sigh of relief, and the white-knuckled grip on the railing loosened as Enoch docked.

Then she saw the bags sitting on the dock. Not that they were that distinctive, Jeannie told herself with sick calm. Just a battered leather suitcase that was possibly almost as old as she was, and a canvas duffel bag that was new and scarcely used. Anyone could have luggage like that.

But it wasn't just anybody coming out of the café, dark glasses pulled over his cold, wintry eyes, barely a trace of a limp marring the stride of those long, lean, jeans-clad legs. He hadn't seen her yet, wasn't expecting to see her. He went over to his bags, then raised his head to look at the oncoming boat—and looked straight into her eyes.

His mouth may have tightened beneath the dark glasses, but she couldn't be quite certain. He just stood there, watching her, as she carefully moved away from the rail, picking her way over the debris that littered the *Morning Star*'s deck, her high heels wobbling slightly. She kept her eyes on him, a steady, accusing gaze, never wavering, as she walked down the gangplank and set foot on the dock.

The rage that was building inside her was awe-inspiring,

burning inside her with a white-hot light that threatened to scorch her innards. Never in her life had she felt like murder, but she felt that way right now.

She walked straight up to him, head held high, proud and as tall as she could make her five-foot two-inch body. Suddenly the deserted docks weren't deserted at all. The entire town seemed to have turned out to watch this confrontation.

"I thought Enoch was lying," she said. Matthew was standing by a pile of lobster traps, looking justifiably wary.

"I'm glad he warned you," he had the nerve to say. "I thought I'd be gone long before you came back. I didn't want it to be like this."

"I'm sure you didn't. You didn't want to have to face me; you wanted to sneak away like a thief in the night," Jeannie said in a cool voice. "Did you bother to leave me a note? Some charming little Dear John letter to soothe my wounded pride?"

"Don't do this, Jeannie."

"'Don't do this, Jeannie,'" she mimicked. "You bastard. I loved you. You sneaking, rotten, lying piece of crud."

She could see his mouth tighten. "Go ahead. I deserve it. I never wanted to hurt you."

"Come on, man," Enoch called from the boat. "No use arguing with the girl."

Without turning Jeannie suggested Enoch perform an anatomically impossible act.

"Don't be childish, Jeannie," Matthew snapped. "You don't need to take your temper out on poor Enoch."

Something red exploded behind Jeannie's eyes, and before she realized it she'd grabbed the nearest lobster trap, hauling it aloft as if it weighed nothing at all. "No, I don't need to take my temper out on poor Enoch at all," she said. "You're the fitting recipient of it."

"Put the lobster trap down, Jeannie," he said wearily, in

a condescending tone of voice that didn't help her hurt and rage. "It's too heavy for you."

"I'll show you what's too heavy for me," she shot back. "Go ahead, make my day."

Then Matthew did the unforgivable thing. He laughed at her.

She didn't remember quite how it happened. One moment she was threatening him with a lobster trap that was almost as big as she was, in the next Matthew Connelly was in the harbor with the lobster trap floating beside him and the cheers of almost every woman on Muscatoon echoing in his ears.

"That's it, Jeannie. Go for it!" Karen shouted from the porch of the Muscatoon Inn.

The red fury faded slightly, and with her hands clasped over her head in a sign of victory, Jeannie turned and headed down the one paved street in Muscatoon, out toward the east end of the island, head held high, the cheers serenading her on her way. Not once did she turn back to look at her waterlogged lover.

She managed until she was out of sight, until the cheers of the village women faded from her ears. She managed until she was halfway along the path, in the midst of the thick pine forest, and then sudden horrifying realization swept over her. Had she really knocked Matthew Connelly into the harbor with a lobster trap? What if she'd knocked him unconscious? What if he drowned?

No, she thought with a curl of her lip. Only the good die young. And for all the number of cheering women there were just as many supportive lobstermen around. They at least would save the trap, and undoubtedly Matthew Connelly along with it.

Well, that was that, she thought, slipping the high heels off and shrugging her shoulders. Everyone made mistakes;

she shouldn't have expected to be immune. Live and learn, no use crying over spilt milk, better to have loved and—

A howl of pain interrupted the last platitude, and it was with a sense of shock that Jeannie realized that howl had come from her own throat. She took the handmade leather shoes and threw them into the woods, as hard as she could, and then she began to run, tears blinding her eyes, pouring down her face, racking her body.

The cats were waiting for her when she raced onto her front porch. She was crying too hard to do more than register their presence, and then she stumbled into the house, straight into the living room, and flung herself down on the wicker sofa in an orgy of weeping.

It was getting dark when she awoke. The events of the last few days had taken their toll—the rush to Vermont, the all-night drive back to the ferry, the onrush of grief at Matthew's betrayal, had all conspired to wipe her out, and she'd fallen into a waterlogged sleep without even realizing it. She opened her swollen eyes and for a moment couldn't remember where she was.

It came back to her. The wicker sofa was hard and uncomfortable beneath her, her feet hurt from her run across the rocky path, and her throat hurt from crying. But nothing hurt enough to get her to move, and she shut her eyes again, willing it all to go away.

The sound came again, the unmistakable sound of footsteps on the front porch. Jeannie raised her head sharply as a sudden, absurd hope rushed through her. He couldn't have left her; he had come back.

"Jeannie?" Karen's voice echoed from the front porch, and Jeannie thanked heaven for the darkness. When would she ever learn?

"In here," she called back, pulling her weary body upright on the wicker sofa. Her linen suit was bunched and rumpled around her, her eyes were swollen and gritty, but the dim twilight of the living room would cover a multitude of sins.

Besides, who did she think she was fooling? "You look like hell," said Karen. "I thought I'd better come out and see how you were doing after that debacle in the harbor."

"Thanks." Reaching for the Depression-glass saucer that held kitchen matches, Jeannie lit the kerosene lamp in front of her, squinting against the sudden bright flame. "Did someone fish him out of the harbor or has he joined the lobsters?"

"Enoch fished him out."

"Too bad," Jeannie said, shoving her tangled hair away from her face. "Did he take him away with him?"

"Yes."

"Well, there's something good to be said for the afternoon. I'm fine, Karen. Sadder but wiser, bloody but unbowed, et cetera, et cetera."

"Now I know you're upset; you always talk in clichés when you're upset." Karen sat down beside her on the sofa. "Do you want to talk about it?"

Jeannie considered it for a moment, then shook her head. "Not right now. Maybe later. Right now I want something to eat, a lot to drink, and then a good night's sleep."

"I've brought you dinner from the inn. With Hal's compliments, believe it or not. I think he's decided to overlook your midnight swim."

"He's not picking up the pieces," Jeannie warned. "I'm going back to celibacy full-time."

"I think he's given up on you, darling. I think he's toying with celibacy himself; he hasn't had a woman in more than a week. If I didn't know better I'd think he was in love."

"Not with me," Jeannie said.

"No, not with you. I can't imagine who it might be; no one new has shown up." Karen shook her head. "I'll just go and heat this up. Why don't you go take a shower and change out of those clothes? You must be..." her voice trailed off in a strangled cry of horror. "What in God's name is that?"

"What?"

The expression on Karen's face suggested she was viewing something very old and very dead and quite possibly smelly. "That painting," she said in tones of deepest loathing. "I have never seen anything so bad in my entire life."

It was there, all right; he'd hung it over the fireplace. If possible, it was even uglier than when she'd first seen it. Swirls of muddy purple and brown warred with a bilious shade of green that presumably represented the ocean, and the one recognizable feature, the spit of land on the eastern end, was so grossly misshapen that Jeannie found herself laughing. "God help me," she murmured. "He would have to leave that monstrosity."

"Did Connelly do that?" Karen asked in awe. "I thought the man was a painter. When he wasn't a crook, that is."

"He wasn't a crook; he was a police detective," Jeannie said patiently. "And as you can see, he most certainly wasn't a painter. I think I'll burn it."

"Don't do that!" Karen protested. She viewed the offending painting, tilting her head to one side. "It sort of grows on one."

"Like barnacles," Jeannie said.

"No, I actually might grow to like it."

"You can have it."

Karen shook her head. "If and when you really decide to burn it, I'll take it for you. But in the meantime I'll make you dinner while you read the note he left you."

"Note?" Jeannie shrieked.

"It's on the mantel under the painting," Karen said smugly, disappearing into the kitchen. "I'll leave you in peace."

She hadn't noticed it when she'd stumbled in earlier, not the horrible painting or the white sheet of paper propped beneath it. Maybe there was some excuse for his leaving like that, maybe she'd done a terrible, unforgivable thing by tossing him into the harbor. She reached for the paper with trembling fingers.

A moment later she wished she'd used a grappling hook to toss him over. She crumpled the sheet of paper in one small fist.

"What's he say? Did he come up with a good excuse?" Karen reappeared beside her, placing a glass of red wine in her hand.

Jeannie tossed it off in a single gulp, took Karen's glass and drained that, too. "Nope. He said he wasn't able to love me the way I deserved to be loved, and he didn't want to use me."

"Noble of him," Karen observed dryly.

"Bastard," Jeannie said succinctly. "Too bad he didn't drown. Wanna get drunk with me?"

"Sounds good to me. We can have a great time cursing men."

"Follow me." They trailed into the kitchen, where the smells of reheating lasagna wafted through the huge room. Jeannie poured them both another glass, then lifted hers high in a toast. "Here's to Matthew Connelly, long may he rot in hell."

"And here's to Hal Vreeland, may he join Matthew Connelly there," Karen offered.

"And here's to the all the rest of the men in this world," Jeannie said. "May they prove to be more worthy of our love and affection."

"Hear, hear," said Karen, and they drained their glasses.

Chapter Fifteen

Schooner Springs, Colorado, was about as far removed from the south side of Chicago as he could get, Matthew Connelly thought as he drove slowly through the busy, tourist-crowded streets of the picturesque little Western town. Even in autumn the place was packed, and winter would bring its own host of problems. Despite the quaint, cow-town quality of the Victorian storefronts, the wide streets, the easygoing ambiance, Connelly wasn't fooled. There were crimes beneath the charming front, there were murders and thefts, and almost as much snow in people's pockets as topped the towering mountains surrounding them.

Still and all, it was a hell of a lot more peaceful than Chicago, even if it lacked the serene charm of Muscatoon Island. He'd always known Muscatoon was a stopping-off place, a spot for R and R until he was ready to face life again. Schooner Springs was another step on his journey back into life. A temporary assignment as chief of police for the resort town would give him enough of a taste for it to see if that was how he wanted to spend the rest of his life. As peaceful, as laid-back as it was, he already knew it wasn't the answer. His ghosts were still haunting him. Only now Jeannie MacPherson had joined their ranks.

The answer didn't lie back on Muscatoon island, he had

to remember that. He'd left because he had to, because he couldn't stand to hurt Jeannie any more than he had already. He wasn't ready or able to fall in love, and he could see her falling head over heels. And he wasn't going to let her get more involved.

The problem was, now that he'd left her, she seemed even more present in his thoughts, his dreams, his fantasies. He'd left her because he couldn't love her. Now, with a puzzling twist of fate, that no longer seemed to be a problem. He spent his free time mooning over her, daydreaming about her until he felt like an infatuated schoolboy.

His anger had carried him through the first few weeks in Colorado. The cracked ribs took longer to heal than the broken wrist, and every time he coughed the pain reminded him of Jeannie MacPherson's white-hot rage and her deftness with a certain lobster trap that caught him just the wrong way. But his anger had healed before his wounds, and for a while he was even glad she'd managed to connect. At least she'd been able to vent her rage, to release it. By now he'd be a part of her past, forgotten, a summertime mistake.

Except that he was feeling more and more as if he didn't want to be forgotten, didn't want to be a part of her past. As he was coming slowly back into the mainstream of life, he was beginning to realize that he could be human after all. Every last emotion that had seemed wiped out of him after the Springside Strangler was moving back in, like fresh blood pumped into lifeless limbs. It hurt at first, it hurt like hell, but the feeling was coming back, coming back stronger than ever. And it was coming back for Jeannie MacPherson.

All right, maybe it was still part of some mid-life crisis, he warned himself. The last thing he should do was drop everything and race back to Muscatoon Island and beg her forgiveness. This might be a temporary aberration, and if he gave her false hope he'd never forgive himself.

False hope? Who the hell was he kidding? If she had any sense at all—and Jeannie MacPherson had a great deal of sense—she'd take one look at him and head for the nearest lobster trap. And it would be no more than he deserved.

Well, he'd give her time, he'd give himself time. His contract with the city of Schooner Springs would be up at the end of December, and then, and not until then, he'd head back to Muscatoon Island and see whether Jeannie Mac-Pherson might be as forgiving as she was sensible, and whether the two of them might find something more permanent.

God, he was getting maudlin in his old age. He could see living on Muscatoon, he could even see babies and commitment and living happily ever after. Surely he was old enough and experienced enough to know those things never worked out. What self-destructive imp was telling him that they could?

Well, he was going to ignore that imp, at least until December 31. And then, come hell or high water, he'd track Jeannie MacPherson down and admit that whether he was capable of it or not, he *was* in love with her, dammit. And what did she want to do about it? And then he'd duck.

The cast had been off his wrist for two weeks now, but it still twinged slightly as he turned the fancy sedan that was part of the sheriff's perks into the rambling ranch house that was another one of those goodies. Three more months, he thought. Well, maybe now he'd know what it was like to do time.

JEANNIE WAS DOING SOME time of her own. Muscatoon Island had never seemed so remote, so barren, so lonely. It fitted her mood perfectly, but it did nothing to lighten it.

Even the amusing stop-and-go courtship going on in the kitchens of the Muscatoon Inn only provided momentary distraction.

Hal Vreeland had finally discovered Karen, or so it seemed. Maybe Jeannie's words had sunk in during their ridiculous boat excursion, maybe not. Whatever the cause, the results were a determinedly celibate summer for the innkeeper as he cautiously pursued his chief waitress.

It had taken Karen a couple of weeks to realize what was happening. When Jeannie had first called her attention to it, she had scoffed and announced that she was almost as loony as Hal. After all, he'd had her and thrown her away. Why should he change his mind?

But after another week of his shy, almost deferential behavior, she had to admit, it appeared that he *had* changed his mind. Particularly when he flat-out ignored the blatant overtures of the most recent high-flying divorcée who came to taste the Muscatoon Inn's various delights.

"So what are you going to do about it?" Jeannie roused herself from her depressive torpor long enough to ask. They were both sitting enjoying the peace that only comes after feeding forty-five hungry tourists breakfast. Karen had her feet up on the scarred oak table, and with a sigh she yanked the kerchief from her head and shook her blond hair free.

"Make him suffer," she said cheerfully.

Jeannie laughed. "Are you sure you want to do that? He might wriggle off the hook if you give him enough slack."

Karen fanned herself with an old copy of *Down East*. "If he wants to wriggle he can go ahead and wriggle. If I take him this time it's going to be on my terms, not his."

"Good for you." Jeannie stared morosely into her coffee cup. "It'll keep you out of trouble."

"Speaking of trouble, have you heard from your cop?"

"Nope."

"Are you ready to get rid of that horrible painting yet?"

"Nope. I keep it in my living room to remind me of what a fool I've been." Jeannie sighed. "I loved not wisely but too well."

"Oh, God, here come the clichés again. You've talked in nothing but those since Matthew Connelly left here," Karen complained. "When are you going to get over him, Jeannie?"

Jeannie managed a wry smile. "Are you trying to tell me there are other fish in the sea?" She ducked as Karen tossed the magazine at her head. "Sorry about that. I'm already mostly over him, Karen. By September I won't even remember what he looks like."

"He looks like Harrison Ford. You can't forget that unless you never go see a blockbuster movie again," Karen said. "Why September?"

"I'm leaving Muscatoon in September. Time to face the real world and all its problems again."

"Since when doesn't Muscatoon constitute the real world?" Karen demanded. "It seems pretty real to me right now."

"It's real to me, too. But I'm not sure it's my world. Sooner or later I have to go back to my old life just to make sure I'm not copping out. And Tom needs me right now."

"I thought Tom was married."

"Of course Tom's married, and very happily so. He needs me professionally, not emotionally. We're going to expand the company, somewhere out West, and I've promised I'll oversee the project, at least in its beginning stages."

"And then what will you do?"

Jeannie shook her head. "I don't know. See how much I like it. See how much I like being in the midst of things again, how much I miss Muscatoon. Then maybe I'll be back, if I can take the loneliness."

"It never bothered you before."

"I'm afraid Matthew spoiled it for me," she said with a sigh. "I used to be so happy all alone out there on the eastern end. Now it feels empty."

"Maybe that'll pass. There's a lot to be said for living alone."

"Maybe. I did it for more than two years, and loved it, but I'm afraid the time has passed. I want someone to love; I want someone to have babies with and live happily ever after."

"Someone?" Karen echoed archly.

"No, dammit," she said on a low wail, "I want Matthew! Much good it will do me."

"Can anyone join or is this all girls?" Hal inquired brightly from the dining-room door.

"Come on in," Karen said with a lazy gesture, not bothering to remove her feet from the table. "Maybe you can cheer Jeannie up. I'm consoling her on her lost love."

Hal strolled into the kitchen, looking like a very handsome, very insecure puppy. "You know what they say, Jeannie. Better to have loved and lost—"

"Oh, God, don't you start it, too," Karen moaned. "One person speaking in clichés I can survive; two will drive me crazy."

Jeannie grinned. "A friend in need is a friend indeed."

"Neither a borrower nor a lender be," Hal chimed in.

"Waste not, want not," Jeannie said.

"A stitch in time saves nine."

Karen screamed, a loud, echoing scream that would have reached clear down to the dock. She smiled sweetly. "One more word," she said, "and I won't answer for the consequences. Did you know Jeannie's planning to leave Muscatoon, Hal?"

"I knew she was going to work on the new ice-cream plant, but I thought it was only temporary."

"I don't know how permanent it will be. Speaking of which, may I use your new telephone? I need to check in with Tom."

Hal sighed, a long-suffering sigh. "I sure will be glad when they finish installing everyone's phones. I have non-stop traffic through my office all day long."

"Oh, it's a tough life," Jeannie mocked. "I doubt they'll get around to laying the lines to the eastern point, so you're just going to have to be neighborly."

"Go ahead," he said wearily. "Karen can keep me company while you finish your business."

Karen grinned a knowing grin. "I suppose I can, at least for a short while. Why don't you make a couple of phone calls while you're at it, Jeannie? I can beat Hal at cribbage while we wait."

"Beat me?" Hal echoed, affronted. "I'd like to see you try."

"Who else should I call?"

"Maybe a certain cop?" Karen suggested slyly.

Jeannie shook her head. "I don't know how to find him. I don't even know what state he's in. All I know is that he didn't go back to Chicago."

"You tried?"

"I tried," she admitted.

"Well, then, why don't you call his sister? She ought to know where her brother went to."

Jeannie stared at her for a long, contemplative moment. "I've been afraid to," she said finally.

"The two of you hit it off pretty well, didn't you? I'm sure she'd tell you."

"Unless Matthew told her not to." That unpleasant thought cropped up, unbidden.

"He wouldn't do that, Jeannie. I have a very real suspicion that Matthew Connelly is no more finished with you than you are with him."

"Hope springs eternal."

Karen grimaced. "Call her, Jeannie."

"Maybe."

She disappeared into the office, and Karen turned her attention back to Hal. "Get the cribbage board."

"What are you doing, Karen?"

"Matchmaking. Can't you tell?" She took the cards from him and began shuffling with a deftness that would have put an Atlantic City dealer to shame.

"Why don't you expend some of that energy on yourself?" he demanded, taking Jeannie's abandoned seat and moving it closer to Karen.

She smiled sweetly. "Oh, I think you're doing a good enough job."

SLOWLY JEANNIE REPLACED the receiver on Hal's brand-new telephone. It was the first one installed on the island, and so far the only one, with the exception of a pay phone down by Ernie's store that no one ever bothered to use. It was a nice phone, she thought absently. A pretty, brick-red shade. And so very helpful.

She sat there in silence for several minutes, leaning back in Hal's oak swivel desk chair and staring out the window toward the sea. She didn't really want to leave Muscatoon, didn't want to leave the ocean and the rocky coast of Maine, but she didn't want to stay alone any longer.

The last of her indecision evaporated, and she leaned forward and began the laborious dialing that would get her off the island. Within five minutes she was talking with Tom Mickelson in Vermont.

"I've thought about it, Tom, and I will oversee the new

factory. But I've changed my mind about Santa Fe. I want Tom and Jeannie's western branch in Schooner Springs, Colorado.'' She held the phone away as the loud squawking threatened to deafen her. ''Schooner Springs,'' she murmured dreamily to no one in particular. ''I bet it's beautiful in the fall.''

''LOTS OF EXPANSION going on around here, Connelly,'' Harry Bateman, one of the town fathers, boomed in a suitably expansive tone of voice, clapping his hand on Matthew's shoulder and jarring his cracked ribs. ''Lots of new industry, lots of growth up at the ski area, lots of new talent and new money streaming in. We've been talking, and we'd like you to be a part of that new growth, that new talent.''

Matthew kept his face blank, not allowing even a small wince of pain to mar his expression. These cocktail parties were one of the less delightful perks that went along with the police chief's job, and as often he could he shunned them. He'd been caught sneaking out that afternoon, collared by Harry Bateman, and he'd had no choice but to go along amicably. The mayor was using the event to make another announcement about a new company moving into the Schooner Springs area, and they were all supposed to express their delight with the move and their eagerness to support it.

Well, as far as he was concerned Schooner Springs already had too much growth and money and talent and industry. Any more would crowd the place past any pretensions to charm or quaintness. But then, it wasn't his business, and it wasn't his place. Only for another three months. He gave Harry Bateman his professional smile, reserved for police commissioners and town fathers and other sorts who helped pay his bills, and took another sip of beer. ''I'm flattered, Harry, really I am.'' He matched Bateman's broad tones. "But I can't really make a commitment at this time...."

"Of course you can't, of course you can't," Harry boomed. "And we wouldn't want you to. But keep it in mind, Connelly. We could sure use a man of your talents out here. Here, let me get you another beer." Before Matthew could protest, Bateman had whisked the half-finished Coors out of his hand and replaced it with a fresh one. Matthew bit back his complaint. One of the things he missed most about the East and the Midwest was the existence of imported beer, something with a bite and a heft to it. Coors tasted too much like water to him.

If Bateman would just wander away, find some other poor slob to brag to, then he might possibly be able to slip out the back. All the area newspeople were in place, scarfing up the goodies, swilling down the Jack Daniel's along with the omnipresent Coors, milling around and paying very little attention to the mayor's pontifications. He was halfway through his current announcement, and everyone knew how long it took for him to come to the point. At least, thought Matthew, it wasn't an announcement about the latest string of murders, or the latest coke bust, or how many derelicts froze to death last night. Schooner Springs would never allow news of derelicts or murders to get into the press, and anything to do with drugs was carefully hushed up. He'd had his orders when he arrived, and it caused him no great pain to follow them. Publicity had never been his cup of tea, and he'd had more than enough with the Springside Strangler.

"This is great news," Bateman was saying beside him. "Great, great news. A shot in the arm for this town."

The rumble from the assembled press corps threatened to drown out the mayor, and Matthew leaned forward. "What's that?"

"Just listen!" Bateman admonished, grinning broadly and digging his elbow into Matthew's cracked ribs with an excess of good-fellowship. "Great news."

The cocktail chatter drowned out Matthew's uncontrollable groan of pain. Without further hesitation he pulled away from Bateman's beefy arm, held up his still-full can of beer with a silent message, and at Bateman's understanding nod, headed off in the direction of the bar. At the last minute he veered off, determined to slip out to his car before anyone noticed. Bateman would happily find another drinking buddy and he could read about the announcement in the morning paper.

A sudden cheer went up, a sound of uninhibited enthusiasm from the assembled, usually cynical reporters, and Matthew stopped by the door startled enough to delay his departure.

"Bunch of sissies," the grizzled old-timer who still served on the city council sneered from his station by the bar. His glass of whiskey was so dark it resembled molasses, and he caught Matthew's curious gaze. "Bunch of wimps," he announced more loudly. "I've never seen so many grown men excited about ice cream."

A sudden foreboding swept over Matthew. "Ice cream?"

"Some fancy Eastern ice-cream company is setting up a factory outside of town at the old Remson place. Bunch of damned foolishness if you ask me."

"What kind of ice cream?" His voice sounded hollow.

"How the hell should I know?" the old codger shot back. "It's too cold up here to eat ice cream. You need something to warm your innards. Like this." He raised his glass and downed an impressive amount.

Matthew had hesitated too long. "There you are, boy," Bateman shouted in his ear. "What do you think about the mayor's news? Great, isn't it?"

He didn't really need to ask. He'd known this was coming for a long time, and right now he wasn't quite sure how he felt about it. "I couldn't quite hear everything," he said. "What ice-cream company?"

"Why, the best, son, the best. Nothing less than Tom and Jeannie's Celestial Ice-Cream Works. And one of the founders is coming out to oversee the factory."

He nodded gloomily. "Not Tom, I suppose.?"

"Nope. The little lady herself," Bateman said cheerfully. "Ain't that great news?"

"Great," said Matthew gloomily. "Just great."

Chapter Sixteen

Schooner Springs, Colorado, was not Jeannie MacPherson's idea of a place to live. Oh, it was quaint all right, she thought as she drove down the wide Western streets that looked so strange to her Eastern Seaboard eyes. But there were too damned many people, too much money, too much self-conscious charm for her tastes. Two years on Muscatoon had taken their toll, she thought. There was always the possibility that she might never become totally comfortable in civilization again.

Mind you, the mountains were beautiful. She'd nearly had a heart attack on her way from Denver that morning, climbing the switchbacks over Berthoud Pass in her little rented Chevette, soaring down the other side with her foot on the brake and her sweaty palms clenched to the steering wheel. If it made her nervous in summer, she hated to think of those incredible mountain passes covered with snow. She could only hope and pray that Matthew wouldn't take too long to come to his senses.

A police car cruised by in the opposite direction, and for a moment her heart leapt into her throat. On closer inspection the driver turned out to be a blond-haired man who appeared to be in his mid-twenties, and Jeannie relaxed. Connelly wouldn't be out in a cruise car, she reminded herself. He was management level; doubtless he seldom left his desk.

She was half an hour early for her appointment with members of the city council. Tom had already sent someone to do the dirty work. An abandoned beer factory had been bought and was already halfway renovated for the ice-cream works. She could drive back out Highway 17 and take a look at the progress, or she could wander around the living quarters Tom had rented for her. Or she could park her car and look for the police station.

She'd already seen the ice-cream works, and she'd already dropped her bags off at the ski-area condominium that Tom mistakenly thought was just her style, with its hot tub and king-size bed and microwave oven just large enough for one frozen dinner. She wasn't quite ready for Matthew Connelly in all his glorious flesh. She needed a few days to psych herself up.

She cast an anxious glance at her reflection in the rearview mirror. It had taken all summer to build up the thin layer of honey-gold tan with its mixed blessing of freckles across her nose, and God only knew how long the October sun in the Rockies would preserve it. She'd gotten her hair cut on her way west, and it now swung just above her shoulders. Her eyes were still clear and blue; the ten pounds she had gained from depression-eating had disappeared rapidly when she made her plans to move to Schooner Springs. In all things that mattered she was the same person Matthew Connelly had first surprised in the seedy little kitchen in Sunshine Cottage such a short while ago.

The Schooner Springs Municipal Building was off on a side street. It looked like any other bureaucrat's office building, square and solid and unimaginative. Jennie pulled the car into the parking lot and stopped, staring up at the red stone facade and the posted list of offices contained within.

It held the town offices, the site of her planned meeting. It held the federal post office, the zoning committee, the planning committee, the chamber of commerce. And it held police headquarters.

Once more Jeannie checked her rearview mirror. There were four police cars parked in the parking lot, three large black luxury cars with municipal license plates, and a scattering of out-of-state license plates. Doubtless one of those police cars belonged to Matthew. Would he be wearing a uniform? Was there any way she could get in and out of her meeting and that building without running into him before she was ready to?

The chances were iffy, all depending on the offices' proximity to one another. Well, she was still ten minutes early. She could head straight for the police, breeze in with a cheery hello, and then go to her meeting as if she hadn't a care in the world.

Just the right touch, she thought, pleased with herself. No need to give the boy a swelled head. He might very well assume that she'd picked Schooner Springs, Colorado, of all places, for her ice-cream works simply because he was there, but he couldn't be certain. It was too much of a quixotic gesture, to be sure, and she didn't know if he realized how quixotic she could be. Nor how determined.

No, she'd play it very cool for the first couple of weeks. At least she had the element of surprise on her side. In the battle of the sexes she anticipated, she would need all the advantages she could find.

The building was dark and cool after the bright, hot sunlight, and for a moment Jeannie stopped, blinded. Maybe Matthew wouldn't even recognize her. She was wearing her yuppie uniform—Liz Claiborne suit, discreet heels, gold chain around her neck. He was used to seeing her roam around in cottons and jeans—or nothing at all, she thought with a reminiscent sigh.

Police headquarters were on her left, municipal offices on the second floor. Holding her head up, she turned left.

And all for nothing. Captain Connelly wasn't in at the moment. Could the graying desk sergeant, who looked like Humphrey Bogart, be of help?

Jeannie didn't know whether to be relieved or disappointed. She let out the pent-up breath, smiled a dazzling smile, and said thank you, no. Maybe later. And headed up to the second floor.

"They're waiting for you, Ms MacPherson," a similarly attired yuppie informed her, opening a paneled door into the inner office. "Welcome to Schooner Springs."

"Yes, welcome to Schooner Springs," boomed Harry Bateman, moving from behind the massive oak desk that he'd commandeered by the sheer force of his personality. "I'm sorry the mayor couldn't be here today, but he's on one of his damned fact-finding missions. Cares more about saving Central America than he does about the future of Schooner Springs."

Jeannie smiled politely. "Maybe Central America needs more help," she suggested in a pleasant voice.

Bateman laughed his big, room-shaking laugh as if she'd made a great witticism. "Maybe it does at that," he agreed. "Harry Bateman here." He held out a beefy hand, and she let her smaller one disappear into its mighty grip. "And we're damned glad to have you here, Miss MacPherson, damned glad. Let me introduce you to the boys. That's Winnie Klein, head of Klein's Feed and Clothing store. Now don't you go thinking that he really sells cowboy clothes, though. No self-respecting cowboy could afford even a bandana at his place." The willowy Winnie nodded a friendly hello.

"And there's Charles Hudgins, president of the ski area, and a personal friend of mine. You be nice to him, you hear?" He gave Jeannie a friendly cuff that almost flattened her, and Charles Hudgins grinned sourly.

"And then behind you is our local chief of police, Matthew Connelly. He's only temporary, but we're hoping we can talk him into staying on fulltime, ain't that right, boy?"

So much for second sight, Jeannie thought philosophically, turning around very, very slowly. "Hello," she said. And then she let her eyes feast on him, as her face smiled a polite smile.

He wasn't in uniform. The jeans were faded, and probably some of the same ones he had worn in Maine, but the rest of his clothes were new. He must have been wearing some of Winnie Klein's high-priced cowboy duds, and he looked depressingly gorgeous.

He also didn't look the slightest bit surprised to see her. She should have realized the efficiency of small-town grapevines. Despite the size of Schooner Springs, it still was, in most respects, a small town. "Ms MacPherson," he said, his tone distant and noncommittal. "Welcome to Schooner Springs."

"We're planning a small reception for you on Friday, sort of a 'welcome to Schooner Springs' little get-together," Harry said in a hearty voice, moving between the two combatants with a singular lack of sensitivity. "You'll be providing a lot of jobs for the people in this area, and big as the ski area is, we can always use new industry. Not to mention bringing us some of the best damned ice cream in the world. This'll be our little way of saying thank you. Maybe his honor might even show up, but I wouldn't count on it, would you, Winnie?"

"Wouldn't count on it," Winnie echoed in a soft voice that matched his pale gray appearance.

"That would be very nice," Jeannie said, "but I don't think..."

"Friday okay for you, Charles?" Harry demanded, and Charles's sour smile tilted upward. "How about you, son?"

It took Jeannie a moment to realize that "son" was Matthew Connelly. She cast a curious glance at him wondering how he'd take being addressed as such, but he seemed inured to it.

"Wouldn't miss it for the world, Harry," he said, and that wonderful voice of his sent its customary shivers down her backbone.

"And bring that pretty little filly with you," Harry said.

Jeannie could feel her face pale. She did her best to appear unmoved, but she could feel those winter-gray eyes on her, eyes she had wondered if she'd ever feel again. "Which one?" said Matthew Connelly evenly.

Damn, she thought, it felt good to be alive. To be so angry she could spit, to be so in love that she wanted to fall at his feet and kiss his brand-new pointy-toed cowboy boots, to be so wound up she could climb Mount Wilhelm and back down again. It was so much better than those deadly weeks in Maine after Matthew had left her and everything had turned a dull gray.

Harry Bateman was laughing again, and Jeannie wondered for a moment if he ever stopped that thunderous joviality of his. "That's right, I forgot. You've got all the young ladies in town in an uproar. You better watch your step, Jeannie. You don't mind if I call you Jeannie, do you? Feels like I know you after looking at your face on a box of ice cream so many times. Anyway, this man's downright dangerous. Even with cracked ribs and a broken wrist he was breaking hearts right and left."

"Cracked ribs? Broken wrist?" she echoed.

"Now, don't you worry, Jeannie. It ain't that dangerous

around here. Connelly came to us in damaged condition, but he mended just fine, didn't you, son?''

Jeannie fought back the feeling of guilt that threatened to swamp her. If he had all the young fillies in town in an uproar, he deserved every broken bone he got. "How did it happen, captain?" she inquired in a bland voice. "I'd think a big strong man like you would be able to take better care of yourself."

Matthew's answering smile wasn't reassuring; there was definitely an evil glint to it, one promising retribution. "I ran into an angry woman, Ms MacPherson."

"And he's been running ever since," Harry bellowed. "My own daughter did her best to get him interested, but no dice. My wife thinks he's nursing a broken heart. Now don't scowl at me, boy. I think Jeannie here needs to know what she's up against."

Jeannie found herself smiling in spite of herself. "Broken heart, eh? By the same wicked woman who broke your wrist?"

"I doubt it," Matthew drawled. "I make it a policy never to take the same risks twice."

"It's a good policy," Jeannie said. "I wish I could learn it."

"Now, now, boys and girls, let's not get all serious on me," said Harry. "We're all going to be working together for the next few months; let's be friends."

It was extremely difficult to send subtle messages to a determinedly distant Matthew with Bateman's bulk between them, but Jeannie did her level best. She raised her head, looked him straight in the eyes, and said in a silken voice, "I have every intention of staying on good terms with the chief of police."

Bateman roared with laughter. "That's usually a good idea, missy."

"It won't do you any good." The words were softly spoken, but Jeannie had no doubt as to his meaning.

She smiled at him. "We'll see about that," she murmured.

"Hear that?" Bateman bellowed. "These two are going at it already. Sounds like it's going to be a lynching or a wedding, or I miss my guess."

"Harry." For the first time Charles Hudgins spoke, and his slow, heavy voice carried a definite warning. It also carried a surprising New York accent.

"I know, I know." Harry put one beefy arm around Jeannie's slender shoulders, another around Matthew's, squeezing them both against his burly body. "Sometime this mouth of mine is going to get me into a hell of a lot of trouble. Don't mind me, boys and girls. I'm a hopeless romantic. Always looking for happy endings."

Jeannie suffered the embrace; she had no choice, given his bearlike strength. When she finally was able to extricate herself she gave herself a brisk shake. "Happy endings are nice," she agreed.

"But they don't exist outside of fairy tales," Matthew said slowly.

"Children, children. One would think you two had known each other forever to be squabbling like that, rather than just met," Harry reproved them.

At that point Jeannie decided she'd had enough for one day. This constant sparring was shredding her nerves. "Look, I have to be back out at the factory by one," she said. "If you'll let me know where and when that reception will be, I'll see what I can do."

"You're up in the Telemark condos, aren't you?" Charles said in that eerie voice. "We'll be holding it in the Svenson Lodge, just about in walking distance."

"If I ever learn my way around the mountain," she said

with a laugh that she hoped wasn't disapproving. She hated the crammed-together condos and nightclubs and ski shops.

"Oh, you'll learn fast enough," Charles promised. "Friday evening, six o'clock. I'll send someone to bring you, so you won't have to worry about getting lost."

"We wouldn't want our chief of police having to send out search parties, now would we?" Harry boomed.

"Especially when they might not be very strongly motivated," Jeannie murmured.

One last time Harry roared with laughter, and Jeannie took quick advantage of his merriment, slipping under his arm and moving past Matthew with a deftness that surprised even her. "See you gentlemen later," she tossed off over her shoulder.

She almost made it. She'd forgotten the lightning-swift moves Matthew was capable of. She was halfway out the door before he caught her, far enough out of sight so that when his hand clamped down on her wrist with biting force she felt safe in kicking at his shins.

But he was too fast for her. "I warned you," he said in an undertone. "I never take the same risks twice."

Harry poked his head around the door. "You two gonna get better acquainted?" He eyed Matthew's deceptively gentle-looking grip on her wrist.

Matthew smiled then, a sharklike smile that boded no good for the likes of Jeannie MacPherson. "I just thought I'd like to give Ms MacPherson a personal welcome."

"Well, good, good," Harry boomed. "Make her feel at home. We want the two of you to stay in Schooner Springs a long, long time."

"I'll do my best, Harry," Matthew promised, his voice like raw silk.

She really had no choice but to follow him. That tanned, long-fingered hand was like a manacle around her wrist, the fingers biting in with unnecessary force as he dragged her down the flight of stairs. She pulled back on the landing, but he ignored her efforts, jerking her forward, almost off her precarious heels, as he continued on down the iron steps.

"Which wrist did I break?" She had the temerity to inquire. "If it's the one you're currently using to torture me, it's clear I didn't cause any permanent damage."

Matthew stopped dead-still at the bottom of the stairs. The doors were closed leading into the hall, and they were entirely alone in the empty stairwell. "You do believe in living dangerously, don't you?" he questioned softly. "What makes you think I won't break your wrist in return?"

Jeannie thought about being frightened for a moment, then dismissed the notion. "You aren't a bully, Matthew."

"And you are. One doesn't throw lobster traps at people who can't very well toss them back."

"I'm sorry about that."

"Are you?" He was plainly skeptical, and he had a right to be, Jeannie thought. She wasn't really sure she was sorry at all.

"Let's say I'm sorry I broke any bones," she temporized.

"That I might believe. Now why don't you tell me why you're really here," he suggested politely.

"To oversee the new ice-cream works," she replied sweetly.

"Sure you are. Why Schooner Springs?"

She smiled. "Why not Schooner Springs?"

"Don't play games with me, Jeannie. Did you know I was here?"

She cocked her head to one side. He still had that grip on her wrist, but he clearly had almost forgotten it. Instead of squeezing tightly, his thumb was absently stroking her, sending shivers of mournful delight down her backbone. "I knew you were here," she replied with a modicum of honesty. "I just decided not to let that deter me."

He smiled then, a slow, skeptical smile. "Uh-huh," he said. "Well, I'll do my best not to get in your way if you do your best not to get in mine. Sounds fair to you?"

Not promising, she thought. But at least he wasn't riding her out of town on a rail. "That sounds eminently fair. I wouldn't want to interfere with your little fillies." She couldn't keep the note of spite out of her voice, and his smile broadened.

"No, we wouldn't want that." His thumb was moving higher, and Jeannie told herself he couldn't realize what he was doing. Suddenly she began to sway closer to him, almost by accident, almost as if he was exerting a gentle pressure to bring her closer to him. But he couldn't be, could he?

"No," she whispered awaiting his lips nervously, "we wouldn't want that." She shut her eyes as they drew closer and closer.

The door at the top of the stairwell slammed open and there was a sound like stampeding elephants clattering down the stairs. As the clattering reached the landing, it turned out to be Harry Bateman, huffing and puffing.

He paused long enough to catch his breath, leering down at them like a benevolent Western Santa Claus. "Still getting acquainted, children?"

Matthew was a foot and a half away, and his hands were no longer anywhere near her. Jeannie had been too bemused even to feel him move away, but the sudden loss of his warmth left her feeling bereft enough to cry.

"Just warning Ms MacPherson about some of the pitfalls of life in Schooner Springs," he said smoothly.

"Like certain lonely police chiefs?" Harry suggested slyly.

"Like certain gossiping businessmen," Matthew returned.

"Like not being late to meetings at the factory," Jeannie broke in. "See you later." She was racing for the door before Matthew had a chance to stop her.

"Maybe," Matthew said in a cool voice.

"Definitely," boomed Harry Bateman.

Chapter Seventeen

Matthew Connelly left word that he wasn't to be disturbed, closed the door of his spacious, old-fashioned office, dropped into the chair and propped his booted feet on his cluttered desk. The pointy toes of his cowboy boots amused him, though they had a bad habit of tripping him up. He should have gone for good old Frye boots, instead of these fancy things. Who was he trying to kid?

Well, he was trying to kid Jeannie MacPherson, for one thing. He still couldn't quite believe his reaction when she walked into the room, the immediate tightening in his gut, the wanting that had been so carefully banked down flaring forth uncontrollably at the mere sight of her. If he'd had any doubts before, the sight of that slender, endearingly vulnerable back had banished them. She looked like a little girl dressed up in her mother's clothes. That suit wasn't right for her, though it was undeniably flattering to her narrow, coltish body. She belonged in country clothes, not in stockings and high heels. He liked her barefoot, bare-legged, running along the rocky beaches of Muscatoon Island, her red hair streaming behind her. He even loved her red hair, he realized with a start. He must be far gone.

But things hadn't changed all that much. He still was a man carrying too much emotional baggage. Every time he'd think he was finally free from the past, the nightmare would start again—he'd be staring at the bloody hole in his groin and then up into the grinning death's-head face of George Kirwin, and he'd wake up in a cold sweat. He wouldn't, couldn't, ask Jeannie to share that nightmare, wouldn't, couldn't use her to forget again. He had to get the Springside Strangler out of his life before there was room for the likes of Jeannie MacPherson. If she couldn't wait, if it was a case of now or never, then he'd have to settle for never.

That was hard to do, when the memory, the scent, the feel of her invaded his sleep and most of his waking hours. He could be patient enough when she was half a continent away, but the thought of her only a few miles up the mountain was enough to shatter his strongest resolutions.

December, he reminded himself. It was the beginning of October already; he'd been in Schooner Springs since August and he'd survived. Two months down, three months to go. But it was a lot easier when Jeannie MacPherson was an idealized memory and not a hell of a temptation.

Of course, there was always the chance that she was simply there for revenge, that tossing him in the bay and breaking three of his bones wasn't quite vengeance enough. He discounted that thought as quickly as it sprang up. Jeannie would do many things in a white-hot rage, but once that immediate anger faded, she'd be a lot more reasonable. It wasn't in her nature to hurt someone in cold blood.

There was also the distant possibility that her coming to Schooner Springs had nothing whatsoever to do with him. He'd never been possessed of an overwhelming vanity before, but maybe it was part and parcel of his mid-life crisis.

Harry had blithely told him how unexpected the ice-cream works were, that he'd heard Tom and Jeannie's had already placed an option on a more suitable factory in Santa Fe and then abruptly changed its corporate mind; and that

Jeannie MacPherson's presence as overseer was also a complete surprise. There was no way Matthew could believe that he wasn't part of the reason for that abrupt change in corporate policy.

Damn, he thought, rocking back in the swivel chair. He felt pressured, angry, determined. He also felt more alive than he'd felt in maybe twenty years. Jeannie MacPherson was there, and it was going to work out, sooner or later. She was going to get what she wanted, what they both wanted, but it wasn't going to be all on her terms. He was going to take his own sweet time to do it right, with no more ghosts lingering. But God, it felt good to be alive.

IT WAS GOING TO TAKE HER a long time to get used to this condominium, Jeannie thought disconsolately, staring out the wide picture window at Mount Wilhelm looming overhead. The view was breathtaking, if you trained your gaze over the rabbit warren of condominiums to the lofty peak above them. The conveniences in the apartment were, well, convenient; but the novelty of the microwave had worn off by the third day, the hot tub was making her skin wrinkled and sloughing off her hard-worn tan, and the VCR was broken.

She was getting absolutely nowhere with Matthew Connelly.

When she first got back to the apartment with its freezer chock-full of Tom and Jeannie's best, she sat on her sofa and shook. Never before had she actually hit someone in anger, at least not since she was seven years old and her best friend had called her a problem child. Her elation over tossing Matthew in the bay hadn't lasted long, and now the knowledge that she'd broken his wrist and his ribs absolutely horrified her.

"Never again," she swore out loud. "Never will I lose my temper."

It had been a useless oath. She'd lost her temper a dozen times in the past four days, had been snappish, restless and bored. The burly construction crew didn't really have any need for an interfering executive nosing about the old beer factory. The specifications were perfect, the workmen experienced, and Jeannie was left feeling like a fifth wheel.

The sight of Matthew Connelly driving around the wide streets of Schooner Springs in his distinctive silver-and-black sedan didn't help matters. She did her best to bump into him once a day, on some trumped-up pretext or other, and it only added to her monumental frustration. He'd be charming, distant, perfectly polite and even friendly. But it was the uninvolved friendliness of casual acquaintances, people who had to work together, albeit distantly. They might never have shared eight nights of monumental passion that still left her knees weak and her palms sweaty at the memory.

She'd only been there four days, and it was iffy how long she could stretch her stay. The factory would be ready to go into production sometime in the new year, but whether Jeannie could stick it out that long remained to be seen. There simply wasn't enough for her to do. The new head of personnel, a boring sort from Denver, was doing all the hiring; the foreman was doing all the renovations; the comptroller in Burlington was doing all the ordering. All Jeannie could do was drive from the beer factory to her condo, back and forth, with hot tubs in between.

It was Friday afternoon, and that damned reception was due to start in another half hour. Jeannie padded barefoot through the thick gray carpeting, cursing and glowering. She hated, absolutely detested, these social occasions, and had avoided them whenever possible, sending a willing Tom in her place. But there was no one to deputize; it was the price she had to pay for being in Schooner Springs. She glared at her reflection in the mirror, at the strange woman staring back at her, and sighed wearily.

The simple black dress had cost a fortune. When she bought it, she was certain that it did wonders for her skinny body, made her look almost tall and willowy, and gave her a veneer of sophistication that would stand her well against anything Matthew Connelly chose to dish out. But now it felt uncomfortable, unnatural, and she couldn't rid herself of the feeling that she was dressing up as someone she wasn't. Her russet hair hung in a shiny cap around her face, her makeup was sophisticated and understated, and she was half tempted to take another dive into the constantly burbling hot tub.

Her doorbell rang, its melodious tones one more irritation on her already raw nerves, and she jumped. It would doubtless be Charles Hudgins come to escort her to the party, or one of his myriad shadowy assistants. She didn't know whom she preferred. Charles made her nervous, with the rough-edged voice and sour expression that was at variance with surprisingly avid little eyes, but his assistants gave her the creeps. They were all tall, dark and menacing, with dark suits, pockmarked faces, New York accents and ethnic last names. She kept peeking to see if they had ominous bulges in their jackets but could never be certain. Still, she couldn't rid herself of the notion that she was surrounded by a private army.

The doorbell rang again as she was slipping on the highest pair of heels she owned. They were the only thing that made the black dress work, they had been very expensive, and they were definitely dangerous on the health of a woman who had a tendency to fall off even the shortest heels. One ankle collapsed under her, and she fell against the wall, cursing, before she hobbled to the door, holding the other shoe in her hand.

"I'll be right with you," she said breathlessly as she flung open the door. "As soon as I get my damned—" of course, Matthew stood there, just as she'd fantasized but refused to admit "—shoe on," she finished, even more breathless. "What are you doing here, Matthew?" *No, that's not the way you were going to do it,* she lamented mentally. *That sounds like an accusation. You were supposed to sound arch, flirtatious, not hostile.*

"I've been ordered to bring you to the reception," he drawled. "Am I supposed to wait out here or are you inviting me in?"

Jeannie remembered the landscape hanging over her fireplace. "You're supposed to wait out there," she said quickly, too nervous to care how it sounded. "I'll be right out." She slammed the door in his face.

When she opened it again thirty seconds later she expected his most thunderous expression, almost welcomed it. If they could just get into a fight, then she might be able to break past that barrier of affability he'd set up.

But his expression was the same—distant, courteous, just slightly bored. Only his eyes suggested they felt any emotion at all, and Jeannie simply couldn't read them, no matter how hard she tried. "I'm sorry, but the place is a mess." The shoes were on, and they brought her eyes level with his mouth. Not a good place to be level with, she thought. "I haven't had time to get organized yet."

"You've been that busy?" The tone was still polite, friendly, but she could hear the skepticism beneath it, and she gritted her teeth.

"There's been a lot to do," she said brightly.

"You haven't looked as if you were overworked when I've seen you," he commented, still not moving.

"I wasn't aware that you were watching that closely."

Stalemate. Matthew looked down at her, and the bland expression faded a bit around the edges for a moment. *One small triumph,* Jeannie thought.

"Are you able to walk in those shoes?" he demanded coolly.

"Why shouldn't I? Have we that far to go?" His silver police car was nowhere in sight, and her own rented Chevette was parked down at the lower lot.

"Not that far. But you've never been good on high heels, and those are ridiculous." The moment the words were out of his mouth he looked as if he regretted them, and Jeannie felt another flare of triumph.

"I'll be fine. If I twist my ankle you can always carry me. That is, if your wounds have healed sufficiently." It was a deliberate dare, but Connelly was back in control.

"My ribs still give me a bit of trouble," he said, holding out his arm. "If you're ready?"

She could feel her face flush. It was going to be a long time before she'd stop feeling guilty about that—if ever. "I'm ready."

They traversed the narrow paved streets without a word between them. She took his arm because she couldn't help herself, couldn't deny herself the chance to touch him, to feel the steely strength of his forearm beneath her small hand. The shoes were precarious, but by concentrating on her balance and on Matthew Connelly's arm she was able to make it to the lodge without sprawling on the cobblestone roadway.

He abandoned her the moment they entered the milling crowds, abandoned her to Charles Hudgins's ominous patronage and Harry Bateman's overwhelming bonhomie without a backward glance. Jeannie watched him go, her face unguarded for a moment, her heart in her eyes.

"Have you known our police chief long?" Charles inquired silkily.

Jeannie pulled herself out of her distraction, shaking her head without the slightest compunction. "Not at all."

"Come along with me, little lady," Harry bellowed, placing a meaty hand on her forearm. "I've got lots of people I want you to meet." He was sweating slightly, his protuberant forehead flushed and shiny, and the look he cast Charles was subtly, surprisingly beseeching. For a moment Jeannie's natural curiosity reasserted itself, and she forgot all about Matthew Connelly. Something was going on between the two men, something apparently unpleasant, and she wondered what she'd interrupted when Matthew had thrust her between them.

A moment later that expression had vanished from Harry's bovine, friendly face, and she was being dragged off faster than her ankles could support her, from one group of Western-style yuppies to another, all the while trying to keep an unobtrusive eye on Matthew and whatever company he chose to keep.

For what it was worth, it didn't take her long to realize that any company he had was not of his own choosing. Bateman had been right; the young ladies of Schooner Springs found Dirty Harry fascinating. And who could blame them? Matthew Connelly had been good-looking on Muscatoon Island when he was pale and limping and bad-tempered. Now, tanned and healthy and mockingly polite, he was positively irresistible. Each time a lithe young creature sashayed up to him as he lounged against the bar and nursed a Coors, Jeannie would feel her nerves tense and she'd lose track of the conversation. Each time said young lady would give up and wander away, Jeannie would breathe a sigh of relief, turning her limpid gaze back to whomever Harry was pushing her on as if she'd never been distracted.

Charles's private army was very much in evidence. She wondered for a moment why he hadn't dispatched one of them, rather than the police chief himself. Maybe it hadn't been Charles's orders at all; maybe Matthew had volunteered, despite what he'd told her.

If he'd been interested enough to choose to come fetch her, that interest hadn't lasted long. Each time she sneaked a look at him he'd be supremely uninterested, either in her or in anyone else. The Coors seemed to hold the greatest fascination, and Jeannie felt her frustration rise.

If she hadn't sworn never to give in to her temper again, she'd go over there and slap the beer out of his hand. But she'd made a promise to herself and she intended to keep it. Matthew was right; she was a bully, to hit someone she knew would never hit back. Even if she wanted to force some sort of confrontation, some sort of emotion out of him, Matthew wasn't the sort to be forced.

Besides, she was here in Schooner Springs to win him over, not to capture him like some prize buffalo. She had to be careful, ladylike, patient, let him see that he wanted her, needed her, loved her if he could only recognize it. And he wasn't going to do that if she made a scene.

The party seemed to drag on forever. Jeannie's face began to stiffen from smiling so much, her neck hurt from keeping it turned away from Matthew, and her ankles were ready to collapse underneath her. The white wine Harry had provided her without asking was dry and tasteless, and she began to have the feeling that if this party didn't end soon she was going to burst into tears.

Not that tears would help matters. Matthew would probably just smile that distant little smile and walk away.

"What's the sigh for, little lady?" Harry inquired.

"That's an awful lonesome sound for a pretty little filly like you."

"I'm not a pretty little filly, Harry," she said in a weary voice. "I'm a hardworking woman who's had a long day."

"Long day, huh? Charles said you were only out at the site for half an hour."

Jeannie stared at him, amazement and the first inklings of uneasiness creeping in. "Who was watching me?" She asked the question in a deceptively quiet voice.

"Oh, you know Charles. His boys are all over the place. Someone must have mentioned it to him." Even Harry had the sense to be uncomfortable.

"I wouldn't have thought my comings and goings would be of such interest."

"Oh, everything a pretty little filly like you does is of interest," Harry protested.

"Harry," Jeannie said in a deceptively gentle voice, "the next time you call me a pretty little filly I'm going to scream."

"What?" She'd startled him out of his overbearing cheer, and he stared at her warily.

"Having a good time, Jeannie?" Charles had appeared out of nowhere, and on cue Harry began to sweat again.

"Just fine."

"Great party, isn't it?" Harry boomed.

"Just great," said Jeannie, looking around her a little desperately. Sometime in the last few moments she'd lost sight of Matthew, and she wondered if he had sneaked out the back, finally taking pity on one of the willing young ladies. Whether he did or not, she knew she was going to believe the worst, and the depression that had been lingering around her head settled in.

"We're getting up a little party for dinner down at the

Rusty Tub,'' Charles said, that low, metallic voice not helping matters. "We're hoping you'll join us."

"Oh, I don't think so," she began, when she realized to her complete amazement that Harry was squeezing her arm. Quite hard, all the while his face had that beatific smile beneath the sweating, nervous brow.

"Now, I'm sure you can't have any other plans," Charles said smoothly. "I'll make certain that you're delivered home safely at the end of the evening. I won't take no for an answer." It was politely done, but Jeannie couldn't rid herself of the notion that it wasn't a request, it was an order, and Harry's pinching hand didn't help lessen that impression.

"Are you ready, Jeannie?" Matthew Connelly's gravelly voice had often been welcome, but never more so. Harry dropped his grip on her arm, Charles stepped back, and the threat was effectively withdrawn.

"You don't need to take Jeannie back, Connelly," Charles said, and the threat was still there, this time for Matthew.

But he was already drawing her away from the older man, his hand on her arm strong and unbearably familiar. "That's all right, Charles. I never leave a job half done." And without another word he was leading her away.

As Jeannie looked back to smile an apologetic farewell she couldn't rid herself of the suspicion that something very odd was going on. Very odd, indeed.

Chapter Eighteen

"You haven't got any sense at all, have you?" Matthew demanded as he half led, half dragged her up the winding, narrow road to her condominium.

"I don't know what you're talking about," she snapped back. "And why did you drag me off without giving me a chance to say goodbye? How did you know I didn't want to go out to dinner with them?"

"Because I already heard you trying to make excuses," Matthew replied flatly. "And even if you were stupid enough to want to go along with them, I'm not about to let you. I don't want you getting into any more trouble than you can help."

Despite his tone of voice, Jeannie felt unaccountably warmed by this first genuine sign of concern. "Why would you care?" she asked in a low voice.

He cast her a measuring glance, not slowing his headlong pace in the slightest. "Because the more trouble you're in, the more trouble I'll have to get you out of, and I think it would be a good idea if I spent as little time with you as possible."

It was a very effective slap in the face. "Why?"

He stopped then, and she almost barreled into him. She

halted just in time, teetering on the high heels. "Why?" she said again, her voice breathless and slightly plaintive.

"Because we rushed into things on Muscatoon Island. You know it and I know it. Neither of us was ready for a relationship—"

"I was," she interrupted, throwing pride to the winds.

"Maybe you were, but I wasn't. I needed to be left alone, I needed peace and quiet and time to think."

"So you're blaming me for everything. I think your memory is a little convenient, Connelly. If I remember correctly it was you who kissed me on Enoch's boat, you who carried me up to bed in Sunshine Cottage. I don't remember bashing you over the head and having my wicked way with you." *Not that that wasn't exactly what she wanted to do right now,* she thought mournfully. In the setting autumn sunlight he looked golden and glorious. And totally unsympathetic, she reminded herself.

"I'm not going to argue with you, Jeannie," he said, his rough voice infuriatingly dictatorial. "I'm warning you to keep away from Charles Hudgins, for your own sake." He started back up the roadway, and she had no choice but to follow.

"You still haven't told me why. I'm not into blind obedience, Matthew. Is Charles dangerous?"

"In my opinion, yes."

"Then why don't you do something about it? You're the police chief around here, aren't you?"

"The moment he breaks a law, I will. At this point he's done nothing illegal as far as I can see." They were almost at her door. The sun was sinking behind the magnificent peaks of Mount Wilhelm, gilding the condominiums and making them almost pretty in the twilight.

"Are you sure you'll do something? After all, isn't he one of those who pay your bills?"

She was unprepared for his reaction. One moment they were striding up the walkway to her front door, in the next she was pushed ungently against the rough wood wall, with Matthew towering over her, glaring down at her in a white-hot fury.

"If you were a man," he said, "or even two inches taller, I'd shove those words down your throat. I worked for the Chicago police department for seventeen years and I was never on the take, I never made deals, I never looked the other way. I'm not about to start for some two-bit deal in some affected little ski town. Do you understand?" His voice was low, dangerous, Dirty Harry to the life.

Jeannie swallowed nervously, nodding her head. "I understand," she said, her voice wavering.

The fury vanished as quickly as it came. She was still pressed up against the wooden siding, with his much larger body intimidating hers, close enough so that she could smell the clean fresh scent of his skin—a scent that brought back a host of erotic memories so painful that she almost wept.

"Do I frighten you, Jeannie?" he inquired in that same low, evil voice.

She wished she could deny it. "Yes," she said. "Sometimes."

She was unprepared for his reaction. He grinned, a simple, infectious grin. "Good," he said, and lowered his mouth to hers.

She should have kicked him. She should have slapped him, shoved him away, told him he couldn't terrorize her like that. But it had been so long since he'd kissed her, and the feel of his mouth on hers destroyed any common sense she had left. Besides, she'd sworn not to lose her temper.

So she moved away from the wall, into the shelter of his strong body, and she slid her arms around his waist, pulling him closer, as she opened her mouth beneath his.

She heard a distant moan of hunger and desire, and couldn't tell if it came from him or her. His arms were around her, holding her against him with unnecessary force, as if he thought she'd try to escape, and his mouth slanted across hers with a hunger that could only come from two months' celibacy and something more. He wasn't kissing just any woman, Jeannie realized. He was kissing her. And he wasn't just wanting any woman. He was wanting her.

As much as she wanted him? Impossible. No one had ever wanted anyone as much as she wanted him. She pressed her body up against his, feeling him strong and hard against her, and a wave of triumph swept over her. It was going to be all right, it was going to be glorious, it was going to be...

A total disaster, she realized as he tore his mouth from hers and pulled away. She let him go, too benumbed to do otherwise. "That was a mistake," he said, his voice even, his breathing ragged.

"Was it?" She was shaking, she realized absently. And that damned man didn't even care. "Then why did you do it?"

"Don't be naive, Jeannie. You know as well as I do why I did it. But I don't intend to do it again."

"You don't?" There was no disguising the mournful quality in her voice. "Not ever?"

"Jeannie, I—" Before he could finish what he was about to say a new voice entered the fray.

"Hey, there, little gal." It was Harry Bateman, huffing and puffing up the hill after them. "Wait up a moment."

Matthew swore then, a short, obscene word, and Jeannie took a deep, shaky breath. "What about Harry?" she whispered in a suddenly angry voice. "Am I supposed to keep away from him, too? Is he part of your suspicions?"

"I'm not sure. I'd watch my step if I were you." He'd

moved away, much too far away from her, and his face was distant.

"Well, you're not me," she snapped, stepping back into the pathway and beaming at the approaching Harry. "Hi, Harry. What can I do for you?"

His smallish brown eyes darted between Jeannie and Matthew. "I'm not interrupting anything, am I?" His high, bald forehead was still sweating, though now it seemed caused more by exertion than nervousness. For a moment Jeannie considered telling Matthew about Bateman's extreme edginess in Charles's presence, then thought better of it. Let Matthew figure things out for himself. He was probably simply paranoid after all his years of big-city crime.

"Of course not, Harry. I was just about to invite Matthew in for a drink." She hadn't planned on doing any such thing, certain that he would have abruptly refused. "Why don't you join us?"

As expected, Matthew shook his head. "I'm afraid I'm going to have to take a rain check. There's something I need to follow up on."

"Tonight?" Harry inquired. "Now, now, my boy, all work and no play make Jack—"

"I don't think Matthew would ever be considered a dull boy," Jeannie said.

"Matthew, eh? I'm glad to see you two are getting along a little better. I'll be glad to take you up on your offer, little lady. That's an offer I wouldn't be fool enough to refuse, not at my age."

"Remember what I said, Jeannie," Matthew said abruptly. "Bateman." That short name was all the courtesy he could muster, and in another moment he was walking away from them, his long legs eating up the distance without a limp in sight.

"Still sighing, Jeannie? I'm getting the feeling that

there's something more between you and our police chief than we thought.''

"We?" she echoed, turning guarded eyes back from Matthew's disappearing figure. "Who thought?"

She could feel the nervousness skitter back between the two of them. Then Harry shrugged. "Oh, whoever I can find to gossip with. You got any Kentucky bourbon?"

Jeannie was still only half there. Her mouth tingled from Matthew's; her body still felt imprinted with his flesh. "What?"

"You offered me a drink. I'm taking you up on it."

"Oh." Belatedly Jeannie pulled herself back to a reluctant reality. "Of course." She moved on ahead, opening the unlocked door of her condominium and ushering Harry's bulky form in.

"Don't you lock your doors?" He was clearly disapproving.

"I got out of the habit when I lived in Vermont and Maine. I can never remember to carry my keys with me." Flicking on the lights, she went over to the bourgeois little bar that came fully stocked and quickly whipped up a drink for her unwelcome guest.

"Just a splash of water, please, and no ice," Harry said, moving to the window to stare out over the little village, the rash of condominiums climbing up the mountainside like an advancing army of square soldiers. "You really ought to lock your doors. I know our police chief would make a point of telling you so."

"Would he?" Jeannie poured herself some whiskey, neat, and drained it. She didn't often drink, but Matthew Connelly had the tendency to put her in need of something to dull the pain.

"I'm sure he would."

"Well, I wouldn't want to put him to the trouble. I'll lock

my door," she said gloomily, kicking off the damnable high heels and dropping down on the modular sofa. "What can I do for you, Harry?"

He moved away from the window, startled, and she could see the nervousness around his eyes, the puffy fingers clenching the glass of whiskey. "What?"

"You came after me," she said patiently. "I presume you wanted something?"

Harry opened his mouth, about to speak, when his eyes caught the landscape over her fireplace. He stood there, mouth agape, and she had to give him at least some credit for artistic taste.

The first thing she'd done when she'd entered the plastic perfection of her condo was to take down the Chagall print over the fireplace and replace it with Matthew's monstrosity. She'd had it framed, much to the horror of the framer in Bellingham. Its muddy colors added a welcome touch of reality to the decorator-perfect confines of her condo, and every time she looked at it she smiled.

It was just as well Matthew had refused her last-minute invitation. He had a fairly good idea of how far gone she was; she didn't want him to have complete proof of her besotted condition.

"That painting," Harry said faintly.

Jeannie smiled into her whiskey, her dark mood lightening. "Do you like it?"

Harry shook his head, dropping onto the love seat opposite her. The springs creaked ominously beneath his bulk. "That's the second one I've seen by the same artist. I can't imagine what you people see in him, but then, I don't know much about art. I only know what I like." He took another glance at the picture, then shuddered. "And I don't like that one."

Jeannie had latched on to the most important part of his

speech. "You've seen another one like it? I thought I had the only—" she cast about in her mind for a suitable name, spied the television set and quickly continued "—the only Victor west of the Mississippi."

"Victor, is that the artist?" Harry took a deep, restoring drink of his whiskey. "No, as a matter of fact, our police chief has a very similar painting hanging in his living room. Same sort of scene, but his has a woman in the picture."

"A woman?" Jeannie held her breath.

"Tall, chubby creature with bright orange hair," Harry said.

Jeannie smiled delightedly. Given Matthew's dubious talent, that tall, fat creature could only be herself. *He must love me,* she thought happily. *Whether he knows it or not, he must.*

"But here, now, I didn't come to talk about art," Harry boomed, some of his usual amour propre returning. "I came to talk to you about Charles. You don't want to offend Charles, missy."

"Why not?"

"Why not? Because, well, because..." Harry sputtered, draining his glass of bourbon. "Because he's a powerful man, little lady. A man who can be a lot of help to his friends."

"And what does he do to people who aren't his friends?"

Harry just shook his head. "I wouldn't want to speculate on that. Let's just say I thought I should give you a word of advice. You don't want to get on Charles's bad side. It just wouldn't pay."

"And how do I stay on his good side?" She asked the question with idle curiosity, having no intention whatsoever of worrying about Charles Hudgins's opinion of her.

"By keeping out of his way when he doesn't want to see you. And by going along with him when he invites you out to dinner. Oh, you don't need to think he's got his eye on you. He has a wife back in New Jersey he thinks the world of. He isn't interested in a little extracurricular activity. But he likes to have pretty ladies around him at times, and it would be wise on your part to go along with it. It won't hurt you any, and not doing so might." He set the empty glass down on the pecan-wood coffee table with a snap, rising to his feet. "Well, that's all I wanted to say. Just a bit of friendly advice to help you get along in Schooner Springs. And Jeannie..."

"Yes?"

"I wouldn't mention this little conversation to our police chief. He doesn't need to know everything that goes on up here on the mountain. He has enough in the village to keep him busy, right?"

"Right," Jeannie echoed, smiling sweetly and making no promises. "Thanks for coming to talk to me."

"Well, I just wanted to make sure you knew how to get on."

"Oh, I'm learning fast," she said blithely.

It was an interesting predicament, she thought as she obediently locked the door behind him. Matthew had warned her to stay away from Charles; Harry was practically throwing her in his lap. Given her own preferences, she would be more likely to go along with Matthew's advice.

But going along with Matthew's advice wasn't going to get her anywhere, and she'd be damned if she'd sit around her condo as she had that week, waiting for him to come to his senses. It was time she did something about the situation, and disobeying Matthew's edicts would be a good start.

As a matter of fact, she might very well disobey more than Matthew's edicts, she thought, stripping off the black dress and tossing it on her king-size bed. There was plenty of innocuous little laws she could stretch, bend and possibly snap, right under Matthew Connelly's nose. He thought he could keep away from her, did he? He would soon learn that Jeannie MacPherson, once she decided she wanted something, wasn't the sort to sit back and wait patiently. She'd waited long enough. And she suspected, from the hungry fierceness of Matthew's kiss, that he'd waited long enough, too. She just had to make him realize it.

She dropped her underwear in the hamper, turned on the whirlpool and stepped in, a dreamy smile on her face. The hell with patience, the hell with waiting till December. She'd have Matthew Connelly admitting he loved her by the end of the month or give up and go back to Muscatoon Island. She'd never been a quitter in all her thirty-three years; she wasn't about to start now.

THE LIVING ROOM OF HIS ranch house was still, dark and deserted when Matthew finally let himself in. He didn't bother snapping on the lights; the lingering sunset gave the uncluttered room enough illumination to enable him to find the leather sofa without tripping.

He tossed his keys on the coffee table, sank down and propped up his booted feet. What the hell was he doing here, alone, when more than anything in the world he wanted to be with Jeannie MacPherson? Was he alone on principle, or out of stubbornness, or out of common sense? Somehow, when it came to the chilly loneliness of an October evening, none of the self-righteous reasons he'd barricaded himself with made much sense, especially with the taste and smell of her still lingering on his hands and mouth.

What was he waiting for? Some magic time when all his memories disappeared, when the Springside Strangler no longer cropped up in his nightmares and reminded him of things he didn't want to remember? It was time to put George Kirwin behind him, where he belonged. He was in jail with no chance of parole, serving three consecutive life sentences for only a small portion of the random murders he'd committed. Serial murderers were the hardest to find, but Matthew had found him, caught him, testified against him, and now should be ready to forget him. God, why couldn't he forget him and think only about Jeannie MacPherson?

He reached up and ran his long fingers through his thick hair, trying to rub away the headache that had plagued him since he left her with Harry Bateman hovering around her. He doubted she was going to pay attention to his warning. She was in a feisty enough mood so that if he said black, she'd say white. He was going to have to make the message a little clearer. Maybe he was going to have to make that message clearer tonight.

He sat forward, sudden energy speeding through his weary body. She would have kicked Harry out long ago, and she'd be alone, and probably just as frustrated by that kiss as he was. Maybe he could put the past out of his mind long enough to concentrate on the very real distractions of Jeannie MacPherson. Even if that was the last thing he wanted, to use her once again to keep his mind off other things, he rationalized that at least he was getting closer. He knew that he wanted her, needed her, maybe more. He just couldn't leave everything else alone yet. Maybe by December.

In the meantime he no longer wanted to be alone. Matthew Connelly, loner personified, no longer wanted the privacy and solitude of his ranch house. He wanted Jeannie. He got to his feet with a sudden surge of energy, ready to head back out to the car, when the phone shrilled suddenly in the darkness.

He grinned. He'd bet anything that was Jeannie right now, as restless and lonely as he was, giving in to it even sooner than he had. She'd have some trumped-up excuse, maybe even a spurious prowler around her condominium. And he'd have to go check it out, wouldn't he?

"Yeah?" He couldn't sound too welcoming on the phone. "Connelly here."

"Matt, is that you?" Tony Tonetti's voice crossed the miles from Chicago. "I've been trying to call you for days. Haven't you gotten my messages?"

A slight flash of guilt swept over Connelly. "Listen, Tony, I told you, I never want to see Chicago again if I can help it. Don't you like your promotion? I'm sure you'll do a better job than I ever did."

"It's not that, Matt. Though God knows I'd love to have you back."

"No way." Matthew's hopeful mood vanished abruptly as he recognized the tension in Tony's voice. "What's going on, pal?"

"It's George Kirwin. They're filing another appeal."

"I thought they filed their last appeal."

"We all thought so. Apparently that idiot lawyer of his has drummed up some new evidence. It looks like he's going to get a new trial, Matt. And you know what that means."

"I'll have to testify." His voice was cool, composed, giving nothing away.

"You'll do it?" Relief was heavy in Tonetti's voice.

"I don't have much choice. Thanks for calling me, Tony. When will you hear?"

"Who knows? It's up to the judges, when they want to hear the motion, and you know as well as I what jerks judges can be. They do things in their own sweet time and nobody else's."

"I know. Keep in touch, Tony. If you need me, I'll be ready."

"I knew I could count on you."

Matthew stared down at the telephone in the gathering darkness. So it wasn't all over. He should have known there was a reason he couldn't get rid of the Springside Strangler, that he'd continue to haunt him. It wasn't just the bullet in the groin. His past was still entwined with his quarry, and even though that quarry was locked away the doors might possibly swing open again.

He dropped his keys on the table beside the telephone and moved back to the sofa. He wasn't going anywhere tonight, and he wasn't going anywhere near Jeannie MacPherson—at least not until he could say goodbye to George Kirwin once and for all.

With a sigh he stretched his long, lean body out on the sofa, wincing slightly as his ribs twinged. No, he wasn't going anywhere. Damn it to hell.

Chapter Nineteen

She gave herself the weekend to think about it. Two full days, Saturday and Sunday, while she shriveled up in her hot tub, tried to figure out ways to be creative with a microwave, and gave Matthew Connelly one last chance. Somehow, even though he'd pushed her away, the feeling of his kiss still lingered, and she vividly recalled the emotion that had swept between the two of them at his touch. If Harry Bateman hadn't come lumbering up, they might have gotten a lot further in their quest for understanding.

Maybe it was only her quest. If so, she couldn't afford to wait around for him to meet her halfway. She was going to have to go out and get him, throw him off balance, make him realize what he needed in his life. She wasn't going to rush into anything. He had left her with the feeling that he would be back, soon, on Friday night, and she'd waited, all night long, all Saturday and Sunday, waited for God knows what.

Monday dawned cool and crisp and clear, a perfect autumn day in the Rockies. The aspens were a golden yellow against the jagged peaks surrounding the small town, and as Jeannie sat by the picture window she began to appreciate what drew people there. She still preferred a half-deserted island in Maine, but Colorado had a certain charm all its own.

She'd given up on the microwave and devoted Sunday to making almond croissants. She ate three of them, washed down with strong coffee, and mentally girded her loins. It was time to do battle.

Finding the perfect opportunity for her first strike was going to prove a problem. It needed to be something flashy, harmless and deliberate, enough to let him know she'd declared war, but not enough to alert other people. For the meantime she wanted it just between the two of them.

Fate was on her side that morning. The main street of Schooner Springs was relatively deserted. Most of the out-of-state tourists were still in bed, the working stiffs had already arrived, and only the early shoppers were out and about. And Matthew Connelly was standing on the corner of the main intersection, a slightly glazed look in his eye as Harry Bateman boomed in his ear.

She gunned her motor, oh, so gently, as she slowed her approach to the red light. He looked up and saw her, that blank mask firmly in place. Jeannie looked around the deserted streets, looked up at the red light, and calmly drove straight through it.

She caught a look at Matthew from her rearview mirror. He was staring after her, all but scratching his head in puzzlement. Humming a little song, Jeannie drove on out to the factory.

Day two was almost as much fun. She'd been heading through town when she saw Matthew's distinctive black-and-silver car parked outside Klein's Feed and Clothing store. Quickly she'd slammed on the brakes, pulled a quick U-turn and parked behind him, directly in front of the fire hydrant.

The good weather was holding. She left the car long

enough to stroll into her competitor's shop for an ice-cream cone. She was waiting for him, leaning against the side of her car and smiling as she licked the huge cone of Heavenly Hash.

He took it all in with one swift glance. The car, the hydrant, the triumphant, naughty expression on her face. Without a word he got back into his car and drove away. Probably hoping that she'd be properly chastened by his ignoring her, she thought. But she'd seen his backward glance, seen the imperceptible tightening of his mouth when he walked out of the store. Tossing away the rest of the cone, she got back in her car, still humming.

Day three was a disappointment. It was raining, and no matter how long she cruised around the deserted streets of Schooner Springs, Connelly's silver-and-black car was nowhere to be seen.

The rain kept up on day four, but Jeannie decided to up the ante. She headed straight for the municipal building, determined to beard the lion in his den. He hadn't arrived yet, and all the parking spots in front were taken. Except the one marked prominently for the chief of police.

Jeannie pulled in, locked the car and went shopping. Three hours later, when she returned there was a bright red traffic citation on her windshield. It had been written up by a lesser officer, but Jeannie wasn't dismayed. Matthew had received the message; his car was parked rows back among the lesser mortals.

He called her that night. She was expecting it, though he'd given in to the pressure a little faster than she had thought he would. His rough voice on the other end of the line brought a wicked smile to her face, and she quickly curled up on the supremely uncomfortable modular sofa and prepared to listen.

"Yes, Matthew?" she replied in a sweet voice.

"Cut it the hell out, Jeannie."

"Cut what out?"

"Don't give me that. Running red lights, illegal parking, harassment of an officer of the law. If you think I won't bust you, you're even more naive than I thought."

"Would you arrest me, Matthew?" she inquired. "That might be very exciting."

"Jeannie..." His voice was a direct warning, a warning she ignored.

"Would you use handcuffs, Matthew?" she murmured. "Please, say you'll use handcuffs," she pleaded with a ghost of laughter in her voice.

Matthew's reply was short, obscene, before he slammed down the phone in her ear. Jeannie stared at the silent instrument for a long moment. "You've lost the first battle, my friend," she said softly. "Now let's see about the whole war."

On day five she managed to jaywalk in front of him, a real coup in terms of timing and opportunity. It left her giggling the rest of the day. Day six she waited until he'd arrived home and was just getting out of his car. She sped by, tossed some litter out, almost at his feet, and drove on, humming. She could hear his curse above the noise of her engine. She wondered how he would react when he discovered the litter was a pair of her sexiest panties.

Day seven was another washout, literally and figuratively. Matthew was nowhere to be seen; his silver-and-black car had disappeared; his house was closed up tight. Day eight was the same, as was day nine. It wasn't until day ten that she found out from Harry that Matthew had been called back to Chicago to testify concerning an old case of his. He was due back on Friday. Was the little lady getting a thing for the chief of police?

Jeannie smiled politely, reminding herself she wasn't go-

ing to lose her temper or even commit violence against anyone, even an overgrown oaf who insisted on calling her little
lady. At five feet one and three-quarters that phrase came a
little too close to the truth.

Well, she had two more days. Her first instinct was to
break into his house and leave a calling card, but she'd
underestimated Matthew's talents. The house was completely impregnable, from the double locks to the alarm-
rigged windows. As far as she could tell, the only way she
could break in would be to smash the sliding glass door,
and that involved a little more vandalism than she cared for.

She contented herself with peering through the windows,
getting her first glimpse at Matthew's second painting. *He
ought to be ashamed of himself,* she thought, staring at the
muddy colors, at the hefty Valkyrie with the orange hair
standing on what was presumably a cliff. Painting it once
was bad enough; twice was a crime against humanity. Still,
it was a good sign, that he'd been haunted enough by Muscatoon and a short, skinny redhead to re-create the picture
he'd left behind.

His parking space was already filled on Friday when she
drove to the municipal building. She blithely pulled into the
mayor's spot, knowing that this particular misdemeanor
would probably be in vain. The mayor had gone from his
fact-finding tour of Central America to negotiating with the
Native Americans on strike in the state of Washington, and
Jeannie began to have the suspicion that she'd be back in
Maine without even meeting his honor. Well, she could survive that, as long as she took the chief of police with her.

Matthew's office was empty when the fresh-faced young
uniformed officer showed her in. She sat down, propped her
booted feet on his desk and waited with an outward show
of patience. It was time to get tough, she'd decided. Like a

show of fireworks, she was setting off all her big guns, and if she couldn't scare a reaction out of him, she'd give up.

"Enjoying yourself, Jeannie?" His rough voice came from behind her, and it took all her self-restraint to keep from pulling her feet off his desk and jumping up.

She turned to smile up at him over her shoulder. "Yes, indeed." She kept the smile firmly in place, but the sight of him put a dent in her determination.

Matthew moved around her, seating himself in the chair behind the desk, and matched her even smile. "What can I do for you?"

He looked like a different man. The grimness was gone, the shadow that haunted the back of his winter-gray eyes had vanished, the lines that bracketed his mouth had disappeared, and he looked ten years younger. Jeannie continued to stare at him, completely at a loss for words. She'd seen him look like that, once or twice—at peace with the world, with his surroundings and himself—but it hadn't been often. Usually only after they'd made love.

That had to be it, she thought with sudden despair. He'd been off seeing someone, maybe that ex-wife of his. He'd fallen in love at last, and it wasn't with her.

"Jeannie? Earth to Jeannie, come in please." Matthew prodded. "Are you still in that scattered brain of yours?"

Instinctively Jeannie pulled herself together, taking her feet off his desk and straightening up. "My brain's not scattered," she said. "Did you have a good time in Chicago?"

He smiled, an inner-directed surprise lightening his expression. "As a matter of fact, I did. In a manner of speaking. How'd you find out where I went?"

"I have my sources," she said loftily, all the while thinking feverishly. Maybe she was jumping to conclusions, maybe all he'd had was sex in Chicago, not true love. While the former was unpalatable, at least it was more acceptable than losing him forever. "You're probably wondering why I'm here."

"Not in the least. You're here to try some more of your little tricks. You must have been incredibly frustrated these past few days, to have your unwilling victim take off. So what's your latest, breaking and entering? I expected to find my house trashed when I got back."

"I'm not into willful destruction, Connelly," she said in a lofty voice.

"That's good. I don't think I'd be so tolerant of vandalism. So go on, Jeannie. I'm waiting. But I expect this to be good." He leaned back, smiling expansively, and Jeannie almost burst into tears. In thirty-three years she knew how to recognize a man in love, and Matthew was that man.

Her plan had been half-formed, an effort to try to talk some sense into him, to offer to stop the conflict if he'd only give them a chance. But a good general knew when to change plans midbattle, and she quickly switched, leaning forward and smiling seductively. He may be in love, but he still might have a weakness for her, a weakness she'd be glad to exploit.

"Speaking of being frustrated," she murmured, glancing up at him out of her limpid blue eyes, "I wondered what the laws were against soliciting in this county."

"Stiff," he said. "Why?"

She moved then, slowly, as seductively as she could manage, rising from her chair and perching on his cluttered desk, leaning toward him. "Because I thought I might offer you my body for the paltry sum of...say, a hundred dollars?"

"A hundred dollars?" he scoffed, his eyes watching her with sudden intentness.

"If that's too much, I could always arrange a discount," she murmured, leaning closer. She'd managed to undo another button on her ecru silk blouse, and while her cleavage was nothing impressive, Matthew had always found it stimulating. "What about fifty?"

He laughed then, a comfortable, amused laugh that effectively destroyed any seductive aura she was trying to project. He shook his head. "It's hard to be a vamp, Jeannie, when you smell of vanilla and fresh-baked bread and look like the girl next door. I'm afraid I can't arrest you for pandering. Better try something else."

Jeannie pulled herself off the desk, keeping her temper only by sheer force of will. "How about ten bucks?" she said lightly.

"Nope."

"You don't know what you're missing."

"Yes, I do," he said, and the last of her seductive act vanished.

"Yes, I suppose you do," she said in a depressed voice. "All right, how about I'll pay you a hundred dollars if you'll ignore my parking tickets?"

"Your parking tickets only come to twenty-five dollars," he countered. "Forget it, Jeannie. I'm not going to bust you for bribery, either."

"So what are you going to do about me?" she demanded in sudden desperation.

He smiled, and if she'd been less upset she would have seen the tenderness and, yes, desire in those usually chilly gray eyes. "I'm going to ignore you," he said, "until I'm finished with this job."

Jeannie didn't hear the latter part, or if she did, she didn't pay any attention to it. A cold knot of anger and determination was forming in the pit of her stomach. "All right," she said evenly. She had turned to leave when his voice stopped her.

"You're keeping away from Charles Hudgins, aren't you?"

She turned and gave him her most quelling stare. "So far," she said, her dulcet voice making no promises. "So far."

He watched her go with an enigmatic expression on his face that turned to a smile once she was out of sight. He shook his head, leaning back in the chair and propping his boots on the desk. She couldn't do it with his aplomb, given the relative shortness of her luscious legs, but she did a creditable job.

God, she looked ready to kill him, he thought wistfully. When he told her he was going to ignore her it looked as if she'd burst. It was a lucky thing there wasn't a lobster trap anywhere around, or he would have been in deep trouble. He laughed out loud, the sound a rusty chuckle in the stillness of his office.

He was a turkey to do that to her, but he deserved some revenge for her harassment. Tonight, or tomorrow night if he could wait that long, he'd show up at her condo and set things straight. Too many things had finally fallen into place in the past few days, and Jeannie MacPherson was a major part of them. Even if he wanted to give her a little of her own medicine back in return, he wanted her even more than a little harmless revenge.

Finally, once and for all, he could close the chapter on George Kirwin. Not forget him, as he'd tried to do so desperately during the past few months. You couldn't forget a human monster who'd been an obsession for more than two years. But you could look at him squarely, know he was locked away for good, that the last possible appeal had been denied after all and that you were part and parcel of that denial, and go on to something new. If remembering and making sense of the Springside Strangler was part of that moving on, so be it.

Thirty thousand dollars was a decent piece of change,

when it came right down to it. Thirty thousand dollars' advance to write the story of George Kirwin for a major New York publisher, the one who'd read his police reports and marveled at their conciseness. He'd always been teased as the one member of the department who wrote in English. Apparently the publisher had seen more than lucidity—he'd seen talent, and an eye for detail. Sherrard & Co. were telling him he'd be another Joseph Wambaugh.

Maybe. He couldn't wait to see Jeannie's expression when he finally told her. Muscatoon Island was the perfect place to put the Springside Strangler to rest. It was a good place to write, a good place to paint, a good place to live. If Jeannie came with him.

He'd walked out of that courthouse a free man. The motion for a new trial had been denied, and Matthew Connelly had come to the belated realization that he could live with the memory of George Kirwin and the presence of Jeannie MacPherson at the same time. Indeed, there was no way he could get rid of the one, and no way he wanted to get rid of the other. To his complete and utter amazement, he'd suddenly faced up to what he had avoided so long. He was in love with her—completely, hopelessly in love with her. It was more than time that he told her.

But not quite yet. She deserved another few hours to stew. Just a tiny bit of revenge for the ignored stoplights, the littering, not to mention a couple of cracked ribs that still weren't perfect. *Just a few more hours,* he thought, leaning back and smiling.

JEANNIE STOMPED OUT of the police station in the white-hot rage she'd promised herself she'd never have again. Ignore her, would he? She'd see how soon he'd ignore her.

The mayor's parking space was right beside the police

chief's. Matthew's silver-and-black car sat there, as smug as its owner, she thought, reaching for her door handle.

It was the end of the day, and the parking lot was half empty. In mid-October the afternoon sun was already setting, and in the gathering twilight not a single soul was in sight. With a sudden cool aplomb born out of sheer temper, she let go of her own door handle and turned to Matthew's.

Of course, he hadn't locked it, not directly outside the police station. She slid into the front seat, reached under the dashboard and opened the hood.

She'd learned to hot-wire cars when she was seventeen and always losing her car keys. It was a talent not unlike that of riding a bicycle—once learned, it was never forgotten. The engine of the black-and-silver car purred into life, and the hood was down and Jeannie back in the front seat in a matter of moments. No one had seen her, but that didn't matter. Matthew would know very well who had done it. She was even kind enough to leave her keys in her car, so he wouldn't be completely without transportation, and unable to find her.

Countless times Harry Bateman had offered her the use of his cabin up by Bellow's Falls. She'd drive to a public phone, call and tell him she was taking him up on his offer, and then drive out there and await her fate.

As she drove off into the gathering dusk she was humming once more, a wicked smile on her face.

Chapter Twenty

It didn't take her long to regret it. Bateman's directions were hopelessly tangled, the darkness was descending with frightening rapidity, and the road was dirt beneath the big tires of Matthew's car. She had to pull over to find the lights, pull over again to find the heat against the autumn chill. The moon was full, a bright, almost eerie beacon against the darkness, and Jeannie shivered as she pushed the heat up further.

The box in the backseat contained the hastily purchased necessities of life—coffee, croissants, a couple of tins of soup and some freshly baked French bread. She'd also had the foresight to stop and buy a bottle of Jack Daniel's and a down sleeping bag. She had the dubious conviction that by the end of the night she was going to need all the warmth she could muster.

She had no idea how long it would take Matthew to track her down or, indeed, if he'd even bother. He might try to hold out, knowing that sooner or later she'd have to return the damned police car. At this point she refused to consider that eventuality. She had enough food to last her a couple of days, and nothing else to command her attention. It was the weekend; no work would be done on the old factory that would supposedly require her help. She could just sit it out at the cabin, waiting to see how good a detective Matthew Connelly was.

Saturday afternoon at the earliest, she figured. Maybe not till Sunday or Monday. She could make a run down into the little mom-and-pop store she'd passed on her way up the mountain, to get more soup and maybe a little junk food to soothe her tortured nerves. She could safely stay away until Tuesday at the latest. If Matthew hadn't found her by then, she'd have to give up.

The police band radio was flashing red lights, squawking terrible, unintelligible noises, and Jeannie turned up the car radio to try to drown it out. As far she could tell there was no on/off switch on the CB; she was doomed to its unwelcome company.

The road was getting narrower. Every time she drove over one of the cattle grates that abounded in Colorado, she jumped. Sleeping cattle loomed out of the darkness, adding to her uneasiness. All she needed was to get to the cabin and be confronted by a maddened bull. If these bovine creatures were bulls. The vagaries of Western beef raising was beyond her, but the subject was a welcome distraction, and she spent the last, tortuous five miles pondering who was gelded and who wasn't, and how they found the cows that were still wandering in the woods when it was time for slaughter.

The road turned into a narrow, rutted track. Jeannie's hands were clenched tightly around the steering wheel, convinced that somehow she'd taken the wrong turn, when a tiny little cabin loomed up out of the gathering darkness— with no rampaging cattle in sight, she realized with a sigh of relief.

She was used to making herself at home in places without the basic conveniences. Muscatoon Island had taught her how to live without electricity or plumbing or central heating, so it didn't take long to get comfortable in the little hunting cabin. The kerosene lamps were trimmed and ready, and in the wavering lamplight Jeannie looked around with less nervousness and more delight.

It was a large, one-room cabin, with a wood stove at one end and a huge stone fireplace at the other. The furniture was rough-hewn and minimal—a table, a couple of benches, and a large bed built into the corner of the cabin. Jeannie tossed her new sleeping bag on it and began to settle in.

Several hours later, sitting cross-legged on the bed and staring at the roaring fire she'd built handily, she was very pleased with herself. Her stomach was pleasantly filled with the soup and French bread, the Jack Daniel's was warming her innards, and the cabin glowed with light and warmth. She'd even managed to locate the outhouse and the nearby stream, so that there was a tub of water heating by the wood stove for dish washing and people washing.

For the first time since she'd left Maine she felt at home. She must be a pioneer reactionary, she thought with a trace of amusement, snuggling down under the sleeping bag she'd wrapped around her. Anyone in her right mind would love microwaves and hot tubs and massive color TVs.

To be truthful, the hot tub was fun for a while, and the color TV had taught her the wonders of ''Miami Vice'' and Sonny Crockett, who might very well replace Frank Furillo in her heart. When she went back to Maine she'd have to give up on that particular fantasy. That would be fine with her, as long as she had her own personal Dirty Harry to take his place.

She took another sip of her whiskey and leaned back against the rough pillows. Thank heavens she'd been wearing jeans and a sweater instead of a suit today; it would have been damned hard being a pioneer in Liz Claiborne. Driving a stolen car, she would have been idiotic to go back to her condominium to change. At least she had the latest Jonathan Gash mystery in her purse, and one night of squinting at a poorly lit book wasn't going to make her blind. She'd have to read slowly, though, and make it last. She didn't want to go back down to the tiny town of Madsen unless she had to.

Lovejoy the antiques dealer was as amoral as usual, and she settled down to enjoy herself. It must be late, but she never wore a watch, and it could be anywhere from nine to midnight. But for the first time since she came to Colorado, time didn't matter. She had all the time in the world.

She stopped when she had read a third of the way through the book, rationing herself sternly. She got up long enough to stoke the fires for the night and pour herself another glass of whiskey. She hadn't made much of a dent in the bottle, but she felt warm and pleasantly muzzy. Until she thought of what she was doing there.

Something had happened to Matthew Connelly in Chicago, something that had given him a peace she'd been unable to impart. Whether she liked it or not, he looked like a man in love. And a man in love with someone else wasn't going to take kindly to an old lover stealing his car.

So what if worse came to worst and she wasn't going to have him? What would she do with the rest of her life? Sonny Crockett and Frank Furillo, though delightful, didn't really exist. And Karen and Hal seemed to have developed an adult relationship finally, leaving the only single male on Muscatoon Island the redoubtable Enoch.

But she didn't want to live in Burlington anymore, and Colorado felt cold and empty. She wanted to go home, to Muscatoon, with or without Matthew. Maybe she could raise sheep.

She slipped out of her jeans and sweater, crawling beneath the sleeping bag in her bra and panties. She was tired, depressed and a little drunk. A good night's sleep would do her wonders.

A good night's sleep was the last thing she was going to have. She'd barely been asleep when the heavy door to the cabin slammed open, and she raised her head to stare at the figure looming there. The flickering firelight provided little illumination, but Jeannie had no doubts who it was.

"Go away," she muttered sleepily. "I don't care if you're Bigfoot or Dirty Harry; go away and leave me alone."

He moved closer into the cabin, and she could see fury radiating through his strong body. "What if I'm a raping, murdering trapper who found his way down to civilization?"

"I would have smelled you coming." She pulled herself upright then, the sleeping bag wrapped around her. "How did you find me so fast?"

He slammed the door behind him, and despite the sturdiness of the log cabin it shuddered beneath the force. "I could have been here waiting for you if I wanted. You forget, MacPherson, that I've been a cop for almost eighteen years, and a damned good one at that. It took me about seven and a half minutes to figure out where you'd gone."

"Bully for you." She flopped down on the bed and pulled the sleeping bag over her head. "Take your car and go away." Her voice came out an unintelligible mumble from underneath the covers.

A moment later she felt the covers ripped away from her. With a shriek she grabbed for them, but he'd tossed them away, and stood towering over her, his face hidden by the shadows. "What did you say?" he asked with deceptive politeness.

She glared up at him. "I said take your damned car and shove...drive it home," she said.

"And how will you get back?"

"I presume you drove my car up here."

"You presume wrong. I had Harry drop me off at the bottom of the hill."

"Then I'll walk back."

"It's seventeen miles to Schooner Springs, Jeannie."

She rolled over on her back, staring up at him, trying to ignore the fact that she was wearing only underwear and failing utterly. At least she could be glad that she was wearing her prettiest silk-and-lace bra and panties. "Then what," she said in her iciest voice, "do you expect me to do?"

He stared down at her, and she felt her skin warm beneath his gaze. She knew him too well not to recognize there was something beneath that impregnable expression. Slowly he reached a hand up and began undoing the buttons on his shirt. "I expect you to move over."

Dead silence reigned in the cabin, with only the hissing crackling sound of the fire penetrating the stillness. Jeannie stared up at him, wetting her lips nervously. "Oh, yeah?" she said with great originality.

"Yeah," he said, stripping off his shirt and reaching for his belt buckle.

The hell I will, she thought rapidly, staring up at him as he pulled the leather belt from his jeans and tossed it on the floor. *He can't just expect me to roll over on my back and welcome him home. Particularly when he's probably come from someone else's arms....*

He'd reached the snap on his jeans and was pulling the zipper down. "Wait a minute," she said sharply.

He ignored her, sitting down on the bench opposite her to pull off his cowboy boots. "No," he said.

"Answer me one question." He looked so beautiful in the firelight, his chest golden in the flickering shadows, that Jeannie knew it didn't really matter what the answer to that question was.

"All right. One question." The other boot came off, and then he was pulling off his jeans.

"Who did you sleep with in Chicago?"

He stopped for a moment in what could have been surprise, and then stepped out of the jeans. "What makes you think I slept with anyone?"

"The look on your face this afternoon. You looked like a man at peace." Which was more than he looked like now, she thought, wishing he'd kept his clothes on. He looked like a beautiful, very aroused male, and she knew there was no way she was going to turn him away, even if he'd slept with half of Chicago.

He smiled, a slow, sexy smile that reached his winter-gray eyes and turned them soft as ashes. "I did, did I?" He reached down for the sleeping bag he'd torn from her so unceremoniously. "Are you jealous, Jeannie?"

She was beyond the point of playing any more games. "Yes."

He tossed the sleeping bag back over her, and it fluttered down with a whispered sigh. "Don't be. I didn't sleep with anything but your ghost."

"Since when?"

"Since I had to leave you."

"Had to leave me," she echoed, miserable and confused and frustrated. "But why...?"

He leaned down, placing a gentle hand on her mouth, stopping her questions. "Not now. Later we can talk. But not now." His mouth replaced his hand.

He slid down on the bed beside her, and his body was hard and strong and warm next to hers. Beneath his experienced hands the last of her lassitude vanished.

"Oh, God, Matthew," she whispered when he moved his mouth from hers to trail soft, damp kisses down her cheekbones. "It's been so long."

"Much too long," he replied, moving his long legs against hers. "Much, much too long." There was no more need for words.

Jeannie had blown out the kerosene lamps when she'd gone to sleep earlier, and the only light in the dim recesses of the log cabin was the golden glow from the fire and the fitful light of the full moon outside the windows. She lay back against the rough wool blanket beneath her, listening to the sounds of the night, the hiss and pop of the fire, the wind in the aspens outside, the rustle of the down sleeping bag above them and the soft rubbing of flesh on flesh. It seemed to her fanciful mind as if she were warm for the first time in months, warm and at peace. Yet peace was the last thing on her mind at that moment, as his deft hands slid beneath the waistband of her panties and slid them down over her narrow hips.

"You know what I did with your litter?" he whispered in her ear, taking tiny, stinging bites of her tender lobe. "I slept with them. I even took them to Chicago with me."

"Did you?" Her voice came out dazed and rusty as his hands moved up to the silken wisp of a bra. It came apart in his hands, as it was meant to do, and then she was naked against him, flesh to flesh, bone and muscle and hot skin all entwined in a silken tangle. "You should have taken me to Chicago with you," she said, pressing her mouth against his strongly corded neck. "You should never have left me, Matthew."

"Shh," he murmured, and the soothing sound was answer enough. "That's over. Don't think about it. Think about now. Think about this." His hand trailed down, over her flat stomach to gently stroke the softly rising swell of her femininity.

She arched against him, the warmth in her turning into a fire. Her hands reached up to cradle his face, and she kissed him, long and deep, telling him without words how much she'd missed him, how much she loved him, how much she hated herself for hurting him. He answered her, his tongue a strong, driving force within the receptive warmth of her mouth, telling her he would never leave her again.

Slowly, carefully she let her hands slide down his arms, past his ribs, down the hard flatness of his stomach to touch him, hold him. His answering groan was reward enough, as he pressed himself into her willing hands, and she gentled and stroked him. His response was to delve deeper into her mysteries, the warm dampness of her telling him how much she needed him.

"I don't know how long I can prolong this," he murmured against her cheekbone. "I don't know if I've ever wanted anyone as much as I want you."

"Really?" The prosaic tone was somewhat shattered by her shivering, gulping gusts of breath.

He laughed, a soft rustle of sound. "Really," he said, his hands magic on her skin. "Would it be too much to hope you feel the same way?"

He was above her, looking down into her bottomless blue eyes, and she smiled up at him, her breathing rough and labored, her lips curved deliciously. "Not too much to hope, at all," she murmured. "I love you, Matthew. And I want you." She twisted up and kissed him, hard, on the mouth. "Now."

"You are the most impatient female I know," he murmured against her mouth, as his deft hands spread her legs around him. "Always in a hurry." She could feel him pressing against her, and she shivered in anticipatory delight. "Always...in...a...hurry...." Slowly, carefully he filled her, a deep deliberate thrust that seemed to penetrate to the very center of her being. By their own volition her hands clenched on his shoulders, her legs tightened around him, and a small, wailing cry escaped her lips.

"Did I hurt you?" He was suddenly still, a worried frown warring with the look of dazed delight that had overspread his darkened features. "Jeannie, are you all right?"

Slowly she let out a deep, tight breath. She smiled up at him, a smile full of love and delight and sheer pleasure with the world in general and Matthew Connelly in particular. "I have never felt better in my entire life," she said fervently. "Never, ever. Ever, never. Oh, God, Matthew, don't leave me." Her voice disintegrated into a rough cry of passion as he pulled back and then thrust into her.

Then there were no more words, only soft, incoherent cries of pleasure from deep in her throat, as she rose to meet him, stroke for stroke, taking all of him and reveling in it with a glory that transcended anything she had ever felt before. She wanted it to last forever, wanted to keep on floating in this sea of delight, but almost against her will she felt her body convulse around him, felt herself shudder and stiffen and cry out against him. She felt him follow, his body rigid in her arms, and her name was on his lips, over and over and over again, as together they drowned in an onrush of pleasure.

She didn't want him to leave her, and she clung to him, a garbled murmur of protest escaping her lips when he pulled away. But he didn't go far, and he brought her with him, cradling her in his arms.

She rested against his side, and she felt his sudden wince. "Wrong side," he said with a quiet laugh, when she raised her head inquiringly. "Those are my bad ribs."

Horror and shame swept over Jeannie. "Oh, Matthew, how could I do that to you? I hate myself!"

He cupped her chin in one strong hand, smiling down at

her. "Maybe you had to. Just don't do it again, okay? I've had enough injuries to last me for years."

"But I could have killed you. My horrible, wicked temper..." she wailed, but he kissed her, stopping all her recriminations.

"Just keep away from lobster traps," he whispered, "and you'll do just fine."

She still couldn't quite rid herself of her overwhelming feelings of guilt, but she snuggled down beside him, guarding his ribs with extreme care. She yawned, extravagantly, and felt her eyes begin to drift closed. "We haven't talked yet," she murmured sleepily.

"Tomorrow," he said, his voice drowsy in the stillness. "But promise me one thing."

"Anything," she said rashly.

"Keep away from Hudgins and Bateman."

"I don't run into them anyway." She raised her head with the last remnants of energy left before sleep claimed her. "Why?"

"I'll tell you later. Just trust me enough to take my word for it. Keep away from them. You promise?"

Jeannie sank back down beside him, curling into his warmth and strength with a blissful sigh. "Promise," she murmured drowsily. A moment later she was asleep.

Chapter Twenty-One

When she awoke he was gone. She couldn't quite believe it, wouldn't believe it. She opened her eyes slowly in the late-morning light, conscious of an emptiness beside her in the bed, and a tenderness in her recently untried body, and a sense of peace that was fast eroding. She sat up, slowly, and looked around her.

His clothes were nowhere to be seen, but that was nothing unusual. He probably was up and dressed ages ago and had gone off to the outhouse. Or to make sure she hadn't done any damage to his silly car. All she had to do was call out and he'd come to her, back to the tumbled bed and her arms.

She believed that, didn't she? So why didn't she call him? Was she afraid there'd be no answer? Was she afraid that if she climbed out of this big old bed and went over to the window she'd find the silver-and-black car gone?

She wasn't afaid. She knew. As wakefulness slowly claimed her, she knew what had pulled her out of a sound sleep. The sound of an engine being started, the sound of a large black-and-silver sedan pulling away from the deserted cabin in the woods. Matthew Connelly had left her.

The water that she'd brought in the night before was cool by the now-dead fire. She moved to the window, long enough to make sure that the car was in fact gone, and then she began mindlessly, methodically, to wash herself in the cool water.

The food from the night before was untouched. She made coffee, nibbled thoughtlessly on a croissant and waited for him to return.

It took her hours to realize he wasn't coming back, not until he'd taken care of whatever mysterious business involved Harry and Charles Hudgins. And that might very well take days.

Jeannie MacPherson was tired of waiting. He'd given her no answers last night, no reasons for his abrupt departure from Muscatoon or his sudden about-face. All he'd given her was a night of love.

If she had to choose between answers and Matthew's lovemaking, she had to admit she'd choose the latter. But she didn't want to have to choose. She needed more than a warm, astoundingly adept body; she needed his trust.

It was a warmish day for October, with the yellowing aspens all around her as she started down the winding mountain road. Enough was enough. She wasn't going to stay put like an obedient child. She was going after Matthew, and going after the truth. She'd had enough of living without him.

Four miles later she was having doubts. The Nikes that had started out comfortable were rapidly proving themselves to be half a size too small, a fact she'd been able to ignore up till now. The sun was surprisingly hot, and even with her sweater tied around her waist Jeannie was getting more and more uncomfortable. The sound of a car in the distance filled her with sudden hope, and she peered ahead, hoping to recognize the silver-and-black of Matthew's sedan.

It wasn't, of course. The huge black limousine advanced on her slowly, the smoked windows ominous in the bright afternoon light, and a sudden frisson of nervousness swept over Jeannie. She could run into woods on either side of the road, but right now she barely had the energy to walk out of the way, much less run. She fixed her fiercest gaze on the car as it pulled up beside her, and with a silent purr the window rolled down.

Charles Hudgins stuck his death-mask face out the window. "Harry Bateman told me you might be out here," he said, that metallic voice a perfect match for his sour smile. "I thought you might be getting ready for a taste of civilization."

Jeannie hesitated for a long moment. Even without Matthew's warning, Charles Hudgins gave her the creeps. It was probably all the power of suggestion, and the poor man couldn't help having an unpleasant face. "How did you know I didn't have a car?"

His smile widened, making Jeannie's skin crawl. "I know everything that goes on in Schooner Springs, Jeannie. You took Matthew Connelly's car last night. Harry dropped him off, and he drove it back this morning. Without you. Therefore it stood to reason that you were left out here without transportation. Can I offer you a ride back to town?"

All of Jeannie's instincts told her to say no. One of Hudgins's goons was serving as chauffeur, another was riding shotgun. Charles's affability was about as reassuring as a rattlesnake's, and the last thing she wanted to do was climb into the cozy backseat of this oversized car for the half-hour ride back into Schooner Springs.

On the other hand, her feet and her head ached, she was hot, sweaty and grumpy, and she couldn't think of one good reason not to accept his ride. Except for Matthew's obscure warning.

She summoned up her brightest smile. "I'd love a ride back to town." Before she could say another word one of his minions had jumped out of the car and was holding the door for her. She climbed in beside Charles, stilling her last feeling of uneasiness, and leaned back against the velour seat. "I don't want to take you out of your way..." she began politely, and Charles smiled his chilly smile, settling a pair of sunglasses back on his nose.

"We came out here specifically to pick you up," he said in that sepulchral voice of his. "Go ahead, Fernand."

Fernand turned the huge car on the narrow road with an impressive deftness, and a moment later they were moving silently back toward Schooner Springs. "Why did you come out here just to pick me up?" Jeannie asked finally.

Charles only smiled. "It will all be clear in a little while. In the meantime why don't you lean back and enjoy the ride?"

Oh, God, not another obscure man, she thought. *Why did they love to be so mysterious?* For a moment she considered pushing Charles, then thought better of it. She'd just as soon have a peaceful ride back to her condominium, where she could climb back into her hot tub and figure out what she was going to do about Matthew Connelly.

She didn't rouse herself until they started up into the rabbit warren of condos and Fernand took the wrong turn. "I'm up in the Telemark condominiums, Charles," she said.

"I know. Drive on, Fernand." Charles's smug expression was hardly reassuring. "There's something I wanted you to see."

"Really?" All Jeannie's instincts were in an uproar. "I want to get home and take a bath, Charles. Couldn't this wait till later?"

"It will only take a few moments. I just wanted to show you a thing or two about our chief of police."

"Why?"

For the first time Charles laughed, a mirthless, chilling laugh. "Why?" he echoed. "For the sheer hell of it, I suppose. Matthew Connelly has been interfering in my life a little too much. I thought it was about time I interfered with his." He smiled his ghoulish smile. "You're about to watch a noble cop take his first fall."

"What do you mean?"

"Matthew Connelly is going on the take."

"I don't believe you. If you're doing something illegal, he's not going to let you get away with it."

"Oh, it's not strictly illegal. Immoral, unethical, perhaps, but not illegal."

"I still don't believe you. Matthew would never—"

"Every man has his price, which I discovered long ago. With some men it's a little harder to find out what the price is, but everyone's got one."

"I don't believe you could meet Matthew's. And why should you want a witness? Aren't you afraid I'd turn both of you in?"

"Why should you? You're in love with Connelly, any fool knows that. If you turn us in Connelly will lose everything. He's got a national reputation as a stalwart lawman, and a fat book contract to write about the Springside Strangler. You blow the whistle on him and he'll lose everything. And you wouldn't want to do that."

"So instead, you think he'll take money to look the other way? I find that hard to believe."

"He wants to buy some land on an island in Maine. Muscatel, was it?"

"Muscatoon," said Jeannie, some of her confidence fading.

"That's it." The car pulled in front of Charles's massive town house, which commanded a central location in the ghetto of condominiums dotting the mountainside. "Come along."

"I'm not going anywhere."

"Of course you are, my dear."

"Not until you tell me what immoral and unethical thing you want Matthew to ignore."

"That would be foolish of me, now, wouldn't it? We don't need another inquiring mind."

"You won't get me out of this car until you do." She crossed her arms in front of her and leaned back against the velour seat.

"I think you underestimate Fernand. He has a great many hidden talents. I have no doubt at all he could get you into my town house with the minimum of fuss."

"I imagine he could. But he'll have to render me unconscious to do so, and then I wouldn't be able to witness your confrontation."

"A good point. Besides, it's nothing so very terrible, nothing Tom and Jeannie's Ice Cream isn't doing. It's progress, pure and simple. We plan to build more condominiums up here on the mountain."

"Yuck. There are too damned many as it is."

"That's a matter of opinion. If I can build them, I can sell them, and isn't that what free enterprise and the American way is all about?"

"So what's the problem? That's tacky, tasteless and money-grubbing, but immoral and unethical seem a bit harsh."

"There's a slight problem with the land I bought from Harry. It's unfortunately quite close to an old uranium mine. I'm afraid the radiation levels are a little high for safety standards. Mind you, they're dropping all the time. By the time the state comes by to check, they should be more than acceptable."

"And when will the state come by?"

"In the normal run of things it won't be for another five or ten years. There's a lot of development in Colorado, more than the state agencies can keep up with. But our police chief has been poking his nose where it doesn't belong. I simply want to ensure he doesn't become too talkative to the wrong people. I've had one of my assistants lay the groundwork with him. All that's left is for Connelly to pick up the money.''

"Won't Harry say something?"

"Harry has been...encouraged not to. Besides, he's making a fair sum of money on the deal. Is that enough information to satisfy you? If it isn't, I'm afraid I'm going to have to rely on Fernand. Matthew is due for his first installment in a matter of minutes, and I need you in place.''

Without waiting for her reply he climbed out of the car, placing his cold, lifeless hand on her unresisting arm. She followed him up the wide redwood steps, keeping an eye out for the silver-and-black car. It was nowhere in sight.

"Fernand, take Miss MacPherson into the bedroom and make her comfortable," Charles said smoothly. "Make her a drink while she's waiting."

"You know what you can do with your drink, Charles."

"Tsk, tsk. You should be grateful that I'm opening your eyes.''

"I still don't understand why you're doing this."

"Revenge and insurance, my dear. I'd like Connelly to know exactly how serious I am about this matter. And I want him to realize that I don't like being interfered with.

"I think he'll get your message," she said dryly.

They didn't have long to wait. Fernand had seated her behind the door to the bedroom, left conveniently ajar so that Jeannie could hear every word. She heard Matthew's footsteps as soon as the others did, and she looked beseechingly toward the silent Fernand.

He smiled, a cold smile as lifeless as his master's, and placed a scarred finger to his lips in a gesture of silence.

She had little doubt that if she leapt for that open door he'd be there before her, and silently enough that Matthew wouldn't have the faintest idea what was going on.

She sat there in complete misery. Would he or wouldn't he? The man she knew, the man she loved, would never take a bribe. But how well did she know him? She had little doubt that Hudgins was right; every man did have his price. Had he found Matthew's? He couldn't have, he simply couldn't have.

"Connelly," Charles's voice was expansive. "I'm glad you were able to make it."

"It seemed important." The rough, sexy voice of Matthew's banished almost every one of her momentary doubts. She couldn't be mistaken about the man she loved.

"Can I offer you a drink? Scotch? Imported beer? I remember you don't like Coors."

"No, thank you," Matthew said politely. "I can't stay long. Harry is waiting for me."

"Now why would Harry be waiting for you?" Even Jeannie could recognize the sudden tension in Charles's chilly voice.

"He's got an appointment with the state inspector. Apparently some land he sold you has a radiation problem that will have to be cleared long before you plan to build. He's got a lot of questions to answer. I imagine they'll be in touch with you in the next few days."

Jeannie couldn't resist any longer. "Yippee!" she shouted, jumping out of her chair and racing around the bedroom door before Fernand could stop her. "I knew you couldn't do it. I knew it, I knew it. I—"

If she thought Matthew could look forbidding before, it was nothing compared to the icy look he gave her. "What the hell," he said in a dangerous voice, "are you doing here?"

Jeannie's steps faltered just short of launching herself into his arms. Arms that certainly didn't look ready to receive her. "It wasn't my fault. He made me come with him."

Matthew's lip curled derisively. "I don't see any signs of force on your body, Jeannie. How'd he get you in the car, hypnosis?"

"Well, I did accept a ride—"

"After I warned you—"

"After you abandoned me out in the woods," she countered.

"As charming as these domestic squabbles are," Charles broke in heavily, "I'm afraid I must withdraw my hospitality. I'm going to have to check with my lawyer on several things. I don't suppose you, ah, feel like telling me how cooperative Harry is being with the state inspectors."

Matthew smiled, a smile fully as chilling as Charles's best efforts. "He's being extremely frank."

"How endearing. Get me a drink, Fernand."

Matthew's hand clamped around Jeannie's defenseless wrist and a second later they were out in the autumn sunshine.

"Why didn't you tell me what was going on?" Jeannie demanded, wrenching her hand free with surprising ease. "And why didn't you tell me about your book contract? You had plenty of chances last night. Why didn't you tell me about the Springside Strangler? And why didn't you trust me?"

"Why didn't you trust me?" he countered angrily. "I told you to stay put, to keep away from Harry and Charles. The next thing I know you're spying on me from Charles's bedroom. Were you disappointed, Jeannie? Did you think I'd be on the take?"

Jeannie shrugged. "Actually, I sort of fancy you like Serpico. Refusing all bribes, that sort of thing."

"Give me strength!" Matthew shouted suddenly. "I would suggest that you take that sweet little butt of yours and go back to your condo and stay there. I'm not in the mood for any more of your fantasies right now."

"And I'm not in the mood for your secretiveness and high-handedness and—and—"

"Fine," he snapped. "That's just fine with me. Why I ever thought you'd be reasonable is beyond me."

"I can only say one thing to you, Matthew Connelly," she said in a furious voice as she started up the steep roadway to the Telemark condominiums.

"What?"

"I wish to God I had a lobster trap with me." With that parting shot she turned and stomped up the hill.

Matthew watched her go, fresh fury simmering inside him. It had only been a matter of luck that Charles Hudgins hadn't chosen to play rough. Matthew had known his sort for all his working life. The Charles Hudginses of this world didn't care whom they hurt and how they got what they wanted, and they usually had the Fernands of this world do the dirty work. From what he'd been able to pry from Harry last night, Charles didn't use that sort of tactic in his Colorado enterprises, keeping it for his more urban developments. But Matthew had little doubt that if he were pushed into a corner he could rapidly turn very mean indeed.

Of course he hadn't trusted Jeannie. With her insatiable curiosity she was bound to get right in the middle of things, and the safest place he could think of for her was stranded out in the middle of nowhere. He had had every intention of finishing up with Hudgins, picking up a huge meal and a great bottle of wine and his mother's engagement ring, the one that his first wife was never able to get out of him, and going back out to that little cabin in the woods to settle their future once and for all.

That was all shot to hell. Right now all he wanted to do was follow Jeannie MacPherson up to her condo and give her the shaking of her life. But he knew exactly where that would lead, and he wasn't ready to get there. He was too damned mad.

Well, let her stew about it for a while. He had enough things to do in the next few days. He'd already given in his notice to the traveling mayor of this fair city, along with his report on the misbehaving city council members. He had to make arrangements to have his things shipped to Muscatoon, check with Hal and Karen to have Sunshine Cottage opened up for him, and find out how long it was going to take for the first part of his advance to reach him. Not that he didn't have more than enough to live on; in the years with the Chicago police department he'd never been into conspicuous consumption. But he wanted to know where he stood financially before he finally met his fate.

He watched her until she turned the corner, stomping all the way, and he shook his head. It certainly wasn't going to be an easy life, or boring. But never again would he be able to hide from life. To his surprise, it felt good, damned good. He headed back down the mountain.

Chapter Twenty-Two

Jeannie slammed the clothes into her suitcases, temper and despair warring for control. She had a reservation on the last flight out of Denver tomorrow night, a reservation she'd be more than happy to cancel. But she doubted she'd have a reason.

In the last week she'd seen Matthew Connelly exactly twice, each time at a distance, and the look on his face had been less than reassuring. The town of Schooner Springs took little notice of the scandal involving two of the city councilmen. A juicy attempted murder was overshadowing that and keeping the local police extremely busy. Jeannie knew and understood that Matthew would be too involved to settle their private difficulties, but she'd given up hope. Her nerves were on the raw edge, her temper frayed, her emotions shattered. She'd needed to get away, back to the peace and quiet of Muscatoon Island, before she'd do something she'd regret.

Not that she hadn't already done a great many things she regretted. She did have one last hurrah planned for this afternoon, she thought as she stuffed her black dress down on top of her muddy Nikes. One last little gesture, and then if that failed she'd be gone. It would be up to Matthew to take the next step.

She snapped the bag closed, reached for her silk raincoat, and paused long enough to check her reflection in the full-length mirror, which was only one of the things she'd be glad to do without once she got back to Muscatoon. She had a great dislike of seeing her skinny, naked body when she wasn't expecting it.

They were having the dedication ceremonies out at the factory that afternoon. Granted, the work was going fast, but the enterprise still wouldn't be operational for another month and a half. However, the absent mayor was making one of his rare appearances, and Tom and Jeannie's Celestial Ice-Cream Works had decided they'd better grab him while they could. Who knew when his honor would next be in town?

Then Jeannie would be free. Tom had agreed that there was nothing much she could do out there until the plant was operational, and then the plant supervisor from Burlington would take over anyway. She might as well go back to Muscatoon and clip coupons. Which was just what she intended to do. She missed the ocean, the rocky beaches, her drafty old house and her friends. The only thing that could replace all that was Matthew Connelly, and he wasn't offering.

She looked good enough, she thought as she surveyed her reflection. Her color was a little high, but then, she was keyed up. It wasn't every day that Jeannie MacPherson became a flasher.

Of course, a flasher in a silk raincoat had a certain style. And she'd chickened out of going all the way. Instead of her birthday suit, she was tastefully attired in a lavender corset and fishnet stockings like a Victorian hooker. She couldn't wait to see Matthew's expression.

She wrapped the raincoat back around her body and tied the tie snugly. Just a brief public appearance, then she'd back the mayor into a corner and flash him, with the police chief a helpless witness. Then she could watch the fur fly.

It was a beautiful day for her last day in Schooner Springs. The sun was shining, the mountains were clear and forbidding in the distance. If only things were different, if only people like Charles Hudgins and Harry Bateman hadn't raped the land and peopled it with hundreds of square boxes at a thousand dollars a foot, then she could learn to love the place. For Matthew's sake she would have been willing to try.

She was late when she pulled up outside the half-completed ice-cream works. Most of the media was there, such as the small town boasted, and even the silver-and-black sedan was in place. She slid from the front seat, the lavender-hued spike heels and fishnet stockings the only clue to what lay hidden beneath the raincoat, and started for the crowds.

"Where do you think you're going?" She'd know that rough, sexy voice anywhere. She stopped where she was, turning to look at him.

He was leaning against a car, his jeans riding low on his narrow hips, the tweed blazer an effective contrast to the black T-shirt. He looked sexy and dangerous, not at all like the chief of police.

"I think this little shindig is in my honor," she said, keeping her coat held closed in tightly-clenched fists. "Besides, I want to meet the mayor."

"He's surrounded by half the town. His appearances are so few and far between that people build up a lot of grudges. Don't worry, if you get a chance to give your little speech at all, it won't be for quite a while. The mayor's real busy campaigning."

"I thought his term didn't run out for another two years."

"The man wants to be president. He's spent all his adult

life campaigning,'' Matthew said with his customary cynicism. "I don't think he's your type, Jeannie."

"I still want to see him," she said in her sweetest voice.

They were curiously alone in the midst of the crowd; no one was within hearing distance or seeing distance. "Why?" Matthew demanded.

"Because I have something for him."

"What?"

She smiled brightly. "This." And she flung open her raincoat.

A second later she was tackled, flung against the nearest car as his arms wrapped around her and the raincoat, effectively covering her from any curious eyes. "That does it," he grated in her ear. "You're under arrest."

"What for?" she murmured coyly.

"Indecent exposure, lewd and lascivious behavior, interfering with an officer in the performance of his duty, you name it." Out of nowhere a pair of handcuffs appeared, and before Jeannie could react they were clasped tightly around her narrow wrists. "You have the right to remain silent," he said dragging her back toward his car. "If you give up that right—"

"Matthew!" Jeannie shrieked. He ignored her, continuing to recite her rights as he pushed her into the backseat of the silver-and-black sedan. "What the hell do you think you're doing?"

"Exactly what you've been asking for," he said as he slid into the front seat and started the engine. "I'm arresting you. That's what you wanted, isn't it?" Dead silence. "Well, isn't it?"

"Sure," she snapped. "Just make sure you put me in a cell with someone reasonably good-looking. I'd been thinking I should try out a criminal next. I've done policemen."

"I'd say you have." Gravel spurted up beneath the tires as he squealed out of the parking lot.

"What are they going to say when I don't show up for the dedication ceremonies?" she demanded as she righted herself after being flung back against the seat.

"With the mayor doing his little act I doubt they'll even miss you," he said unsympathetically. "If they do, I'll be glad to inform them of the charges against you."

"You might as well add grand theft, auto, to the thing," she offered. "Lock me away for a nice long time. That way I won't keep getting in your way."

"Don't tempt me," he growled, stepping on the gas.

The car surged forward, tossing her against the seat once more. It was surprisingly difficult to keep her balance with her wrists chained together, so she contented herself with one final glare at her captor before settling back against the seat. Once more her plans had backfired. Or had they? She'd wanted to galvanize Matthew into some sort of action, and she'd certainly done that. It wasn't her fault that it wasn't the action she'd intended.

She was so intent on feeling sorry for herself and trying to pull her raincoat around her that she didn't pay any attention to their route back toward town, didn't notice when Matthew turned off the main road. The car pulled to a screeching halt, and Jeannie looked up.

"What are we doing at your place?" she demanded hotly. "If I'm under arrest I expect to be taken to prison."

Matthew yanked open the back door of the car and pulled her out, albeit with more gentleness than she expected. "I hate to tell you, Jeannie, but the arrestee isn't in charge of where she's going. Come along."

She had no choice but to stumble after him, into the ranch house, past all the boxes and crates packed for shipping, past the—

"Where are you going?" she demanded suddenly. Even his suitcases were packed and waiting.

"Back to Muscatoon Island." He'd released her, moving away to turn on a light against the gathering gloom. The sunny day had turned cloudy, but Jeannie didn't even notice.

"Why?"

"I have a book to write, for one thing. I've also got a part-time job providing law and order on Muscatoon. Normally, I would have thought there wouldn't be much to keep me busy, but if you're coming back I doubt I'll have a free moment. Unless you're planning to relinquish your life of crime?"

"I'll make your life a living hell," she snarled. "Take off these damned handcuffs, you pervert."

"Why?"

"So I can hit you."

"Now that would be perverse," he said, the smile lighting his eyes. "You don't have to come back with me, you know. I can pass you on to my replacement and he'll be more than happy to arrest you. Half the department knows what happened to my car last Friday. You won't have any trouble convincing people you're a dangerous criminal."

Jeannie sagged against the wall, weary of the battle now that she'd almost won. Or lost; she wasn't quite sure. Even the horrible landscape was gone from the wall. "What do you want from me, Matthew?" she asked in a quiet voice.

He appeared to consider it for a long moment. "I want you to come back to Maine with me. I want you to marry me and have my babies and love me."

A blissful peace settled over Jeannie's ravaged heart. "And what will you do in return?"

"Marry you and give you babies and love you," he replied, and she wondered how she could have ever thought his mouth was grim. It was smiling and sexy and enough to die for.

"On one condition."

"Name it."

"That you never pick up a paintbrush again. I saw your second painting through the window, Matthew. It was even worse than the first."

"All right," he said, the warmth in his eyes sizzling her through the silk raincoat and the French underwear. "But the world's losing a great artist. What's your answer, MacPherson?"

"Unlock the handcuffs, Connelly," she said in a husky whisper. "And I'll show you."

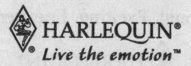

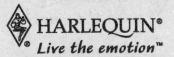

Harlequin Historicals®
Historical Romantic Adventure!

*From rugged lawmen and
valiant knights to defiant heiresses
and spirited frontierswomen,
Harlequin Historicals will
capture your imagination with
their dramatic scope, passion
and adventure.*

*Harlequin Historicals...
they're too good to miss!*